Hounded

Also by Margaret Sherlock

Non-Fiction
SEVEN SISTERS DOWN UNDER

Fiction
AGAINST ALL ODDS
BLIND TRUTH

Margaret can be contacted through her website
www.margaretsherlock.net

Margaret Sherlock

Hounded

Shorelines  Publishing

First published in 2014

by

Shorelines Publishing

3 St. Marks Drive, Meadfoot, Torquay, Devon.TQ1 2EJ

Cover artwork tracey.turner@blueyonder.co.uk

Typesetter elainesharples@btinternet.com

Printed by Short Run Press Limited, Exeter

Dedicated to Emma and Leigh
My pride and joy

Each man is his own absolute law-giver.

Chapter 1

Thursday morning—Bovey Tracey

Isabelle Thatcher turned left and was halted in her tracks by what she saw. Rooted to the spot she raised a hand to shade her eyes from the glaring sun, blinking several times, as if this very act could change what lay before her. Instead of the comforting familiarity of green grass and wild flowers — an amenity that had been a joy for as long as she could remember — a cloak of doom had descended and spread like the black death across the whole field and as far as the eye could see, there was nothing but dark, undulating earth. *So*, she thought, *the rumours weren't idle after all*, this lovely piece of naturalness that had once belonged to her ancestors, was soon to be covered in boxy, brick-built houses.

Today was a special day and Isabelle's time had been meticulously allotted. She'd planned to gather enough blackberries to add to the apples picked yesterday from her own garden for baking three pies — two of which she would sell to the local pub. Determined to continue with her plan, she removed the container for the fruit, hitched her rucksack onto her shoulders, pushed open the wooden rickety gate with one hip and marched through. After a few steps she realized how difficult this usually pleasant task was going to be. The well-worn path that ran alongside the hedge was now almost obliterated, apart from a narrow ledge of firm ground barely wide enough to accommodate her sandaled feet. Gritting her teeth, she contemplated the challenging passage between the ripe fruit and the deep furrows of dark soil. Anger propelled her on.

After moving several yards along the hedge, plucking and dropping the fruit into her plastic bucket, another thought hit her. Where would she spread her blanket to enjoy a cup of coffee later? The blanket had a waterproof underside, bought two months earlier after the wet summer had left the ground permanently damp, but it would be impossible to use it here. After cursing aloud, she carried on picking.

Coming upon a curvature in the hedge, the hint of a smile pulled at her lips. About ten meters ahead, the stump of the old ash tree, cut down after lightening struck it years ago. *Perfect*, she thought, *for taking a well-earned break*. Raising her face to the sun, appreciative of the unseasonably warm weather for October, reminded her of why she was here. It was her son's 14th birthday and blackberry and apple pie was Robert's favourite dessert.

With a steady rhythm of plucking and dropping, plucking and dropping, plucking and dropping, Isabelle's plastic bucket started to feel satisfyingly heavy and her progress more sure-footed. Leaning into a gap in the hedge, reaching for a particularly tempting bunch of fruit, her rucksack became snagged on a web of matted brambles. Turning to untangle them with her free hand, she was rewarded with a cutting swipe across her cheek.

"Damn!"

The sudden outburst silenced the birds. And Isabelle was

still caught up. Carefully, she pressed the bucket of fruit into the furrow of soil behind her before sliding her arms, one at a time, from the straps of the rucksack. With both hands gripping hard, she gave a hefty pull. Bad mistake. It gave way suddenly, and without room behind to step back, she landed on her backside with a thud that reverberated to the top of her spine.

"Shit!" She shouted, annoyed that her flailing arms had upended the bucket and scattered the fruit into the furrow alongside her. She very rarely swore — thought that people who constantly used foul language had no manners, no self-respect and no self-control — but lately she'd been driven to swearing more and more.

Near to tears she sat motionless, legs bent over the front of the furrow and her back supported by the next furrow behind, wondering if it was worth the effort carrying on. Instead, she reached into the rucksack and grabbed her flask. Whilst she was seated, and she had to admit, she *was* quite comfortable, she may as well make the most of it. The coffee, milky and sweet, began to calm her jangled nerves.

She refilled the small cup absentmindedly, her attention locked on to an industrious robin who had been harvesting worms from the newly disturbed soil. Suddenly, her eyes fixed on a glint of, what looked like bright metal reflecting the sun. It had been revealed by the robin as a piece of brown debris was pecked at and flicked out of the way. Isabelle stretched out her hand to touch it but it was just beyond her reach. *Sod it*, she thought, enjoying the comfort of her strange seat and continued to sip her coffee, trying hard to keep her eyes from being drawn to the glinting metal. Curiosity finally got the better of her. Grabbing the upended fruit bucket, she stretched out again as far as she could and scooped up half a bucket of soil. Then scanning the area, found no sign of glinting metal or the brown debris that had lay beside it. Both were now in the bucket.

The robin reappeared, attracted by more disturbance and the sight of a fat, wriggling worm exposed in the bucket. Quick as a flash he swooped, gathered and flew into the hedge, the worm dangling from its beak.

Isabelle looked half-heartedly at the damp mass in her bucket wondering what on earth she was doing? She'd come here for a specific purpose, not to mess about in filthy soil. On the verge of flinging the bucket and it's contents into the hedge, she realized how sentimentally attached she was to it. She'd bought it years ago and had always used it for blackberrying — its bright orange colour with matching lid making it easy to spot wherever you stopped along the hedge. Wrapping her arms around it she whispered an apology, then used its base to smooth out an area of ground in front of her before carefully tipping out the contents. Gingerly her forefinger leveled out the mass until the glinting metal was revealed, her eyes widening in astonishment. It was a ring! A ring of bright gold! She pushed her soiled forefinger through its aperture, marveling at how new it looked. On lifting her finger to inspect the ring more closely, something dragged from the soil. It was the brown debris she saw laying over the ring before the robin had flicked part of it to one side. It was filthy, sodden and weighty and hanging on the ring by a single, disintegrating strand.

Fear and excitement coursed through her body. She looked about her. No one was in sight, just the robin giving out his sweet song as he waited for more signs of food. She reached into her rucksack and fumbled for the polythene carrier bag, always there for emergencies. The ring, and the sodden, disintegrating leather, for she was sure that's what it was, were carefully lowered into the bag. Trembling with emotion, she sifted through the remainder of the soil. But there was nothing but soil and worms.

Chapter 2

Torquay

Vinny Conway looked around his hub, releasing a sigh of frustration followed by a mouthful of foul language. "I need more fucking space", he spat into the claustrophobic room, toeing two boxes of files out of his way. In an effort to create a bit more room around his desk, he decided to remove the extra chair — placed for clients but seldom used — and carted it off to the spare bedroom.

He'd bought the small basement flat a year ago from his neighbour — a solicitor who worked and lived next door. At the time, it seemed more than adequate for a one-man private investigator. The upmarket address had been the main attraction. In a business like his, location was everything if you wanted to be taken seriously and become successful. Trouble was, being successful brings its own problems. In just twelve months, he had accumulated enough paperwork to sink a battle ship. What he needed was a secretary, preferably a redundant voluntary worker — an old biddy with years of experience keeping books but who still had all her marbles and understood what could be shredded and what needed to be kept. There must be thousands of them here in Torquay, looking for something meaningful to do especially if their hubbies had kicked the bucket.

He looked around the simply furnished spare bedroom, which had been used as the main dumping ground for everything from files to reams of printing paper he'd bought cheap on eBay, and realized he needed to buckle down and get organised. He unlocked the window, allowing the morning sunshine to filter into the stale air, before returning for the two boxes of files. As he squeezed along the narrow passage, between office and spare bedroom, balancing one box on top of the other, a loud knocking on his front door stopped him in his tracks.

"What?" he shouted, turning to face the door and scraping the paint off the wall as the top box decided to dismount. The knocking continued, even louder. He slammed the remaining box down on the floor, took two long strides and swung back the front door. Lyn Porter stood there with her hands on her hips and a look of thunder on her face.

"You're in my parking space and I need it. Now!"

"Good morning, Lyn. The door was unlocked, why didn't you just walk in, save me having to repaint the fucking wall?" Vinny stood to one side and caste a thumb in the direction of the scraped wall.

"I'm not in the habit of just walking, uninvited, into someone's private space. If you had hollered, come in, or shouted, doors unlocked, I would have

taken that as an invitation. For all I know, you might have just got out of the shower."

"In your dreams, lady." he said displaying a coarse leer. As you can see, I'm in the middle of reorganising, the parking space will be free after lunch."

"Vinny, we had a deal. I let you have the biggest space

because sometimes you need to park your van there, and the smaller space was more convenient for my car because it was shaded from the sun, which, when loaded, kept my flower arrangements from wilting. Nowhere in this deal was there any talk of you commandeering both spaces, for any amount of time. So please move it. Now!"

"Look, there's a space right outside the front door, big enough to park a fucking bus, and, not so far for you to carry your bunches of flowers or whatever they are."

"The sun is beating down out the front. Your car is in my space which is shaded. Move the van into this massive bus space, then shunt your car into the space where the van was, then I promise to leave you in peace."

Vinny knew in his heart that the bossy cow was determined, but he wasn't prepared to give in that easily.

"I tell you what, just put those spilled files back in the box, while I hunt out the van keys, as you can see I'm all over the place here."

Lyn reluctantly stepped over the threshold as Vinny disappeared down the passage, calling as he went. "Just bring the boxes through here into the spare room."

Ten minutes later, after carrying two more boxes into the spare bedroom, Vinny still hadn't managed to locate the van keys. Lyn started to smell a rat when he casually asked if she'd like to make the coffee and take a break.

"If my parking space isn't free in the next five minutes, I'm going out there and letting down every single tyre on both the van and your car."

"That's madness, you'd be hours away from getting your space back."

"It'll be worth it." She marched out of the front door and slammed it behind her. By the time she'd walked the fifty yards to her own car and driven it around the back to the graveled parking area, Vinny was already backing the van out with a broad grin on his face. But that grin disappeared when he drove round to the front of the terrace and found that the space large enough for a bus, now had two cars squeezed into it.

James Fairbank popped his head around Lyn's studio door.

"Coffee's almost ready, sweetheart." The room was empty. She'd mentioned earlier that their shared coffee break might be a little delayed. She needed to put some finishing touches to several floral arrangements before loading them in her car in preparation for transporting them to London.

Suddenly, Lyn bustled through the door. "I know I'm late and I'm sorry, but I'm still not loaded up, thanks to that bastard below."

"Calm down, have a coffee and biscuit and then we'll load the car together."

Although Lyn appreciated the offer, the last thing she needed right now was a lesson on how to make maximum use of a cars interior. "There's just two more to load up — both fragile — you go and set up the coffee, I'll be with you in less than five minutes."

The solicitor retreated back to his own office and resisted the urge to pour a cup of the freshly percolated coffee until the five minutes had passed. He'd been engaged to Lyn for almost a year and in the first flush of their commitment it had been assumed, by both parties, that they would marry on or around the first anniversary of that commitment. But the year had flown by and both of them had been extremely busy in their respective businesses. On top of this, Lyn's daughter, Sarah, had emigrated to Australia, leaving Lyn in a quandary about where her loyalties should lie — taking time off to visit and help out where she could, or concentrate on her own business and personal affairs. A months trip to Australia, back in April, had been decided upon, with the view that there was still plenty of time for marriage arrangements. Unfortunately, due to his own business commitments, James hadn't been able to accompany her. His office door swung open, abruptly cutting his train of thought.

"Good morning, Vincent, said James, as you can see, I'm just about to take my coffee break, how can I help you?"

"Well, thats decent of you, Jimmy. Save me having to interrupt my reorganising, two sugars, as usual."

The solicitor opened his mouth, but unusually for him, couldn't think of an appropriate response, unlike Vincent, who, whilst plonking himself down in the chair opposite, reaching for two of the four chocolate biscuits and waiting for his cup to be filled, launched into a series of questions about Lyn.

"Your, wife-to-be, is in a fiery mood this morning, what've you been up to that's upset her? If you ask me, I think she's getting frustrated about you not naming the day."

After reluctantly half filling Vincent's cup, James poured his own coffee and took a huge gulp just as Lyn appeared at his office door.

"All done, sweetheart? Come and sit down," he croaked as the coffee burned his throat, "Vincent is just leaving."

Vinny swigged his coffee in one go, grabbed another biscuit and stood up, offering Lyn his chair with an exaggerated bow at the waist and a sweep of his hand. When he reached the door he turned to the solicitor and tapped the side of his nose. "Think about what I said, Jimmy."

Lyn looked at her watch. "Six minutes, exactly, what was all that about?"

"You know Vincent, full of mischief, but he's harmless enough. I'll just get more biscuits."

Lyn sat on the abandoned chair, then changed her mind as the warmth, left behind from Vinny's backside, permeated through her skirt. The man irritated her. He was rude, foul-mouthed, untrustworthy and had almost succeeded in conning her out of forty thousand pounds. And yet, James, who was a stickler for truth, honesty and integrity, clearly regarded him as…As what? A friend? Since Lyn's first trip to Australia, a year ago, she'd broached the subject of their developing friendship several times, but had eventually given up when it always seemed to end with them arguing and *her* sounding paranoid.

"So, you're fully loaded, what time are you leaving?" James asked as he walked back into his office with the replenished coffee pot and more biscuits.

Lyn sensed the tension, it was unlike him to speak until he was seated and looking squarely at the recipient of his well-thought out words.

"Why? Are you and Vinny planning on doing something that I wouldn't approve of?" She instantly regretted her childish peevishness and smiled to make it appear as a joke but his eyes were now looking into hers and he wasn't fooled. "I'm sorry," she said, "But I find it very hard to like him. In fact, I find it hard to even tolerate him. But, there is a glimmer of hope on the horizon, he desperately needs more space, so he may well be searching for larger premises soon."

James carefully rested his cup in its saucer and gently took hold of both of Lyn's hands, caressing them as he lifted them to his lips. After kissing each in turn, he smiled, but the lovely green eyes that bore into hers were tinged with sadness. "Sweetheart, you are the most important person in my life and I know it's been a busy year for both of us. When you return from London, we will discuss one thing only. Where and when we will marry!"

Chapter 3

Isabelle's stomach was grumbling for attention but she carried on regardless. With a soft, worn toothbrush, she gently cleaned the soiled items under running water from the scullery tap. Shaun would have a fit if he could see her now — profligately adding to the soaring water bills — but she didn't care. At long last, she could see light at the end of the tunnel of despair. Despair brought on by a feckless man who cared only about himself and his lustful desires.

Her eyes wandered over the pieces she'd cleaned and set drying on a piece of kitchen tissue on the sunny window sill. So far, including the ring, five items had come to light. A gold coin, the size of a modern 10p, bright and clean as the ring. Two smaller 1p sized coins, which she hoped to be silver but had several ugly patches of black coating on them which she couldn't wash off. And finally, a tiny, extremely fragile coppery coin covered in bright green corrosion, which had all but disintegrated as she'd tried to clean it. The slimy, rotted hide, was obviously once a purse. A purse, quite possibly lost by a distant member of her own family.

Isabelle was fascinated, and all she wanted to do for the rest of the day was to submerge herself in finding out as much as possible about her finds. But that would have to wait. She picked up the ring again and turned it slowly between thumb and forefinger, holding the magnifying glass close enough to read the words engraved on the inside and the small stamp mark showing two letters. She'd done this a dozen times already, but now she needed to write down the information, making absolutely sure of the spelling. She reached for her pocket-diary, and on todays entry, she neatly wrote.

Providence divine hath made thee mine NP

With the polythene carrier bag gaping open, the soil from the field had been left drying in a patch of sunshine outside the scullery door. After pressing the dried, fine earth through a coarse sieve, satisfied that nothing had been overlooked, Isabelle sprinkled it, one handful at a time, around her herb bed.

Back in the scullery, she wrapped each of the coins in fresh kitchen tissue and placed them in the bottom of her sewing box. But where to hide the ring? A piece of jewellery had gone missing from this cottage; Shaun insisting she was careless and forgetful, but she knew better. The missing bracelet was an antique— inherited from her grandmother and of great sentimental value — how could she have misplaced it? It was always kept in the same special place. Shaun must never find out about this ring. This ring that slipped easily onto her thumb. This ring that was heavy and appeared to be the same rich colour as her grandmother's 22ct gold wedding ring which, since the disappearance of the bracelet, was worn on a chain round her neck. She read the inscription again, captivated by the mystery of it and wondered if it belonged to a man or a woman.

Conscious now of the afternoon slipping away, she dropped the ring into a small polythene bag, and on impulse, pushed it firmly into the soil of a potted Basil that stood on the windowsill, feeling confident that it would be quite safe. After all, *she* was the one who did all the cooking in this house. Glancing at her watch, she reached for the local directory, taking it to her favourite seat at the bottom of the garden. Here, she would now enjoy a pot of tea and a sandwich, before taking the first step of one of the most important decisions of her life.

Shaun Thatcher emptied the dregs from his mug of tea onto the ground and flicked the stub of his cigarette into a nearby bush. *No danger of setting it alight,* he thought, *not after all the pissing rain we've had this year.* But today, well today was gloriously sunny. Just his luck that he had to be working. Jules was probably lying somewhere in the sun, stark naked, if the bronzed colour of her skin was anything to go by. The very thought of her sent his pulse racing. What he wouldn't give to spend an hour in her company right now. He leaned back against the warmth of the outside wall, intent on a little daydreaming, when an aggressive voice cut through the peace and quite of the sunny afternoon.

"Thatcher if you value your job you'll get your arse back here and get some work done! And next time you take longer than you're entitled, it'll be docked from your wages."

Shaun had worked for the ceramic tile company since he'd left school, there wasn't a great deal of choice round here, unless you worked unsociable hours stocking shelves at Tesco. The fine white dust, which sometimes covered him from head to toe, was just part of his life. A life that was becoming increasingly harder to cope with. Still, he thought, as he wandered back to the warehouse, Friday tomorrow — pay day. A picture of Jules, young and carefree with a body to die for, flashed across his mind, putting a swagger in his step and a whistled tune on his lips.

Lyn drove at a steady seventy-miles-per-hour along the M5 heading for London. Needing to make up for time lost, she was grateful that traffic was light. Even so, her cargo of flower arrangements were fragile and although secured on wire shelving with cool air circulating in the back section of her car, any sudden braking could prove disastrous.

Three parallel vapour trails cut across the cloudless, blue sky, remnants of planes heading to warmer, more exotic places. Watching, as the vapour slowly began to dissipate, reminded Lyn of promises made. Promises about taking a late autumn break to somewhere sunny and relaxing, where conversations, unfettered by day to day problems, would consist entirely on planning their wedding day. How she longed to just lay down by the sea and relax. Today was sunny and more was promised but this was the kind of weather that promised warmth, when sheltered from the wind, but the minute you stepped into shade, you found yourself reaching for a jacket or even a scarf to keep the chilling breeze at bay. The summer had been wet, so wet that even now, with more than a week without rain, partial flooding could still be seen in many low-lying fields and night time temperatures dropped to just above freezing — the price you paid for clear blue skies. No, you had to go south, much further south to get guaranteed good weather.

She had spent April in Australia — their autumn and her ideal — with temperatures averaging seventy-five degrees. Sarah and Fergus had been busy settling into their rented property and driving here and there to view parcels of land where they could build a home and base for their stud farm. Lyn had been more than happy to temporarily become housekeeper and child minder to her grandson, Martin. The rented property was large and had a fenced-off swimming pool, and while the toddler napped in the afternoon, Lyn swam and soaked up the sun.

On her final weekend, they'd all travelled to Twin Waters to spend time with her parents — Jennifer and Pierre Beck — parents, whom she had only met six months earlier, and before then, had presumed to be dead. As before, the reunion was emotional, especially with the first meeting of their granddaughter and great-grandson to fuss over. Lyn's father — cursed with the worsening effects of Alzheimer's — again failed to understand who she was; but on seeing little Martin, clung to him with such tenderness that it brought tears to all their eyes. In spite of everything, Lyn sensed the building of family bonds and it was with great sadness that she'd bid them all farewell.

Lyn could see the merging of motorways onto the M4 was almost upon her. She eased into the left-hand lane, harnessing all her concentration for the next leg of the journey, if her precious cargo arrived damaged, God knows what she'd do!

Torquay

Vinny swept an appreciative eye around his office. It was just how he liked it; clean and tidy with everything put away, leaving a clear desk and blank spaces around his printer. However, the spare bedroom now housed most of his paperwork — cardboard boxes stacked high and pushed against one side of the room. Stefan, a Bulgarian friend who worked in London, was arriving soon to help him carry out some security work, and kipping down at Vinny's place was part of the deal. *Too bad, mate,* thought Vinny, as he thumbed through the morning's mail, *I'm sure you've slept in worse situations.*

All the brown envelopes, which Vinny knew to be bills and meant even more filing space, were shoved into his top desk drawer. A strong cardboard box, approximately 20cm square by 10cm deep was the last to be inspected. Vinny had been aware of it since it arrived but had vowed not to check the mail until his reorganisation was completed. He flipped the package back and fourth trying to work out what it could be. He hadn't bought anything from eBay for ages, taking himself in hand after realising that bargain hunting was becoming an obsession. His name and address were correctly printed on the front but no indication who had sent it. Soon tiring of the guessing game, his chubby fingers grappled with the tape and tore open the box. Inside, was a smart-looking device which, on reading the accompanying letter, described it as an 'air purifier'. The polished, stainless-steel panel had several rows of venting, each angled in a different direction. Vinny pressed his nose against it but smelt nothing. The letter went on to say, that several businesses had been chosen to receive this complimentary piece of equipment as part of their market research for this simple, but revolutionary new product. After six weeks, when the cartridges would be due for replacement, a member of the marketing team would make contact…etc, etc, etc.

Clutching the box and the letter, Vinny left his premises and mounted the steps to the solicitor's office next door. The office was locked. A high-pitched drilling noise, coming from

Lyn Porter's studio, enticed him to follow the sound. Jimmy, red in the face, was perched on a step ladder, as he pressed forward on a cordless power drill.

"She's getting you well trained then?"

"Damn!" Startled by the intrusion, James' normally steady hand had faltered, snapping the drill. "Pass me those pliers, Vincent. As you can see, this is not the best time for a chat."

"Just wanted to know if you've had one of these sent to you?" Vinny held up the shiny panel of metal before passing over the pliers.

"If I hadn't, I wouldn't be in this fix now." Lyn had been there when he'd opened the package. After a sweeping glance of the contents, he promptly regarded it as unnecessary. She on the other hand, thought it a brilliant idea, especially as some of the foliage required for her more unusual arrangements gave off smells that were quite unpleasant. As a peace-offering for his earlier misjudgement regarding Vincent Conway, he'd offered to mount it on the wall before her return.

"So if I use it, they can't come on to me for any money, seeing as they sent it off their own back?" Vinny enquired, making no attempt to leave.

"It says quite clearly in their letter that the device is complimentary, which means, free of charge. But, I suspect the cartridges, just like most ink cartridges for printers, cost more than the device itself. Do you really want to clutter your life with more appliances, Vincent? I can understand where Lyn is coming from, I've walked into her studio on several occasions and detected malodorous air coming from her stock room. But you don't use anything that gives off an unpleasant odour."

"When I've had a curry the night before, *I* can give off an unpleasant odour, and it's a bit embarrassing when you have a client, especially a female, sitting in the same tiny office. Anyway, why bother going to all that trouble fixing it on the wall when you can stand it on the side there?" Vinny pointed, enviously, to a long run of working surface that was absolutely clear of anything.

"There are no sockets there to plug it into." From the look on Vincent's face, James realized that his neighbour hadn't yet fully unpacked the box or read the fitting instructions.

"Well, I intend to position mine where it will reach a socket, I've had enough DIY for one day. Didn't Lyn get one sent to her?"

"No, and I wish to God that I hadn't had one sent to me! Have you got a 5mm drill bit I can borrow."

Vinny returned about ten minutes later, gripping a toolbox in his hand and wearing a satisfied grin on his chubby face. "It's a great piece of gear. Sitting on the corner of my desk it easily reaches the double socket of the answer phone. Every fifteen minutes, it releases a puff of scent — nothing flowery or poncey — it smells more like the sea on a fresh sunny day. I'm really chuffed with it. Tell her you've changed your mind, Jimmy. Your office could do with freshening up. Get rid of the stench of leather, polish and coffee."

James was in no mood for arguing the point. In his frustrated effort to remove the broken drill bit, he had chipped out a chunk of plaster the size of his thumb. Which meant filling the hole, leaving it overnight to harden, and then completing the task tomorrow. He voiced all this to Vincent, expecting him to now show signs of leaving but instead he removed a steel tape from his tool box and was running it the length of Lyn's studio.

"What on earth are you doing, Vincent?"

"Just gathering facts and figures whilst I've got the opportunity. Lyn never lets me in the place."

"Facts and figures for what?" James asked in a voice that sounded like a screeching seagull.

"Keep your hair on, Jimmy, I'm just forward planning. When you and Lyn finally tie the knot she'll be moving in with you, which means this place will become available. I just want to let you know that I may well be interested, provided of course that we can agree on a price."

The solicitor was speechless as he tried to assimilate what his neighbour was implying. Suddenly becoming animated, he picked up the ladder and Vincent's toolbox and carried them out into the corridor.

"As you know, Lyn will be back in a couple of days, I feel sure she intends to keep her business up and running after we are married, but you'll need to get that confirmed by her. Now I really must get back to my desk."

"Come on, Jimmy, It doesn't make sense, especially in these economic times, to keep two large premises for just two people. Besides, why would she want to mess about with all these flowers and twigs when she has a well-paid husband to keep her, isn't that the whole point of getting hitched?"

"Lyn happens to enjoy what she does. She finds it very satisfying." Making sure everything was switched off, he edged his neighbour out into the corridor and locked Lyn's studio.

Vinny picked up his toolbox and swaggered toward the front door. Before leaving he turned to the solicitor. "Maybe if she got more satisfaction in the bedroom department, she wouldn't need to get it elsewhere."

Chapter 4

Thursday Evening—Bovey Tracey

As usual, Shaun Thatcher entered the cottage by the back door. But unusually, there were no delicious smells of home cooking. It was already dark and he was famished.

"Izzie? Izzie where are you? Has there been a power cut? I need to be out of here in an hour, what's for…"

"We're having fish and chips and Robert's gone to fetch them," Isabelle said, cutting short his question as she sauntered into the kitchen.

"That's a fine dinner to give your son on his birthday and I suppose there's no apple pie either? So there's been another bloody power cut, I'm sick to death of this old place."

Isabelle, determined not to rise to Shaun's building anger, replied evenly. "There hasn't been a power cut, I've spent the afternoon trying to arrange a smear test. They phoned to tell me the last one was unclear and needs re-doing. I've been worried sick! But I managed to get an appointment for tomorrow morning so I'll need the car. I've explained this to Robert. He's more concerned about my health than his stomach. Besides, the meadow's been ploughed up. Can't get near to the blackberries."

"You've still got apples and it is the lad's birthday." Shaun untied his boots, eased each one off and after giving his wife a quick glance, threw them down by the kitchen door. He'd been given a 'particular' place outside the backdoor for keeping his working clothes. But what the hell.

Holding her tongue and refraining from gathering up the filthy boots and tossing them outside, Isabelle closed her eyes and allowed the image of the gold ring to calm her. Intuition told her that this item was meant for her. And, it was the key to improving her life. Shaun's aggressive words sliced across her feelings of calm.

"And how am I supposed to get to bloody work if you have the car? Can't you have this test done at the health clinic?"

"No! Not if I want it done quickly. You can get the bus, just this once. In fact you could probably walk it in half an hour; they give fine weather for the next few days. I'm worried, Shaun, and I want to get it over with, OK? Robert will be back soon. It's his birthday, let's not argue."

London

Lyn smiled as she accepted the glass of chilled white wine from her partner, Jill, allowing the sweet feeling of relief to encompass her. The floral arrangements had survived the long journey without any damage. Tomorrow morning they would make a short journey to Clifton House to decorate the tables of the wedding feast and *her* role in the celebration would be completed. Most of their commissions came from the London area and Lyn knew how fortunate she was to have Jill — whose long-standing contacts secured the majority of up-market events and weddings — but she hated the stress that came with the transportation. "Cheers!" Lyn lightly tapped glasses and took a large, appreciative gulp.

"The arrangements look gorgeous, Lyn. It's very cool in my studio, in spite of this warm spell. I've sprayed the whole lot, again, so you can stop fretting and tell me what's new."

"Candy phoned this morning, asked if we'd like to meet up for lunch tomorrow. As you know, she's not far from Clifton House. You don't need to rush back, do you?" Lyn was thinking of Jill's eight-year-old twin boys, who tended to dominate most of her time.

"Are you crazy! You think I'd pass up an opportunity to have lunch with Candy. Hubby won't mind picking up the kids if I'm not back. Talking of hubbies, have you and James got any closer to naming the day? Unless you intend to have a very quiet and informal do, you don't need me to tell you that you ought to get things moving asap."

"We've agreed to thrash things out this weekend."

"I've been hearing that for the last six months. What's the problem?"

Lyn knew there was a problem, but couldn't quite put her finger on what it was. "I think it's mainly to do with where, rather than when. As you know, all my relatives are in Australia. It's impossible for my parents to come here, because of the way Dad is. Plus Sarah couldn't afford it. And if we get married in Australia, because James's mother is so frail…" Lyn didn't need to say more.

"If it were me, I'd just decide on a nice exotic location and bugger off there without telling the family. Keep it simple. As much as I would like to be present at my best friends wedding, in your position, it's the perfect solution."

"You are forgetting one thing, Jill. James is a traditionalist. It's inconceivable for him to get married and not have his family present."

"Committing to a partnership is all about give and take. He gives you what you want, and you take it — graciously. Cheers!"

Torquay

Vinny felt nervous and couldn't understand why. He knew it had something to do with the phone call he'd had earlier — some bird wanting her husband trailed and photographed as evidence against him — but she didn't sound like the usual type. After giving him her name, Ms Thatcher, and a brief run down on what was required, she'd announced that this phone call would be the only one she'd be making, and furthermore, she'd continued, there would be no correspondence by mail. Her voice had reminded Vinny of one of his primary school teachers who, at the tender age of five, had given him several smart slaps across his legs. He couldn't remember what he had done wrong but he could remember bursting into tears and running home, only to be returned, after being given another slap from his dad — for not taking his punishment like a man.

When Vinny had asked Ms Thatcher for her email address, thinking that this modern chick only communicated electronically, she announced that she didn't have one and she would like to meet the following morning to set everything in motion. His gut reaction was to yell down the phone and enlighten her about the 'real world' and how a profession such as his usually required more time for setting appointments.

But instead, he'd flapped a few pages of the magazine in front of him and told her he could squeeze her in at ten-thirty.

He was now having second thoughts. Stefan was arriving tomorrow afternoon, by train, and he'd promised to pick him up at Exeter after collecting an assignment of security locks there. He also needed to shop for food and booze. Thinking of food, Jimmy usually invited him in to share a meal when Lyn was away but it was almost seven, so no chance of that now. He was starving. Only one thing for it, a take-away curry.

On cue, his newly acquired air filter, emitted a breath of fragrant sea air. Pushing aside all nervousness and thoughts of strident school teachers, Vinny grabbed his keys and jacket, announcing to the night air, "Take your punishment like a man!"

James Fairbank absentmindedly lay the phone back in its cradle and remained seated in the chair by the window. His face reflected concern and on noticing this, he closed the drapes. His sitting room clock chimed seven, fragmenting his thoughts and releasing him from painful memories.

"My God, was I really on the phone that long?" he asked the empty room, checking that his wristwatch showed the same time as the antique clock. It did.

He'd been looking forward to enjoying a relaxed meal and a couple of glasses of wine on his own before the phone rang. Expecting to hear Lyn's voice, he was surprised to hear Helen, his sister, sounding very upset. Their mother, now in her mid-eighties, had just been diagnosed with 'shingles' — a disease where painful blisters form along the path of a nerve or nerves. Fate had chosen the worst possible area to inflict its damage. Her left eye and all around that side of her head was affected, reducing her sight capabilities to less than 20%. Already semi-crippled with arthritis, this additional setback, in a woman whose fierce independence had enabled her to remain in her own home, meant that some outside help would be needed for her day to day needs.

James understood the guilt that Helen was feeling. Being the only female architect, in a busy practice of twelve, had made her obsessively keen in keeping time off to a minimum. Having fought her way successfully, through the years when Jack first started school, she was now faced with a situation that couldn't be conveniently passed to a husband whose work allowed flexibility. Mother was a traditionalist, and as such, expected her only daughter, rather than strangers, to administer to her needs until the disease abated.

Resisting the urge to pour wine, James decided to walk into town in the hope of rejuvenating his lost appetite.

Bovey Tracey

The fish and chips weighed heavy in Shaun Thatchers stomach. Not because he'd rushed his meal, he was used to doing that, it was the stress of having to hold his tongue on things that needed saying. Izzie hated confrontation and refused to see what was staring her in the face. They couldn't afford to go on living where they were. A three-hundred-year-old cottage with thatched roof was fine if you had the money to maintain it. But with household costs spiraling and wages stagnant, the sums didn't add up. All he wanted was for her to see reason and talk about the alternatives.

"Penny for them."

He looked up into the bright, smiling face of his favourite barmaid. Jules was always happy and ready to listen, at a cost, but what the hell.

This was the third time Isabelle had been to the bathroom to relieve her bladder. And the third time she had felt the compulsion to check on her finds. She still couldn't quite believe that finding this treasure had really happened. After slipping on her thick dressing gown, creeping down the narrow stairs and retrieving each item from its hiding place, reassurance calmed her. She was bursting to tell someone about her good fortune but that would spoil everything. No, it had to remain *her* secret.

She'd had a warm bath and gone to bed early, knowing that neither Shaun nor Robert would be back before eleven. In fact Shaun would probably be much later.

After their meal, Robert had accepted his £25 birthday gift with a smile and a brief announcement that he was off to the pictures in Exeter. Isabelle had wanted to know who he was going with, what time would he be home, and what film was he going to see? But Robert had left the room before she'd had the chance to ask anything. She knew full well he was saving for an Iphone, all his friends had them, and he was probably hoping for more money. If his father spent less in the pub, maybe…no, no more maybes. Pulling the covers around her ears, she closed eyes and willed herself to relax.

Waking from a dream she could hear church bells in the distance. She counted ten strokes and looked at the alarm clock beside her pillow. Was it really only ten o'clock? She tried to recover something of the dream but all she could catch was the dissipating image of a tall stranger, offering something to her. Again she needed the toilet. Stress, that was to blame. She'd read somewhere that stress is not only caused by worry and overwork. Excitement and pleasure, especially when you're not used to it, can bring on similar symptoms.

Chapter 5

Friday Morning—London

Sunlight streamed through spotlessly-clean windows imprinting bright chevrons of light across crisp, white table linen in the venue hall of Clifton House. The sight of this evoked Lyn Porter's worst nightmare. It was impossible to guarantee the freshness of her floral arrangements when strong sunlight was allowed to bear down on them for long periods. It was nine o'clock, hours away from the wedding feast. Yesterday, Lyn had phoned the head organiser of Clifton House, Phillis Tompkins, and voiced her concerns about keeping the table centerpieces pristine. Phillis had promised to make sure all the blinds were closed on the left side of the hall. But this had not happened and Phillis wouldn't be arriving until at least ten o'clock. Jill had tried, without success, to find one of the porters. *They* were the only ones allowed to mount the ladders and drop the blinds.

Resigned to the wait, Lyn moved her car to the deepest shade she could find in the Clifton House car park, then walked the short distance to the coffee shop across the road where Jill was already ordering two cappuccinos.

"This doesn't bode well for the rest of the day," she

grumbled, squeezing in alongside her friend on the narrow two-seater bench after making sure she could see the car and any sign of the sun's rays onto it.

"Calm down, everything's going to be fine, assured Jill, tucking into a piece of chocolate cake — her way of dealing with stress. Candy will understand if we're a bit late."

Lyn shook her head when Jill cut a section from her cake and offered it. She knew her friend was hoping to impart the same feeling of peace and satisfaction that she was enjoying but Lyn had explained many times, that eating under stress, was more likely to give *her* painful indigestion. She'd hoped to be out of London before the Friday afternoon exodus. Fine weather was predicted to continue over the weekend, guaranteeing all routes to the west country would have bumper-to-bumper traffic.

Torquay

Isabelle walked slowly past the Georgian premises hoping to catch a glimpse of the gentleman she had arranged to see. His offices were on the lowest floor of the four story building, in fact, they were below ground level. Peering down a short run of steps, one of the windows were visible, but vertical blinds in an almost closed position, prevented her from seeing inside. Shrugging off the disappointment, she concentrated on her main concern, keeping her intentions secret from everyone, except this one person who had promised complete confidentiality. It was for this reason that she'd chosen Torquay instead of Exeter. Both towns had several Private Investigators advertised in the Yellow Pages. But Exeter was only ten miles away from where she lived. Much too close.

Especially for a small town like Bovey Tracey, where everyone knew each others business.

It was twenty-five past ten when Vinny finally settled down at his desk. He'd spent nearly an hour flicking a duster across all the surfaces in his office and making sure that he, and the air within the small space, were devoid of any remnants of last nights curry. Each time the new air-filter coughed out its breath of sea breeze, he'd shouted, "Yes", into the freshened atmosphere. With a well-timed stroke of luck, the air-filter performed its task just as he heard a firm knock on his door.

Introductions and hand shakes were exchanged before Vinny, pointing to the chair opposite his desk, asked his prospective client if she would like a cup of tea or coffee. She declined, saying she'd just had a coffee in Debenhams. Vinny felt relief wash over him, remembering that he had no biscuits to offer. Jimmy, his neighbour, lay great store in offering biscuits with tea or coffee, God knows why, but *he* was the educated one.

Within the few seconds it took, for the woman to walk round to the vacant chair and park herself in it, Vinny had assessed her age, occupation, and why her husband might be driven into the arms, and between the legs, of another, probably much younger and much more carefree, bit of skirt. With her ramrod-straight back, she sat perched on the edge of the chair with one hand gripping the thumb of the other. With mousy hair and dull clothes, she looked to be in her mid forties, but he reckoned on ten years younger. Very uptight and very much reminding him of the dedicated teachers of years ago.

"Mr Conway?"

Vinny suddenly realised that he was being addressed.

"Mr Conway, before we go any further, I'd just like to make absolutely sure that what is said between us stays between just the two of us. What I mean is, do you have colleagues working in the same offices?"

"No. No there's only me." Vinny was still getting used to being addressed as Mr Conway. And he liked the feeling it gave him. He looked down at the scribbled notes in front of him, clearing his throat before he asked. "Mrs Isabelle Thatcher, is that your real name?"

"Yes, do you think I should use a false one?"

"No, that's won't be necessary. Shall I call you Isabelle or…?"

"Mrs Thatcher will be fine," she interrupted with an air of impatience and a reluctance to acknowledge the historical importance of such a name.

Before Vinny got too involved in the nitty gritty of a case, he always made sure of two things: firstly, and most importantly, that he would get paid for his services, and secondly, that he had the means to contact the client to make sure that he got paid. If either were in doubt, he would ask for the money up-front or tell the person in question to sling their hook. Aware that diplomacy wasn't one of his strong points, and this woman wasn't the usual riff-raff who sought his services, he decided to tread carefully.

"Mrs Thatcher," he said, coughing to stifle a strong urge to snigger, "Before we begin the discussion on how I can be of service, I will need to know how I can contact you. I understand your need for secrecy but it's obvious we'll need to communicate at some point. Can I take your mobile number?"

"No, I don't have one and as I said on the phone, I don't have an email address either. The only computer in our home belongs to my teenage son and I'm not prepared to risk him finding out what I'm up to and, as I haven't got the use of the car, except for emergencies, I can't keep coming here. So what do you suggest?"

Vinny scratched the back of his head, which was usually *his* prelude to telling someone to, piss off, suddenly remembering that they were the very words that had earned him the sharp slaps across his legs from a teacher when he was in primary school.

Needing to gather his forces, he made a point of looking at his watch saying, "I'm going to fix myself a coffee. I'm sure we'll sort something out. Are you sure you wouldn't like anything, maybe a glass of water?"

"Thank you, Mr Conway, a glass of water would be very nice."

After sipping the last of the water, Isabelle relaxed back into her chair with a smile of satisfaction. She had done it. She had set the ball rolling and Mr Conway was the perfect gentleman to help her achieve her goal.

First of all, he'd suggested buying a mobile phone which she wasn't pleased about and told him so. She let slip that money was too tight to spend on unnecessaries. At this point, Mr Conway had looked a little concerned. She'd understood what he'd been thinking. Wanting to assure him that his fees would get paid, she'd delved into her handbag, and with an air of reverence, removed the gold and silver coins from their wrapping and placed them on his desk.

He didn't say a word but she could see he was impressed. Then the questions came. His excitement matched her own as she relayed exactly what had happened on the previous morning. She hadn't intended to be so forthcoming but she'd wanted to be honest and thought this was a man who could be trusted. She realized there were laws about reporting the finding of buried treasure; but selling the coins was her only way of paying his fees and he was very understanding about this. As to the ring, she'd sat nursing it on her right thumb throughout their earlier conversations about her husband, and felt momentarily bereft on removing it. But when he'd offered to try and solve the mystery of the letters 'NP' as well as finding out the current market value of the coins, she'd handed over the lot.

Mr Conway's suggestion of setting up a personal email account, an account that only the two of them knew about, was perfect. He'd proposed shortening her name and she'd interrupted telling him her husband called her, Izzie, and that she hated it. Mr Conway had smiled and said that *he,* was more inclined to shortening it to Bella, which in Spanish, means beautiful. With a blush on her cheeks she'd nodded in agreement. He'd carefully read aloud the email address and password whilst Isabelle copied it onto a piece of paper and tucked it into the back of her purse. Within no time at all, Mr Conway had turned on his computer and set up a hotmail account in the name of, bella-bovey@hotmail.co.uk, explaining that now she could walk into any library, contact him and retrieve his emails to her.

"It's such a relief to know that they are in safe hands," she said as she rose to say goodbye. She held his proffered hand with both of hers, and for a moment, had a strong urge to wrap her arms around him in gratitude but instead, squeezed again his large hand. Isabelle had shared her secret and she felt so much better.

Vinny closed the door on his new client. Rubbing his hands together he returned to his desk. After looking over the photograph and details connected to Shaun Thatcher, he clipped them together, placed them in an envelope marked Bella, and dropped them in his filing cabinet. His desk was now clear except for the coins and the gold ring, which he'd promised to place in his safe without delay. A smile creased his chubby cheeks as he pushed the ring onto his little finger and slipped the coins into the breast pocket of his shirt. Making sure his door was securely locked, he stepped out into the warm sunshine.

James Fairbank swore under his breath as seagulls screeched above his head. He was clinging to the near top rung of a ladder, trying to reach a trailing ribbon of seagull mess that ran down the outside of his office window. His cleaning lady wasn't due until Monday and the window cleaner had performed this task only yesterday and because he'd been finishing off the job of mounting Lyn's air filter, he hadn't noticed the filth and now the morning sun had baked it hard. At least the ladder was to hand.

"Good Morning, Jimmy! If you're looking to make a few bob on the side, *my* windows could do with a wash."

James glanced at his watch and twisted precariously to look down at his neighbour. "Actually, it's three minutes into the afternoon, Vincent. Were you coming to see me?"

"Just wanted to let you know that Stefan's coming for a few days, if you're on your own tonight maybe…" Vinny didn't want to throw away the chance of an evening's free food and drink if Jimmy could be coaxed to offer.

The solicitor looked tired but smiled when responding, "Lyn was really keen to get back this evening, but she's not sure she'll manage it. Maybe I'll consider it. Thank you, I like Stefan."

Before turning back to the window, James asked, "Vincent, can you do me a favour and hold the ladder steady, I need to reach up a little further."

Back on terra firma and glad that the odious job was done, a sense of fair play compelled James to invite Vincent in and offer refreshment. But to his great surprise, Vincent declined, saying he'd already drunk too much coffee and he had a very busy afternoon ahead.

"But, I would like your advise on something, Jimmy, if you could spare a few minutes. Do you know anyone who knows about old coins?"

"As a matter of fact, my father used to collect coins going back to medieval times is that old enough for you? I inherited his books and several are good for identification purposes. Mind you, the values they give will be out of date.

"What happened to his coin collection? You got that too I suppose."

"I'm afraid not. Along with many other things, the coins got sold to pay school fees."

"What a waste. I mean, what with the price of gold and silver rocketing, you'd have been quids in." He lay the coins on the solicitor's desk and removed the ring from his finger.

James picked up the ring and was impressed by its weight. His eyesight was excellent but he needed the extra light from his lamp to read the engraving and the makers mark. "This is a seventeenth century posy ring, Vincent, how did you come by it?"

Vinny's sense of worth had expanded throughout the morning, and he wasn't about to let it deflate. "This." He gave a casual wave across the objects in question. "Will be part payment for an assignment I've been given."

With raised eyebrows, the solicitor asked, "Is it legal? This stuff is subject to strict treasure trove laws, Vincent."

"I know all about that. My client is from a long-established family in Bovey Tracey. Back in the seventeen hundreds, her ancestors owned the field where these were found."

"But they still need to be declared, especially if these items were found after nineteen ninety seven, or eight, I'm not quite sure which."

"Doesn't apply, these belonged to my client's grandmother. I'd be very grateful if you could find out anything about them. I'll be back in an hour."

Chapter 6

Friday Afternoon—Torquay

With a pile of books to his left, and a page full of notes in front of him — none of which had anything to do with the business he should have been attending to — James Fairbank gave a sudden gasp of satisfaction. He had found the owner of the makers mark. NP were the initials of Nicholas Payne, a goldsmith who held premises in Exeter during the late 17th century.

Thoughts skipped through his mind. Again, unrelated to the subconscious pull of the Property-Sales Contracts that needed his attention. He'd done his utmost for Vincent regarding cataloguing the coins, even made a phone call to Spink — publishers of Coins of England — in order to obtain a more up-to-date valuation. James' most recent edition of their catalogue was published in 2000, indicating his father had still continued to subscribe long after his collection had been sold. In fact, right up to the year he had died. This realization saddened him.

But it was the ring that really interested him, forcing his mind back to the present. Unbeknown to Lyn, he had searched, without success, in many of the local jewellers for 22ct gold wedding bands. According to his father, presenting your new bride with a ring containing less gold, was being a cheapskate and invited penny-pinching tendencies to creep into all aspects of a partnership that would eventually crumble.

James' first marriage had crumbled very quickly, in spite of both of them having 22ct gold bands, specially commissioned. Even back then in the early 1990's, 22ct gold wedding bands were not available from stock. He had never been a wearer of jewellery but *she* had insisted. Stating, in strong terms, if a man chooses to marry, he should wear the proof of it with pride, just as a woman does. He could still recall the eye-watering cost of the two rings and how little wear they got. But for the life of him, he couldn't remember, nor did he care, what happened to the rings after the turbulent eighteen months they'd been together. *She* (he preferred not to use her name) eventually married his best friend, the friend who had mysteriously turned up at their honeymoon hotel in Venice.

This time things would be different and maybe this ring would prove to be just what he was looking for.

He crossed the hallway which separated his office from Lyn's studio and unlocked her door. An unfamiliar smell assailed his nostrils causing him to frown. Then he remembered, it was the air filter he'd recently installed. His clandestine intrusion into her private workspace was justified by the need to compare the size of the posy ring to the diamond ring he had given her almost a year ago. She always removed it whilst she was working on her floral arrangements — apparently the sap from certain plants left disfiguring patches on the shank which were difficult to polish out — and, she was uneasy about wearing it whilst working away in London. Fear of being robbed still held a tight grip on her after a thief stripped her of all her money whilst she slept during a long-haul-flight to Australia. Knowing Lyn, she would have a special place for it within this area. A smile pulled at his lips as his eyes swept the room and paused on a decorative wooden cabinet that held gift cards and ribbons. In the bottom drawer, underneath a froth of colourful bows, sat the ring. He was about to compare the size with the 17th century posy ring, when a noise from behind stopped him.

Vinny pushed open the solicitors front door, glanced into his office and on seeing it empty, strode purposefully down the hallway towards the open door of Lyn Porter's studio. On reaching it, he sauntered in, inhaling deeply on the sea-breeze scent that permeated the air.

"Bet you regret not hanging on to the air-filter panel, hey Jimmy? Sorry to rush you, mate, but I need to get moving. Any luck with the coins?"

With both rings concealed in the closed palm of his right hand, James ushered his neighbour out of the room and locked the door. He didn't speak until they were both sitting, either side of his desk.

"Yes, Vincent, I have catalogued your clients coins. The two silver coins — both half groats from the reign of Charles 1st, and judging from the condition, had been in circulation for some time — won't be worth a great deal, perhaps £100 or so, depending on who's buying. But, she'll be very happy to learn that the gold coin — a Unite of Charles 1st reign in Very Fine condition — is particularly valuable. My most recent catalogue is out of date but all three coins are there. I took the liberty of phoning Spink of London and spoke to…"

Vinny held his impatient tongue as the solicitor ran a manicured finger down the list in front of him. "A Mr Jarvis.

Back in the year 2000, a Nicholas Briot's hammered issue — which this is, see the flat top shield — in similar condition was valued at £5,250. Mr Jarvis, who seemed quite excited to hear of its existence, says it may well have tripled in value. He suggested that you take the coin down personally, if you want an accurate up-to-date valuation. He also added, if your client wanted to sell, in confidence naturally, they could suggest one of the top collectors. Obviously, this would incur a transaction fee…"

"I bet it would," Vinny interrupted, unable to hold his tongue any longer. "Well I really appreciate your efforts, Jimmy, but they're not for sale. These," he nodded towards the coins that he was carefully loading back into their respective wrappings, "are better than money in the bank. And the ring…" Vinny was about to say, was not his to sell, but now it was the solicitor's turn to interrupt, which was very unusual for him.

"I would be interested in buying the ring. Unless you feel inclined to present it to Lyn and myself as a wedding gift? No I thought not. Only teasing, Vincent but I am interested, if we can agree on a price." James slipped the two rings off his little finger, where side by side they had sat in perfect harmony, and handed one over.

Vinny twirled the ring between his fingers, wanting to know more. Frustrated with his lack of knowledge. Isabelle Thatcher felt a strong attachment to it. Jimmy, he could tell, wanted to possess it. What was he missing here?

"Can I ask you something, Jimmy?"

"Of course."

Vinny was running late. But knowledge was money. Settling back into his seat he anticipated the short lesson on his next question.

"What the fuck is a posy ring? Sounds like something very poncey."

Due to the time of day, traffic was reasonably light as Vinny raced towards Exeter. He'd made two phone calls before leaving and both of the recipients had responded favourably. He was definitely on a 'roll' and spending that little bit of extra time at the solicitors, had been well worth it. HIs status was heading in an upward direction and he intended his bank balance to soon follow. He checked his watch. It was two thirty-five. Should make it to Taffy's place in ten.

Taffy the jeweller worked from a small unit at the edge of one of Exeter's many industrial estates. His address and telephone number were to be found only in Vinny's 'special' contacts book. Because of the nature of Taffy's work — producing items in precious metals — he was ex-directory and only accepted commissions from people he knew or had been introduced by someone he knew.

Vinny had contacted Taffy about eight months ago after a visit from a business man named Len. Len had been attending a weekend seminar in Torquay and become infatuated with a single woman, known only as Carol. Before inviting Carol to join him for dinner, Len removed his wedding ring and the heavy, gold cross and chain — items, he'd sworn to his wife he'd never take off — and slipped them into his bedside cabinet. After a meal in the hotel's dining room and a night of Champagne-fueled-passion, he awoke to find that Carol had gone. It was only after showering and starting to pack that he found the two gold items had also disappeared. Len's concern, whether to accuse Carol or the hotel staff of the theft, paled into insignificance compared to the threat to his marriage. When Vinny was asked for his advice on how to proceed in such a delicate matter. He'd told Len straight. The jewellery would never come to light. Either fake a mugging — which involved the police and knocking yourself about a bit, or, replace the items yourself. Len chose the latter. There and then he brought up detailed photos of the items from his laptop, which Vinny printed off, allowing Taffy to make and replace within a few days.

Vinny screeched to a halt in front of the metal-clad door and gave three short hoots of the horn. After hearing the sound of heavy bolts being drawn back, the door creaked open and a narrow, lined face, topped with wispy, grey hair, peered out. A boney arm followed and waved him inside.

As before, Vinny was fascinated by the vast range of hammers and hand tools that were neatly held in racks around the purpose-built jewellers bench. But unlike last time, Vinny was very pressed for time. He placed Isabelle's ring in Taffy's outstretched palm.

"Like I said on the phone, Taffy, I can't leave the ring with you, so measure, weigh and write down all the info you need to make a perfect copy."

"I've told you before, I'm no faker!" The elderly man declared in a sing-song Welsh accent."

"I know that, Taffy. This is a job for a lady, landed gentry, almost. It was found on her land years ago but she wants to donate it to her local museum. All she asks is for a copy — same size, same weight and same writing inside. How soon can it be done and how much?" Vinny ignored Taffy's tuts and sighs as the jeweller pressed a high-magnification loop into his left eye and studied the ring. Vinny checked his watch, picked up the morning paper from the spare chair and flicked it open — he had neither time nor inclination for any further verbal, too many plans were formulating in his head.

London

Good food, good company, two glasses of sparkling wine and the satisfaction of a job well-done, put Lyn in a much better frame of mind. They'd decided to eat at, Toni's, an Italian bistro within walking distance from Jill's house; a place they'd been meaning to visit for some time. Candy was on one of her, no-alcohol bouts and didn't mind the drive over, or picking up the bill. She could afford it, she'd said, adding that the pleasure she got from an afternoons chit-chat with them was priceless.

"Ladies, would you like to move to the terrace for more coffee?" asked the handsome, Italian waiter as he started to clear their table. Three pairs of eyes followed where he indicated. An outdoor area, barely noticeable when they'd arrived, was now transformed into an enticing oasis of dappled-shade. During the two hours engrossed in eating and talking, the sun, inch by inch, had crept across the outdoor terrace. Instead of umbrellas, palms and other exotic plants served the purpose of creating shade.

"I need a holiday", murmured Lyn after she'd edged her chair into full sun, turned her face to the heavens, scraped off her three-inch-high heeled shoes and propped her feet on a vacant chair.

"Well take one. Isn't that the point of being self-employed? And now is your best chance because we've got nothing on for two weeks, and even then it's only Candy's lingerie do. Don't mean to be rude, Candy, but you and I could manage that with our eyes closed." Jill was loosing patience with Lyn. It wasn't so much that her friend needed a break, she needed to make up her mind about this wedding. When and where it would be held.

"Jill's right," agreed Candy. We can easily manage without you, provided the stock you hold for me is still good. I thought I remembered you saying you and James were taking a holiday abroad during this month to discuss the wedding and also to celebrate his 50th birthday." Isn't that why you made extra silk-florals, as an emergency?"

Lyn opened one eye and squinted at her friends. "Do we *have* to talk about this now, it's such a lovely afternoon?"

"Yes!" They barked, in unison.

"When did you say his Lordship's birthday is?" asked Jill, taking a pen and her pocket diary from her bag. "Handy you staying an extra night, I can grab a card and a little something from the Pound Shop, wrap it up this evening and you can take it back with you." She looked over to Candy and winked and waited for Lyn's reaction. It didn't come.

Lyn's mind was miles away. The mention of James' fiftieth birthday, was another thing she still had to sort out. His family were bound to want to make a big thing of it. And then the inevitable would happen. Questions about the wedding.

She was brought screeching back to reality as Jill grabbed her foot and starting tickling. "OK! OK! You've got my attention. His birthday is in nine days time —a week on Sunday — and I haven't got a clue what to get him. Any bright ideas?"

"I know just the thing," said Jill, checking her watch. "And we'll get it sorted this evening. Hubby's taking the boys for a MacDonald's at five, provided I pick them up from school. We've got fifteen minutes left."

The waiter arrived with a tray of complimentary coffees and liquors. Even Candy couldn't resist accepting. All cares were laid aside as they watched the coffee beans disperse their flavour into the burning Sambuca.

Exeter

Vinny reached into the glovebox of his car, rummaged around till he found a plastic bag containing an assortment of foreign coins. Slamming the door he made his way to the car park's Pay and Display stand, grinning as he slid

two of the heavier coins into the slot, plucking at the emerging ticket below.

He entered Exeter St. Davids railway station just as an announcement was being made. "Brilliant!" His fist punched the air. The posh, nasal voice was apologizing for the thirty-five minute delay of the Paddington train which had just shunted to a halt on Platform One. *Still on a roll*, he thought. Within seconds, Vinny spotted the tall, angular frame of his Bulgarian friend, smiling as their eyes made contact.

Stefan climbed into the passenger seat and was about to fling his sports bag over the back when the sight of something familiar stopped him.

"I see you interested in hunting treasure, Vincent."

Vinny half turned and cast his eye over the state-of-the-art metal detector which lay partly exposed amongst two blankets.

"You've seen these before then? When I spent that week with you in Bulgaria, most of the stuff I saw was ancient. The sort of rubbish you buy at car boot sales here."

Stefan didn't respond until his friend had maneuvered out of the tight parking space and into the flow of traffic. "In Bulgaria, criminals have nearly all money. They can afford latest and best of everything. This gold-finding machine is more than five years old. Two later models already exist in my country."

"Bastard", Vinny hissed, recalling how the guy who hired

out the detector spouted that it was the hottest thing on the market.

"I wouldn't have thought there'd be much call for them over there. I mean, do you have much of a history? Is there any treasure to be found?"

"Yes, much treasure, Vincent. But can only search if you pay big money to gang leader. And when you find treasure, you also give half to him."

"If I'd already paid him and then he wanted more, I'd tell him to get stuffed!"

"Then he shoot you and have it all."

Vinny coughed and wriggled in his seat making a mental note not to visit that part of the world again. But still needing to know, he asked. "So, I take it you're familiar with these machines, Stefan?"

"Yes, I use that kind of machine before."

"Did you find anything?"

"I find what I look for, yes."

"You and me are going treasure hunting this weekend, and I promise you, what we find will be all ours."

Chapter 7

Friday Evening—Bovey Tracey

Isabelle was annoyed. In fact she was livid. As a rule, Shaun would always go down to the local pub on a Friday night. But not tonight. Oh no! Tonight, father and son had decided to watch a football match at home, which meant she was banished from her own sitting room. Even more galling, was creeping around her own home, waiting for an opportune time to make a phone call to Mr Conway. He needed to be informed that her husband wouldn't be in the Carpenters Arms after all. She would have to think seriously about accepting the mobile phone Mr Conway had offered her. He'd said it was an unregistered, pay-as-you-go, whatever that meant, and would lower the risk of Shaun discovering what she was up to. He'd also said it would only add a few pounds to her bill and, he'd be prepared to buy it back after his services were over. Such a nice man.

She'd got back to Bovey Tracey at Twelve-thirty, half an hour before the library closed for the day — Friday was now a half day, thanks to cut backs — but it had been time enough to try out her new email address and confirm to Mr Conway where she expected Shaun to be over the next couple of evenings. She'd supplied a recent photograph. No need for him to ask questions. No need for local nosey-parkers to get curious.

Mr Conway had wanted to start trailing, that's what he'd called it, trailing Shaun as soon as possible. That suited her just fine but now, the trailing wouldn't start until tomorrow.

London

A squeal of delight permeated the downstairs computer area of Jill's home.

Above, a bedroom door opened. "Mum! Keep the noise down! I'm trying to get through my homework."

"Sorry, Lauren, thought you'd gone with Daddy and the boys to MacDonald's." Jill heard her thirteen-year-old daughter's grumbled response —I'd rather die and go to hell" — before the bedroom door slammed shut.

Lyn and Jill had spent over an hour on the computer with a bottle of wine within easy reach. With Jill's inspirational idea as a jumping off point, it hadn't taken long to find what they'd wanted. But, as in most things, the devil was in the detail, and as the stress levels to complete the transaction went up, the contents of the wine bottle went down. By the time everything was completed, confirmed by email, and copies printed out, the wine bottle was empty and they both had the giggles. They'd been surfing the net for James's birthday present. Found the perfect thing, according to Jill, and had just committed to it. A squeal of delight from Jill. A squeal of apprehension from Lyn.

Bovey Tracey

Shaun Thatcher flicked off the TV in disgust. There was still half an hour before the program was finished but the game was over and who needed to listen to three overpaid wankers giving their views on why England had lost.

He'd showered and changed earlier but sniffed his armpits. There had been a few tense moments in the game. And, he'd been eating cheese-and-onion-flavoured crisps. He headed quickly to the bathroom and almost collided with Izzy.

Her eyes scanned him from top to toe making him feel like a piece of shit, then asked accusingly "Where do you think you're going?"

"It's Friday night, where do you think I'm going?"

"But you said you were watching the football…I…I wish I knew where I stood with you."

"Now don't fucking start! The match is over, and I'm off down the pub and because I'm late going, it means I'll be late getting back, so don't wait up." Shaun moved to push past his wife but she blocked his escape.

"Don't you dare use such foul language," she hissed. "Robert can hear you."

"He can hear your constant nagging, as well, and I know which grieves him most."

Shaun headed into the cold, cloudless night, taking deep breaths of the autumn-scented air which held a mixture of wood-burning-smoke, freshly turned soil and a slight hint of manure. *I hope Jules finds it more enticing than cheese-and-onion crisps,* he thought, as he pulled up his collar and plunged his hands into his jacket pockets.

Torquay

For the third time since he'd arrived, Stefan was made aware of the new air filter. Vincent was very proud of it. He'd spoken of it whilst driving back from the station before showing Stefan a list of security jobs, each for fitting stronger locks on doors and windows. They all needed to be done before his return to London next weekend. He was also told of Vincent's new client, a wife looking for proof of her husband's adultery — which Vincent would carry out, alone and after dark.

Vincent was becoming more excited as he explained the reason for hiring the treasure hunting machine. "I picked up all the door and window locks before meeting you at the station, Stefan, so that sets us free to start work first thing Monday morning. Which means, you and me have got the whole weekend off, except for a bit of evening surveillance work."

Vincent opened his desk drawer and removed a small polythene bag. Four items were carefully unwrapped and placed in full view.

Stefan reached toward the ring but first sought a nod of approval before picking it up. From the colour and the weight he knew it was quality; old quality. He squinted inside and saw words that were new to him. "What is the words about, Vincent?"

"This, my friend," said Vincent as he leaned back in his chair bringing his palms together, reminding Stefan of James Fairbank, "Is what is known as a 17th century Posy Ring. A Posy has nothing to do with flowers. It's a motto or a line of verse engraved on the inside of the ring, as in this case, or, on the outside of much earlier rings. This particular posy, *Providence divine hath made thee mine,*" Vincent looked at

Stefan expecting a response. Stefan remained silent. Vincent continued. "In plain English means, this guy got lucky in securing the bird he fancied. There is also the initials, NP, which my research confirms is Nicholas Payne, a goldsmith who at the time was based at Exeter. "

"I impressed with your knowledge, Vincent, and this?" Stefan picked up the gold coin and gauged its weight in the palm of his hand."

Vincent bent nervously towards the open palm fearing the coin might fall and be damaged. "Careful! That's a fifteen grand coin you're tossing around."

Stefan carefully replaced the coin alongside the others. "This is reason for you hire treasure machine, no?"

"This is reason I hire treasure machine; Yes! And you and I are all set for finding more."

"You have permission for searching this place?"

"Just let me worry about the details, Stefan. All I ask of you is that you keep shtum about everything you've heard in this office. We've been invited to eat with Jimmy. Not a word about treasure hunting, OK?"

Stefan never repeated anything to anyone, and rarely asked questions. He found that most of his knowledge came from patiently watching and reading the language of the body. Language that didn't lie. Language that crossed all borders.

James struggled to unlock his porch door. He was balancing a piping hot parcel of fish, chips and mushy-peas whilst the incessant ringing of his mobile phone, left on his office desk, demanded attention.

He picked it up just as the ringing stopped and saw that it had been Lyn. Checking his watch, he pressed 'return call'.

"Hello, sweetheart, I thought you'd said you wouldn't be

phoning until after nine. Is everything all right?" Lyn answered in the affirmative saying it was just a quick call to ask a favour.

"Ask away, but I *am* about to eat, is it something I can call you back on?" He listened to what she wanted, scribbled a few notes on his pad and promised to call back, within the hour. Vincent had told him, emphatically, that he had business to attend to later and couldn't stay long. No sooner had he laid down the phone, than the chink of bottles signaled the arrival of his guests.

Three long strides and James stood before Lyn's studio. After unlocking the door he ushered his guests in. Both stood silently watching as the solicitor unwrapped three inner packages, steaming and smelling of the fish and chips shop he'd just visited. With the wrapping open, he placed each portion in front of the three stools, positioned for this purpose. Reaching for a tray, containing condiments and a plate of bread and butter, James broke the silence.

"Welcome gentlemen to a typical Friday evening supper of fish and chips. Take a seat and get stuck in before it gets cold. I didn't bring any glasses, Vincent, I know you and Stefan prefer to drink beer straight from the bottle and on this occasion, so will I."

Vincent's dropped jaw lifted to enable him to ask "Does Lyn know you're using her pristine studio as a makeshift cafe?" While waiting for a response he wrung the neck of one of the bottles of lager and poured half of it down his throat, releasing a loud belch.

James offered round the plate of bread before answering. "It's the perfect opportunity to try out the new air-filter, which as you know, I gave to Lyn. I've been extremely busy catching up on paperwork and outstanding contracts so that when Lyn returns we'll have the rest of the weekend free and, the last time I took the trouble to cook fresh fish with a sauce, you made the point that you prefer fish cooked in batter and eaten out of paper, 'like in the old days,' I think you said. Also, I know you're busy this evening, so when we've eaten, all this" James waved an arm over the scattering of food, paper and polystyrene trays. "It can be swiftly put in the bin. No washing up, and no unsavoury odour left behind, thanks to that little contraption." As he looked across to the newly-installed panel, it gasped fresh, scented air.

Stefan handed James one of the beers before dipping a piece of battered fish into his pot of mushy peas, swallowing it appreciatively. "Is very good, Mr Fairbank, I eat this every Friday in London, but this fish is very fresh, maybe caught today, no?"

"Thank you, Stefan. Yes, the fish is brought in fresh from Brixham every day."

After twenty minutes of lip-smacking, chomping, finger-licking and all the noises allied to guzzling beer from the bottle, Vincent scrunched his place setting into a diminished mass that fitted neatly into his chubby hand and aimed it at Lyn's polished, stainless steel bin. It missed. He looked at James for a reaction. And when none was forthcoming, he sighed and slipped wearily off his stool.

"This bin is clean enough to eat out of, Jimmy." Sure you want me to drop this greasy paper in it?"

James finished chewing his mouthful of food and wiped his lips on his paper napkin before answering. "It's not a waste bin, Vincent. It holds water for cut blooms while Lyn is working on an arrangement. There's a black bin liner by the door, I'd prefer you to drop it in there." James checked his watch.

"We're not keeping you from anything are we?" Vincent asked as he gathered up the redundant wrappings and empty bottles to place them in the black bag. "The surveillance job I'm working on, doesn't start until tomorrow, so no need to rush on our account. It's nice to get together, blokes only, if you know what I mean? After all, you'll soon be shackled in wedlock. Make the most of the freedom, man."

James resisted rising to the taunt. His mind was more fixed on returning Lyn's call; first he needed to carry out the favour she'd asked and wanted to be alone for that. He needed to change the subject.

"What was your clients reaction to the value of her coins and is she happy to sell the ring?" The questions clearly embarrassed Vincent. He turned to Stefan and then back to James but no words were forthcoming. Suddenly, the phone rang in James's office and he found the capability to speak.

"You see to your call, Jimmy, we'll be off as soon as Stefan's finished his beer."

James snapped up the phone, heard Lyn's voice and said he was just about to call. That he was in the middle of counting them and if she'd give him five minutes, he'd get back to her." Lyn insisted on holding. All he had to do was open the racked-out tall cupboard in her studio, and count the amount of silk, floral arrangements and their colour. "Right, I'll just be a minute." He lay down the phone and grabbed the note book and pen before quietly closing his office door.

He marched back into the studio and quietly closed the door behind him — placing a finger to his lips to indicate silence. Vincent and Stefan watched as the solicitor pulled out tray after tray of floral arrangements of varying shades of pink and purple. He counted and made notes on his pad before leaving the room.

Stefan, making sure the studio was cleared of rubbish, led the way out of Lyn's studio. The solicitor's office door was open and he gave a silent salute of thanks as James, still on the phone, caught his eye. Vincent followed, calling out "Thanks for the hospitality, Jimmy, give my best to Lyn."

Bovey Tracey

Isabelle awoke suddenly unsure whether it was a noise or the dream that had dragged her from slumber She lay motionless for what seemed like an age. Nothing. Relaxing, her mind groped for the disappearing fragments of the recurring dream — a tall stranger offering her…something? She turned to her bedside clock. Two minutes after midnight. The other half of the double bed was cold and empty. That wasn't unusual these days. Maybe Shaun was on the sofa. Or, more likely, he was with his tart.

I HAVE CONNECTED. I HAVE FOUND A LINK. BELLA! BELLA! BELLA!

Chapter 8

Saturday Morning—On Route to Torquay

It wasn't yet nine o'clock as Lyn hugged the outside lane of the M5 motorway towards Exeter. She'd woken early. Very early. Her every thought bound up on what she had committed to. And her desperation to allow as much time as possible for the necessary preparation, propelled her frenzied actions. Jill had been right. Lyn's underlying stress was due to uncertainty. Uncertainty about the future. Hopefully, after the next seven days, all those uncertainties will have been dealt with.

She pulled into the Exeter Services, looking forward to her first coffee of the day. She'd risen at six o'clock, drinking only two large glasses of water to stem the dehydration before hitting the road. But now, she would allow herself the luxury of a proper break, maybe even a bite to eat, while she ran through the paperwork of James's gift. She grabbed the weighty, A4 envelope from the glove compartment and padded across the sparsely filled car park, heading towards the aroma of freshly-ground-coffee.

Torquay

Vinny relieved Stefan of one of the mugs of instant coffee he had just brought into his office. He took a sip and gasped his disapproval. "What the fuck! There's no sugar in it, Stefan."

"You tell me last night you want to lose weight and not put sugar in your coffee."

"Did I? I must have been drunk or I'm going fucking senile."

"You also say, you want to no swear anymore. And if you forget, I to make sure you put £1 coin in that box." Stefan pointed to a 'Save the Children' charity box perched on the shelf above Vincent's desk. "You say your new lady client doesn't like men who swear."

"Just get me some f..f...flipping sugar, will you. We've got a fair amount of trudging around to do this morning and I need the energy. All right?"

By the time Stefan returned with the sweetened coffee, an ordinance survey map of Bovey Tracey was spread across Vinny's desk and a fat finger was tracing it's way around the nucleus of the town centre.

"Shouldn't take too long to find," mumbled Vinny as he reached for the coffee.

"You mean gold or place where gold is hidden?"

"I mean, the field where the gold was found."

Stefan lowered his head to the map. "This town has fields all round, how you know which one?"

"I know enough to be able to find it, Stefan. We will locate and survey it in daylight. Then rape and pillage it after dark!"

Bovey Tracey

Isabelle paced the small perimeter of the library's interior. Unaware that it was customary to prearrange a time for the use of computers, she'd arrived at 10.00am, opening time, only to be told that a computer wouldn't be available until 10.30am.

Glancing again at the library clock her stomach clenched — twelve minutes to go and only thirty minutes to write what she needed to say. Dragging over a chair she sat and checked the notes she'd made on the folded piece of paper: email address, password and the salient points of what needed to be communicated to Mr Conway. Basically, Shaun would be in the Carpenters Arms that evening and after closing time, he and a bunch of the regulars would be going on to a local party to celebrate someone's 30th birthday.

Shaun had been already up and ready to leave for work when she'd ambled into the kitchen, bleary-eyed from lack of sleep. He'd mentioned the party, and actually invited her along, if she wanted to go. She'd given him a certain look that made answering unnecessary.

Her thoughts returned to the computer and her list of notes. Absentmindedly tapping her teeth with the pen, she decided to add one more thing. She wanted the ring back. She hadn't really wanted to part with it in the first place. She would ask Mr Conway to return it as soon as possible.

Seeing the old man packing his papers into his folder, meant her allocated computer would soon be free. She shoved the notes into a pocket and headed toward the private corner. In no time at all, Isabelle was looking at her own mail page. She clicked 'new message' and started to enter Mr Conway's email address. She glanced around her. No one was about as she slowly tapped in the message. Suddenly a clear, audible 'ping' interrupted her flow. A message had arrived for her. Without thinking she clicked onto it, feeling sure it was Mr Conway using one of his other mail addresses. She read and reread the few words several times. Intrigued but nervous. *Who…? What did it mean?* She wondered as she read the message again.

DEAREST BELLA, THE RING IS OUR LINK. TAKE BACK POSSESSION OF IT. NP

What should she do? What could she do? She deleted it.

Time was ticking away. Isabelle returned to the unfinished email to Mr Conway. After informing him of Shaun's whereabouts for that evening, she finished with.

PS I'd like my ring back as soon as possible. Considered, and decided it sounded like she didn't trust him. It was deleted and amended.

PS Please would it be possible to meet soon. I know it sounds silly, but I need the comfort of my ring.
    Thank you, in advance, for being understanding.
    Isabelle.

Torquay

James heard Lyn's car reversing onto the gravelled parking bay and skipped down the back steps to greet her. After a long, passionate kiss he released his hold to arms length, searching her face for indications of how successful the two-day-trip away had been. "You look flushed with excitement, sweetheart. Do we need to empty your car straight away or is there time for coffee first?" James had worked hard catching up to date with all his outstanding contracts and was determined to keep this weekend as relaxed and amicable as possible and to hold to his promise about discussing their future wedding plans.

"I've not long since had coffee," said Lyn as she reached into the car for the A4 envelope and her handbag. "I've got a surprise for you," she smiled teasingly. "So what's it to be first, coffee or surprise?" She knew James hated surprises and mentally planned her release of information around the usual intimacy of sharing coffee.

"Mm, surprise, I think. Then we'll toast the surprise with the coffee."

Caught unexpectedly, Lyn almost blurted out, maybe he wouldn't want to toast this particular surprise, but the memory of Jill's insistent drilling of keeping positive, kept her silent. She walked ahead of him clutching the envelope, trying to remember the subtleties that her friend had rammed home to her. Once in the security of her own studio, she smiled sweetly and handed him the envelope. "Happy Birthday, darling."

Without taking his eyes from hers, James reached for the plain, manilla envelope and wondered why it should be presented, unceremoniously, a week before the actual day of celebration. He sensed the uncertainty but her face gave nothing away. "Shouldn't I wait for next week to…?"

"No! No, you need to open it as soon as possible," she interrupted before clamping her lips shut, afraid that she would start gabbling and ruin everything. She lowered her tense body into a nearby chair, and determined not to say a word, began to take deep, silent breaths whilst waiting for the reaction. It came on the third, quivering inhalation and without knowing it, she held that breath for almost thirty seconds.

"Lyn, this flight is for tomorrow. I have commitments to fulfill, I can't just, just jet off with only a days warning."

"Why not? It's called being spontaneous. Isn't that what surprises are all about?" The slow release of the held breath kept the control in her voice and her smile in place. She watched as James' long fingers flicked from the cover of the glossy magazine — showing palm trees framing an idyllic scene of golden sands, blue sea and cloudless blue sky — to the flight confirmation stapled to the inside cover. No sign on his face of excitement at the thought of a weeks subtropical sunshine on an Island paradise. The only thing that loomed out of his reaction was the word, 'warning'. Why use that particular word? Anyone else would have said, 'with only a day's notice.' His next words interrupted her flow of psychoanalysis.

"Was this Jill's ideas? I know how impulsive she can be." James waited for the berating that would surely follow. It didn't, and because it didn't, he knew he was already half caught in the trap. He lay down the magazine, placed his hands on either side of Lyn's chair and said. "Thank you, sweetheart, for such a thoughtful, and generous present. While we are drinking coffee, we'll discuss if it's at all possible to leave for this holiday tomorrow. If it proves impossible, then we'll simply change the flight and I'll pay the difference." James planted a soft kiss in the centre of Lyn's forehead before leaving for the kitchen.

Lyn's rising frustration was halted by a strange sound in her studio. And the strange sound (reminiscent of a heavy sigh) was followed by a strange odour. Not unpleasant, but unfamiliar. She'd been half aware of a lingering smell when she'd first walked into her studio, but other matters had taken precedence. She slowly turned to the area where the heavy sigh had emitted it's breath, smiling and drinking in the simple offering of a whiff of fresh sea air. Almost simultaneously, the scent of freshly-ground coffee overpowered it.

Another deep breath. This time her own, and she was back on firm ground. "I've just had a demo from the air-filter and I love it. Thank you for finding the time to install it for me. Hope you're not wishing you'd kept it for yourself." Lyn moved the holiday paperwork to one side, but still clearly in view, to allow James to place the large tray between them on her desk.

"No, you know me, I'm quite content with the familiar. Besides, my guess is, when you eventually learn of the cost of running it, the refreshing smell of sea breezes may well rapidly lose it's appeal. Until then, I'm pleased that you're pleased."

Lyn watched in silence as James, in his usual precise way, poured two coffees, positioned two chocolate digestive biscuits on a crisp, white table napkin and placed each on either side of the desk. He lifted his coffee and held it out. Without thinking she did the same.

"Here's a toast," he announced as though 'best man' at a wedding, "to spending a week's relaxing holiday in warm sunshine where we can plan our future." A slight pause. "And if it proves to be impossible to fly out tomorrow, then we will leave as soon as possible."

Lyn's frustration returned. She carefully lay down the coffee cup, which hadn't been chinked to seal the deal, and said in a calm and controlled voice. "I have a business too, James, and next week is the only chance I can get away until March. I've been carefully planning this for weeks, taking into account your commitments as well as my own. You've already admitted that your paperwork is bang up-to-date so what's the problem?"

James didn't get the chance to answer.

A loud rap on the unlocked back door, followed by it's opening and Vincent Conway's coarse voice demanding the solicitors attention, served only to increase Lyn's impatience. A heavy sigh before James rose and left the room. Lyn marched over to her studio door and slammed it shut. This was *her* space and she had no intention of allowing Conway to contaminate it.

Vinny shoved the large, polished, stainless-steel garden spade into Stefan's hand and said, "Is that big enough for you?"

Stefan nodded as he inspected the immaculate tool, feeling concern that it wouldn't be returned in the same way. "This, I think is new, Vincent."

"So? New broom, sweeps clean. Hopefully, new spade, digs more gold."

They had been all set to leave over an hour ago. Then two things had intervened. On impulse Vinny had decided to check his emails whilst Stefan rinsed the coffee mugs. Amongst the junk mails he'd noticed one from Isabelle and curiosity had got the better of him. Initially the message was bringing him up to date on Shaun's expected whereabouts on Saturday night. That was fair enough and showed that the communication route they'd set up was working. What followed made him bristle. She was whining about missing her ring and could they meet up soon just to hand it back.

Didn't she trust him? And, didn't she realise that a 'covert operation' is to take place secretly. If he was seen meeting her, his cover would be blown. He had wasted over twenty minutes replying to it, only to delete it because he couldn't get the tone right. Stefan hadn't helped. The looks and jibes he'd made such as, "Maybe, Vincent, she is losing her heart for you," and then, "Isabelle is having good impact on you Vincent, why you not meet her and ask where is field, then we have more time searching for treasure?"

When finally they were ready to leave, Vinny handed Stefan the detector and a small rucksack. He'd looked at Vinny in that 'knowing', annoying way of his and asked, "Where is digging tool?" Starting to get really pissed off, Vinny had upended the rucksack and several objects clattered to the floor: a 500ml plastic bottle of water, two Mars bars, a black plastic bum-bag for the finds, a torch containing new batteries and last but not least, the all important garden trowel for digging. Stefan picked up the trowel and giggled, something Vinny had never seen him do before and it was not a pretty sight. Between bouts of this girlish behaviour, Stefan had explained that nothing smaller than a full-size, long-handled spade, would be any use for searching on a ploughed field. Vinny was left with no choice. He wasn't prepared to cough up the money for a garden spade he was never likely to use again, so he'd gone on the borrow to Jimmy.

The unseasonable warm weather of the last few days had ended abruptly. As Vinny and Stefan carried their gear to the parking bay at the back of the premises, grey sky bore down and a bitterly-cold, easterly wind cut across their path, causing each, in their own language, to curse out loud. With head bent low, Vinny almost collided with Lyn Porter as she struggled to hold onto a tray full of ribbons and bows she'd just removed from her car. She grunted an apology and veered off in the direction of her own back door. They heard the slam of a car boot and James Fairbank came into view. He was carrying the remainder of his woman's possessions from her car, and acknowledged the presence of the two men with a simple nod of the head.

Vinny sensed an atmosphere that was chillier than the east wind and responded, "Back to winter, Jimmy. If I were in your position mate, I'd take a nice little holiday in the sun. Do you both a world of good."

Chapter 9

Saturday Afternoon—Bovey Tracey

The ferocity of the gusting wind seemed to chill Isabelle to the bone as she struggled to gather the sheets and duvet covers from the garden washing line. The sky was darkening fast and the bedding was almost dry. She'd be foolish to risk leaving it any longer. Reaching frantically for the pegs that held the last duvet cover she felt the first splatter of fat raindrops. Then the heavens opened. She ran for the scullery door with her laden basket, unaware that one of the sheets had half spilled out and was being dragged along the ground.

Not caring that it would cause a row, she turned up the thermostat on the boiler — the kitchen was warm but the rest of the house, especially the bedrooms, were cold. Shaun would be back from work in ten minutes, starving hungry and demanding his lunch, but she needed to sort the washing first.

"Shit!" She shouted on noticing the king-sized duvet cover streaked with grass and mud stains. Lack of sleep over the previous two nights was beginning to take its toll. As well as feeling chilled, her head felt as though a tight, metal band had been placed around her temples, and by gradual increments, some malicious force was tightening the hold. She needed her ring. Needed to feel reassured by it. The association brought back to mind the mysterious email. Had it really happened? How could it have? No one else knows her email address. Maybe she was becoming a little confused because of the overexcitement.

After shoving the soiled bedding in a bucket of hot suds, placing the last of the beef stew on the Rayburn and cutting several doorsteps of wholemeal bread, she sat in the rocking chair close to the stove hands gripping a mug of hot chamomile tea, waiting for her husband and the inevitable anger.

Shaun Thatcher cursed aloud as he kicked the scullery door shut and discarded his outer garments on the mat. "It's bloody horrible out there!" He entered the kitchen, heading straight for the warmth of the Rayburn, accidentally nudging his wife's arm as she stirred the contents of the saucepan. Izzy remained silent as she wiped the drips from the jogged spoon, sighing wearily.

"Robert not back yet? he asked, pressing his backside against the warm metal.

"He's agreed to do extra hours each Saturday until Christmas. By then he should have enough saved for the Iphone. Do you want any pickled cabbage with this?"

"What is it?" Shaun peered into the saucepan. "Oh, not that beef stew again! Christ, Izzy, you made that nearly a week ago."

"We would have eaten it up by now if the weather hadn't turned so warm. What do you expect me to do, throw away perfectly good food when we can barely afford to pay the bills?"

"Well, it's nice to bloody see that you're starting to take notice of what I've been saying for the last twelve months. Believe me things are going to get a lot worse." The sound of wood shifting across uneven slate filled the kitchen as Shaun dragged his chair to the end of the table. He was only two foot from the stove, but he still didn't feel warm.

"I tell you, Izzy, everyone at work, except for the bloody management and office staff, are desperate for overtime. I'm lucky being in the warehouse, I can work Saturday mornings, but the tighter things get for everyone, orders will start dropping off and who knows, they'll be forced to make redundancies or cut the hours. The bills are piling up, Izzy. What we need is a modern two-bedroomed house in Exeter. Cheaper living costs, more opportunities for work. Not just for me. Think about Robert and you could help by going back to work and lift the burden a bit. We can't afford to live in a three-bedroomed, thatched cottage. Everybody thinks because you don't have a mortgage, you must be rollin' in it. This place is a money pit. You know it and I know it."

Isabelle had heard it all before. She didn't have the energy to argue. Her headache was getting worse and all she wanted was a bit of peace and quite, to feel warm and catch up on sleep. "I've turned the boiler up a bit," she said clearing away his empty dish. I think I'm coming down with something, so if you don't mind I'm going for a lie down."

"And I'm gonna contact one of the local estate agents. Get an indication of what this place is worth. You can't bury your head in the sand forever. We can't afford to go on living here."

Clutching a hot water bottle under her arm, Isabelle paused on her way to the bedroom. "You're forgetting Shaun, this is my house, left to me by my grandmother. And I have no intention of selling it. And If you spent less time in the pub, we wouldn't be having this conversation."

With clenched fists, Shaun remained silent as he heard the latch of the door leading up to the bedrooms, the creaking of the stairs and the giveaway 'clonk' of worn bed springs. All familiar sounds but he hated every one of them.

Torquay

James lay the phone carefully back in its cradle and drew a line through the last of the three names on the pad. He still hadn't fully committed to the weeks holiday. Without first feeling uncommitted to others, how could he? Both Sara, his part time secretary who only worked two mornings a week and Sadie, his cleaning lady, who came early on Monday mornings, seemed quite happy about the sudden cancellation of their services. Each said that a short holiday would do him and Lyn a world of good. However, the third commitment was far more complicated and not so easy to wriggle out of. And even after accomplishing it, instead of relief and the happy expectations of a weeks relaxation with Lyn, he found a veil of guilt marring the anticipation.

He hadn't visited his sister in weeks, in spite of promises to the contrary. On hearing about his impromptu holiday in the sun, *she* wasn't filled with similar good wishes as his secretary and cleaner. Mother was still battling against painful shingles, which, due to the affected area around the hairline, had caused severe impairment to her vision. This, coupled with the arthritis that had worsened as she'd aged, meant that Helen's help was needed more and more. James' weekend promise of wedding discussions with Lyn, had kept him from agreeing to visiting Helen and his mother until Tuesday morning when his secretary would be in the office to take any phone calls. However, he'd found himself thrust into the uncomfortable situation of making yet another excuse why he couldn't get over there.

Helen was a good person and extremely talented in her profession as an architect. And she too had commitments. Weeks ago James had offered to pay for a private nurse to alleviate the problem. Mother would have none of it; *she* felt it was a daughter's place to do the caring and if that wasn't forthcoming, she'd manage on her own. All his sister wanted from James, was a little moral support and his company from time to time. Helen had also expressed disappointment that he wouldn't be sharing his important birthday with his family. James had pointed out that leaving his visit for at least another week, meant that Mother should be further along the road to recovery and he and Lyn could turn the visit into a double celebration — his birthday and the decided wedding day. His mother had made it clear on several occasions that seeing him happily married before she died was her greatest wish. This, had gone some way to appeasing his sister. The next promised visit was arranged for the following Tuesday. Two days after their return from Lanzarote.

Noises above caught his attention as Lyn shifted furniture in the room above her studio. Not for the first time, James wondered about how much would change, once they were married.

Feeling confident that they would be leaving for a sub-tropical holiday in just a few short hours, Lyn, with the help of a chair, removed the small suitcase from the top shelf of the wardrobe. She was in her spare bedroom with summer clothing spread across the double-beds bare mattress. A mattress that had never been slept on.

As expected, James hadn't been overjoyed with her unusual and extravagant gift but as Jill had drilled into her, once he was there, unwinding and soaking up the fantastic weather, he'll be wanting to do it more often. However, he hadn't been the easy pushover that Jill had led her to believe. 'He had his commitments for the coming week and if he couldn't reschedule those commitments, the holiday would have to be postponed...' At this point in their strained conversation, Lyn had remembered cutting him off and blurting out that changing the date of the holiday wasn't an option. The package, inclusive of flight, hotel suite and breakfasts, was non-negotiable and nonrefundable due to booking it so late. She'd almost added that if he couldn't go, rather than waste the money, she would ask Jill to join her. But she had reigned in her frustration, knowing in her heart that she wanted and needed this time with James. Their love for each other was far more important than anything, or anyone else. She'd wrapped her arms about him and conveyed these thoughts through words, smiles and long meaningful kisses.

"How did it go?" she asked, popping her head around the door of James' office and finding him running a duster over the empty, highly-polished desk. She made the excuse of wanting to know who's car they'd be using to drive to the airport — knowing James liked to be the driver rather than the driven — but a good excuse to find out how things were progressing on the commitment-front.

"All sorted," he said with a smile, but Lyn wasn't fooled. She knew Helen and his mother would have wanted to share his, 'big' birthday and as this holiday was a surprise gift, it must have seemed like the whole thing was engineered by her to shut them out. It wasn't true. She was fond of his family but the truth of the matter was, she hadn't even given them a thought. And she wasn't about to beat herself up over it.

Bovey Tracey

Staying clear of the Carpenters Arms — the pub that Vinny would acquaint himself with later that evening — they had first entered an inn at the lower end of the town, confident they'd get the information they needed while chomping their way through a ploughman's lunch. However, neither the barman, nor the two surly old men hugging the bar, had been forthcoming. In fact, from the blank stares Vinny received in answer to his question, he doubted whether they had a brain cell between them. Moving away from the bar to sit at a table near the open fire — in Vinny's opinion the only welcoming feature — Stefan had said in a low voice, "They country people, Vincent, suspicious of strangers."

"Yeah, well I think they're all fucking inbreds. I'm just sorry I didn't ask about the field before paying for this lot," Vinny had responded, without lowering his voice.

Forty five minutes later, they'd entered another pub, again keeping well away from the Carpenters. This time Vinny had ordered two pints of the local brew, figuring, quite wrongly as it turned out, that this would encourage a little more openness from the locals; the half pint of lager they had each had with their ploughman's was probably a dead giveaway that they were not only outsiders, but wimpish outsiders.

A few nods, smiles and a bit of small talk later while still sitting at the bar, Vinny had enough confidence to approach John, the barman. "Tell me, John, there's a field on the outskirts of town that has just been ploughed up in preparation for development, am I right?"

"Aye, tha's right."

Vinny waited for more. Waited in vain as John continued to rinse, polish and suspend the clean glasses above the bar. He took a gulp of beer, cleared his throat and asked, again in a forthright manner. "Where exactly is this field, John?"

The barman stopped in mid-polish. "Now why would you be wan'ing to know tha'?"

Vinny looked at Stefan, not for help, he'd already primed the Bulgarian to keep his mouth shut; an outsider was bad enough, a full-blooded foreigner would be disastrous. He'd looked at Stefan because he was stumped for words. Grasping for a response that might add credibility to his questioning, he'd finally stammered, "I'm, I'm interested in local history and…and thought I'd take a few photos for my, for my research, and that."

Blatant sniggers, from several of the drinkers that had been listening put an end to Vinny's feeble attempt to rescue the situation. He was now marked out as the idiot who tried to get one over on the locals. He needed to get out of there, fast, before too much attention was drawn to them.

"I have idea, Vincent."

Stefan's broken English cut into Vinny's reading. They were standing outside the post office and Vinny was running his eyes over the dozens of posters and notices that covered everything from bus times to the selling of peoples rubbish. But nothing about the controversial issue of development in the area and the loss of a local amenity.

"Well it had better be a good one, Stefan, we need to find this field before dark.

"Is better I show you."

Vinny followed, as his friend marched purposefully up the steep incline of Bovey Tracey's main street. After a couple of turns to the left, and what seemed like two miles of arduous hiking uphill, they arrived at a church high above the town. Vinny was still bent double, waiting for his breathing to normalise, when he heard Stefan call out.

"Vincent, come see!"

Still panting, Vinny dragged himself across the road to where Stefan was standing. Before him lay a panoramic view of the countryside surrounding the town — a patchwork quilt of greens and browns.

"See? There, close to town?"

It was very unusual to see Stefan excited and as Vinny followed the direction of his friends pointing finger, the excitement became contagious. On the edge of the green and brown quilt, not far from the centre of, what looked like a toy town from this height, a long triangular section stood out. This section was as black as coal.

Chapter 10

Saturday Evening—Torquay

Apart from the sound of cutlery connecting with porcelain, silence reigned in the dining area of Lyn's kitchen as they ate their roast.

James had booked a table at one of the local fish restaurants as a relaxing prelude to their weekend of wedding-plan-discussions. But like many other things, last minute changes had to be made in order to accommodate the surprise holiday. The flight was early next morning. Suitcases were packed and all business matters dealt with. By six o'clock, the only thing left to do, was to sort through their respective fridges and discard, or freeze, anything that wouldn't keep until their return.

It was a half leg of locally produced lamb that had been the cause of the stunted conversation. Lyn had bought it from the butchers in Wellswood on Thursday morning, reckoning that it would be perfect for eating come Sunday lunchtime. "It's a shame to freeze it," she'd said as James chatted on about the reservation at the restaurant. He'd then suggested giving the joint, along with any other unneeded food to Vincent, who had Stefan staying with him for a week and was sure it would be appreciated. Had it been anyone else, Lyn would have agreed. Who needs to be cooking a main meal hours before your due to jet off on holiday? But when it came to Vinny Conway, rational behavior flew out the window.

"Thinking about it, James," she'd said, averting her face as she carried on rifling through her fridge. "It would be much more sensible staying in. It'll be too tempting in the restaurant. We would probably drink too much, eat too much and arrive back too late. I'll get this on the go while you sort out your kitchen. Dinner will be ready to serve by seven-thirty, which means we'll be eating much earlier than if we ate out."

James had placed his hands on her shoulders and gently turned her round. Feeling compelled, she'd looked him in the face. Piercing green orbs searched for answers she couldn't give. A smile softened the hard angle of his jaw, but didn't quite reach the sadness in his eyes. "See you later," he'd said. Then he was gone.

James had arrived at exactly seven-thirty. For him, punctuality was a sign of good manners. However, an informal meal shared with the woman who was to become his wife, didn't, and shouldn't, fall into a category that was normally reserved for more formal occasions or business meetings.

His intention had been to arrive earlier with a pre opened bottle of red wine. But after clearing out his fridge, he too found several items that couldn't be frozen and likely to spoil within seven days. What to do? Like Lyn, he hated wasting good food. His first instinct was to place them in a plastic shopping bag and drop it down to his neighbour. Unlike Lyn, he didn't bear a strong grudge against Vincent. Pouring himself a glass of wine he sat down to reflect.

Satisfied with his conclusion, he'd dialed Vincent's number, only to be greeted by the answer phone. The familiarity of Vincent's curt command to leave a message or contact him on his mobile, the number following, loud and clear over the airwaves. Not wanting to disturb his Saturday evening out, James opted for leaving a message, explaining, as briefly as possible, about the spontaneous week away and that a bag of perishable foodstuff had been left on his back door step, adding that he should feel free to throw away anything not wanted.

As James had opened his back door, carrying the plastic shopping bag of foodstuffs, the sudden cry of an overhead seagull reminded him that leaving the unprotected bag outside might not be the best idea. He'd quickly returned to his kitchen, already having an answer to his problem. But he couldn't find what he was looking for. Twenty minutes had flown by and he was still looking for the missing item. Returning to his seat of reflection, he'd topped up his wine glass and closed his eyes. Gradually it came to him. When and where he had last used his hard-cased, cool box. The single chime of his antique clock, reminded him that he was out of time. He'd grabbed the wine bottle, now half empty and hurried to Lyn's apartment.

She'd left the door ajar and the delicious aroma of lamb cooked with Rosemary floated through the narrow gap. James had breezed through to the kitchen, just as Lyn was about to carve the joint.

"Hey, that's my job!" he called out before placing the half-empty bottle of wine on a mat in the centre of the table. "Smells good," he said, planting a kiss firmly on her lips.

"Mm, tastes like you started before me," she'd said, "You should have come earlier and we could have shared a glass." She'd deliberately avoided opening wine, knowing that James would bring one of his favourite, expensive reds.

"I'd intended to, sweetheart, but I got delayed looking for something, which I then remembered *you* still have."

"Oh, and what would that be?" Lyn had asked absentmindedly, as she'd carefully removed two, extremely hot plates from the oven and placed them in front of James.

"Remember a couple of weeks ago?" he said, "We did a shared shopping expedition to one of the local farm shops. I unloaded my chilled and frozen stuff first and then you carried off the cool box to unload the rest. I don't recall seeing it after that."

Lyn had paused for moment before saying, "Yes, I remember, It's downstairs in one of my store cupboards. Do you need it straight away?"

James was expertly carving slices off the lamb joint and laying them neatly across the top plate. He stopped, carefully thinking about his response before explaining that he'd need it after they'd eaten. Need it for the several items of food in his fridge that he wasn't prepared to just throw away, especially when there was a neighbour who would appreciate them. Taking hold of the top plate to hand it to Lyn, he realised too late, the burning intensity of its heat. Cursing under his breath he let it go. It fell to the table, knocking over Lyn's glass of wine and shattered the congenial atmosphere.

"Well *you* can do as you like," she grumbled, frantically dabbing at the spreading pool of red liquid. "Conway has caused nothing but havoc in my life and quite frankly, I wouldn't give him the time of day!"

Bovey Tracey

A light tapping on the bedroom door brought Isabelle back into the world of reality. She'd spent all afternoon and part of the evening in bed curled around a water bottle that had been refilled twice. However, she hadn't been able to get the quality of rest that she knew her body and mind needed. She'd slipped in and out of several cat-naps and each time something strange, something quite disturbing seemed to be waiting to take hold of her and she still felt chilled. Chilled to the bone.

The tapping returned, louder, more insistent. "Mum? Mum are you OK? I've brought you a brew."

Isabelle heard the concern in her son's voice and guilt enveloped her.

"It's alright, Robert, you can come in." She had brought her son up to respect the privacy of his parent's bedroom — always knock and only enter if invited. It had never seemed to bother Shaun that their son could just wander in while they were making love. Not that there'd been any danger of that for a long time now, but it was nice to see that Robert still remembered and respected her wishes.

"Dad left for the pub about half an hour ago and I'm meeting my mates soon, can I get you anything before I go?"

Isabelle studied her son as he carefully placed the mug of tea on her bedside cabinet. A tall, sensitive, hard-working boy who rarely complained about anything. The very opposite to his father. One day he would make some lucky girl very happy. "You're a good boy, Robert. Thank you for the offer but I'm not the slightest bit hungry. I'll drink the tea then go downstairs, otherwise I won't be able to sleep through the night, will I?" The last two words came out high pitched and strange, as if she were talking to an infant.

Robert smiled weakly and looked about him, uncertain what to do. His mum looked pale and frail. Very unusual for her. "Dad turned the thermostat down before he went out.

Said it'd be a waste as you were lying in a warm bed. I'll turn it up a bit, shall I?"

"Don't worry, love, I'll see to it. You enjoy your evening and don't be too late."

"Oh, before I forget. This bloke came to see you."

"What bloke? When?"

"Just after Dad left. He knocked on the front door — 'twas obviously a stranger, the only thing that comes through the front door in this house, is the mail."

Isabelle, heard her son slip into the local dialect. This happened when he felt cornered. "Just calm down and tell me exactly what he wanted and who he was."

"Like I said, he was a stranger, a weirdo if you ask me. Asked for, Bella. Didn't know who he meant, till he said, Bella Thatcher, the lady of the house."

Isabelle suddenly realized that Mr Conway, eager to return her ring, had had the sense to wait until Shaun had left but hadn't realised her son would be home.

"What did he say? And what makes you think he's a weirdo?"

Robert, impatient to be off, was almost out of the bedroom door but his mum insisted. "He was dressed weird, tha's all, a long scummy cloak with a hood pulled right over his head. Oh, and he smelt weird, unpleasant, sort of earthy."

"What did he say? Can you remember, exactly?" She felt nervous and she knew the nervousness was transferring to her son. She would have to make it clear to Mr Conway that on no account is he to visit her home again. She understood the reasoning behind the visit, after receiving her email he was anxious to return her ring, and obviously the strange mode of dress was to disguise his appearance. But it mustn't happen again.

"After I got it, that it was you he was after. I told him you were in bed 'cause you were ill and could I give you a message but his message was weird." Robert scratched his left ear, an annoying habit which seemed to help him concentrate. "What he actually said was, Tell Bella she needs the ring back. Obviously what he meant to say was, Tell Bella she needs *to* ring back. I asked him his name. I was talking polite to him, honest Mum, expecting a proper answer or a business card. But all he said was, Nicholas, then turned and disappeared down the front path. Gave me the creeps. Mum, I know you don't usually lock the back door, Dad locks up after he gets in. But seeing as you're not well, I'll take my front door key and unlock for Dad. OK? I gotta go now."

Isabelle heard the muffled slam of the front door. She shuffled across to the bedroom door throwing her dressing gown around her and carefully descended the narrow stairs. She felt old and worn out. She must have picked up a nasty bug from somewhere. *I'll be fine once I've had a decent nights sleep,* she thought, *but first there's something I need to do.*

After turning up the heating and dragging her rocker as close to the Rayburn as possible, she punched in Mr Conway's telephone number, not caring that it would show on the phone bill. She would find a way to overcome that later. For now, it was more important to stop any more intrusions at her home. "Damn!" she uttered, on realizing he wasn't there. No point in leaving a message that wouldn't be picked up until Monday. She scribbled down his mobile number, determined to confront him before her resolve evaporated. "Please God, don't let him be in the pub watching Shaun." The spoken prayer preceded her cold fingers carefully stabbing at the phone. Her head was aching and the spasmodic shivering didn't help. After making this call, she decided she'd take a couple of Paracetamol and return to bed.

A sigh of relief when she heard his mobile ring. But the ringing went on and on.

Vinny and Stefan had just settled in the corner of yet another of Bovey Tracey's pubs. But this one was heaving with people, well-to-do people, considering the mainly posh-sounding voices and the high prices on the menu; but fortunately there were no gormless faces suspiciously watching their every move. The fact that it was ten overcoats warmer than outside, swayed them into staying.

They were running down the list of 'Traditional Home Fayre' when Stefan nudged his arm.

"Is your phone, Vincent?"

"I can't hear it. Mind you I can't hear myself think with all this racket going on. Order two of them." Vinny's chubby finger pointed to third down the list, *Devon Produced Pork Sausages with Mash and Thick Onion Gravy,* "I need the bog anyway, I'll take the call in there."

"Vinny Conway?" A short pause. "Oh, hello Isabelle. This is a surprise. I thought you only wanted to use email for contacting." Vinny listened, totally confused by what she was saying. "But I haven't been anywhere near your house, Isabelle. That's not how it works." He could barely hear her as she rambled on about getting back her ring. Desperate to relieve his full bladder, he entered one of the empty cubicles, clamped the phone between ear and shoulder and unzipped his trousers. Blissful relief, as a gush of hot liquid hit porcelain, was banished when Isabelle's voice, filled with emotion said, "Mr Conway, I must have the ring back as soon as possible! Can you bring it to me tonight?"

"Are you OK, Isabelle? You sound a bit strange. I mean you don't sound the same as when we met yesterday. Shaun hasn't been getting rough, has he? Oh I'm sorry to hear that. You go back to bed with a warm drink, I'm sure you'll feel a lot better tomorrow. Your ring is locked in my office-safe. I'll be keeping watch on Shaun later on, and I'll email you tomorrow. We'll sort something out. Bye for now."

Vinny returned to see two half pints of lager being placed on their table and a lovely looking young woman poised with her pad for the food order. Before Stefan could utter any broken English, Vinny intervened. "Bangers and mash twice, darlin', and a smile to warm the cold evening."

The smile came with the words. "I already taken order from Stefan. He speak better English than you." She winked at Stefan before turning and walking away with her head held high.

Vinny waited for an explanation and when none came he said. "I hope you weren't trying to get off with her, Stefan. You've got a very busy night ahead."

"She from my country. Is good to see she get work in this small town, no?"

"What's this?" Vinny picked up one of the paper napkins, a number scrolled in black ink across its folded surface.

"Is Marie's mobile number. I think is good to have outsider on inside." The subject abruptly changed when Stefan asked, "Was phone call important?"

Without realising it, Vinny was already half way down the glass of beer. Half a pint was all he'd allow himself when he was working and the same went for Stefan. He pushed the glass a few inches away, clasping his hands as he confided the gist of Isabelle's call. Then lowering his voice he said, "I reckon her husband's got wind of the gold finds. He probably knocked her about a bit to get the info and because he can't get his hands on the stuff, he's got someone keeping an eye on her, She didn't say as much but I'm sure that's it. Well, I'll soon be keeping my eyes glued on him. In the meantime, Stefan, I want you to be extra careful on that field, you may well have company. Keep your mobile on vibrate and I'll let you know if I hear of anything going down. Then we'll meet, as arranged, back at the van."

Vinny clammed up as Marie arrived with the food. It was only after she'd left, he noticed that Stefan had an extra sausage.

Chapter 11

Midnight—Bovey Tracey

EVERYTHING IS FALLING INTO PLACE. MY PURPOSE IS LAID BARE. SOON REVENGE CAN BEGIN.

The wind had subsided but Stefan still felt a rising chill as he slowly swept the metal detector from side to side. He halted as bells rang out the midnight hour, the chiming reminding him of home. Reminding him of the time when he last used one of these machines. He hadn't been searching for gold on that occasion. The treasure he sought, on that dark night over four years ago, was the gun his father had buried at the end of the great war. He'd searched night after night for that gun, unable to gain knowledge of its exact resting place because his father was dead. Murdered by the same bastards who had raped his sister and sold her into sex-slavery. Stefan had promised his mother that his emotions were under control. Swore on his younger brother's life that he'd left behind the desire for revenge. But as memories reared, so did the stirring of the coiled snake within.

Under Vincent's instruction, Stefan was working systematically along the bottom hedge of the field. In daylight it had been easy to work out, from what Isabelle had said, where she'd made her find. They hadn't had a lot of time to walk the field before darkness fell, but both had agreed that this was the best area to concentrate on. He was well hidden from the road. Headlights from cars sweeping arks of light across the black, furrowed earth would be totally unaware of the searcher in the field.

Suddenly, a hint of movement up ahead; thinning cloud parted across a segment of moon. Diffused light fell across the trunk of a felled tree and for the briefest moment, the nebulous shape of a hooded figure. Anxious, Stefan looked behind to see how far he was from the field gate. He turned back, eyes searching, then riveting on the tree trunk but there was nothing to see.

His earphones registered a sharp "beep", dissipating the nervous imaginings and bringing his mind back to the job in hand: heavy boot on spade, flick of the soil, pinpoint the metal and then fingers feeling and retrieving. He didn't need the aid of the torch to show him what he'd found. It's weight, shape and smell told him all he needed to know. This was the fifth lead musket ball to be found in this area — signs of violence committed in centuries past.

Danny, landlord of The Carpenters Arms, swore under his breath as once again a crescendo of drunken voices stumbled through, Happy Birthday to You. You, happened to be Jules, his barmaid. A London lass who had been in his employ for over four years, a good length of time considering how most of the young women he'd employed soon tired of the late hours and were gone inside a year. But Jules was a different calibre of woman. A grafter, and smart with it. She wasn't working for pin money, or, as a necessity to get her through college. Jules had lofty plans. Her horizons spanned much further than most of the young women of these parts. As well as doing hard graft six nights a week behind the bar. She had a nice little earner from three properties she rented out. Her ultimate aim included buying a piece of land and doing a self-build. And at just thirty years old, Dan happened to know that she was close to achieving it.

Last orders had been called over an hour ago and by now all glasses should have been collected and washed. Close friends of Jules had offered her a bit of a party at their place after work, but one of them had come down with the bug that was picking its nasty way through the town, and they'd had to cancel the offer. Jules hadn't minded too much. But the punters were devastated, especially the men who poured out their hearts and problems to her over a pint. The pints kept coming, so long as there was a pretty face who would smile and listen. Oh yes, the takings of the pub had risen year on year since taking on Jules. To soften the blow of the cancelled party, Danny had allowed double orders when calling time, as well as relieving Jules of her duties — after all it was her birthday — the extra hour of celebration enhancing the nights takings even more. However, if they didn't shift after the next call, he'd grab his largest broom and sweep the lot of 'em out the door.

Vinny had had enough and he could see that the landlord felt the same way. It had been an eye-opening experience, tucked away on a corner table near the main bar with full view of what was happening. His intention had been to just wander in, use the bog and return to his car, strategically parked so his mirror showed all comings and goings into and out of the place. However, once he'd made sure that Shaun Thatcher was one of the men downing pints, he thought, *why sit for hours in a freezing-cold van?*

Except for three people, everyone in the place seemed to be reeling from the intake of alcohol. Vinny had made his situation clear from the start when he'd asked the landlord for a non-alcoholic-beer. He'd said he was on his way to an old friends funeral in Cornwall, so wouldn't be much of a customer on account of the driving. He went on to say that he'd once spent a fortnights holiday in these parts with this old friend and the Carpenters Arms had become their favourite watering hole. So now it seemed fitting to spend an hour or two rekindling the happy memories. The landlord had been understanding and Vinny had offered to buy him a drink. He'd shook his head and confessed that he didn't touch a drop of alcohol these days.

Jules, the barmaid who was the cause of the celebratory atmosphere and had had at least one drink bought her from every bloke in the pub, including Vinny, was also sober. Absolutely, stone-cold sober. She'd played the part well, singing along and laughing with the crowd. In reality, she was accepting the drinks but pocketing the money. Vodka and lime was her tipple and if she had drunk only a quarter of the drinks bought her, she would have been under the table long ago.

Vinny had watched carefully. Watched as each time one of the competing bulls had called out, 'and have one for yourself, darling', she'd slipped the price of the drink in a pot beneath the counter. Nothing illegal in that. But the glass of water with a dash of lime that was hoisted in a toast of thanks to the giver was, to put it mildly, fucking deceitful. Vinny had bought her a drink out of curiosity — he'd wanted to know the unit cost of each deception. Jules reminded Vinny of Charlene, a crafty-cow who used to work for him. She'd talked her way into sharing his flat then flaunted her body and shared his bed.

Charlene however, didn't understand the true meaning of sharing. Free board and lodgings hadn't been enough for her, she was also skimming the takings. And when the time was right with a more lucrative offer in sight, she'd taken off. Vinny came home one day to find no trace of her, or the few hundred quid he kept as an emergency fund. He remembered feeling very hurt at the time but you live and learn.

Shaun Thatcher was on the move. Reminiscences were banished as Vinny grabbed his jacket. He slowed his pace on seeing that Thatcher's movement had been a few steps across the bar to the vicinity of the birthday-babe. She was enchanting the pants off a guy who was old enough to be her dad. Without apology, Thatcher grabbed Jules's wrist and she was pulled to a quieter area of the emptying bar. You didn't have to be up close to know what was going down. Thatcher wanted what he felt he had paid for in drinks — her undivided attention and maybe a bit of slap and tickle later on. Neither of which would be forthcoming tonight and Vinny doubted if it ever had been. To be on the safe side he'd tail the sad bastard until he arrived back to his own front door. Then at last, he could meet up with Stefan and rummage through the finds.

It was 1.48am as Vinny pulled into the parking bay and came to a halt beneath a street light. Stefan had insisted on leaving the site before going through what he'd found. In a way, this made sense to Vinny. It was pitch dark there and torches and car lights would only arouse suspicion. But as they'd left the scene and headed towards home, Stefan had remained quiet. Too bloody quiet, even for him. Five words, I no like this place, was all he'd spoken after Vinny's prompting and cajoling and the words told him nothing of what he'd found.

"Right, mystery man, get the goodies out." The cold seeped into this van the minute you turned off the engine, so all Vinny wanted was a quick look at the best, and the rest could wait until they got home.

Stefan lifted the bum bag from the foot well. After unzipping the front compartment, he lifted out a mud-smeared polythene bag — the type that banks use for coinage — and unfolded the top to gain access. Very slowly and very carefully five items were placed on his palm which was held, almost sacrificially, towards the light.

Vinny was tired, he knew that. It was only the rush of adrenaline keeping him awake. The slow deliberation of Stefan's action cut the rush to a slow meander and almost lulled him into sleep, until the sight of what lay in his friend's hand jerked him back to life. "What the fuck are they? Lead marbles or what?"

"These are musket balls, Vincent, all found in same place where Isabelle find her gold."

"So what? Isabelle's stuff came from a definite period, the coins and the ring are dateable."

"These are same as bullets from guns. They show their time in history."

"I'm not interested in a fucking history lesson, Stefan, did you find any gold?"

"No."

Vinny fired the engine, turned the heater to full and screeched onto the road.

Chapter 12

Sunday Morning—Torquay

James loaded the final bag into his boot and closed the door as quietly as he could. He'd brought the car around to the front of his premises the night before. The street lighting here made loading the car much easier. It also ensured that his neighbours wouldn't be disturbed. Their flight departed at 7.00am which meant they needed to arrive at the airport by 5.00am. Not for the first time, he wondered if all the disruption was worth a few days away. Putting aside the cold, dark, early start to the day and looking ahead to warm sunshine, relaxation and having Lyn all to himself for a week, brought on a smile and a playful rendition of Happy Birthday to Me.

"How can you be so bright and cheerful at this time of the morning?" Lyn had barely said two words, apart from a grunted, "Good Morning" when James had knocked on her door, asking if she was ready. Both had agreed that sleeping in their own beds would guarantee more hours of sleep. But Lyn's rest had been fitful. She desperately needed this holiday. "Sorry to be such a miserable old crab."

Registering her pale sleepy face he pulled her into an embrace, kissing her cool forehead. Seat belts snapped, mirrors were checked and soon they were coasting along towards the Babbacombe road.

The sound of screaming was everywhere. In his head, a memory from years ago. A dream that was already becoming lost to him. Stefan opened his eyes, realizing the screaming was here also. He untangled his sweating body from the bed covers and moved stealthily toward the bedroom window. Moving the blind a little, revealed a centimeter strip of window. Suddenly, white wings flapping in rhythm to a high-pitched screeching, engulfed the narrow view. He stepped back in fright. Shame washing over him. Again he reached for the blind, instilling courage by cursing aloud in his own language — a ritual he'd learned from his father. But before he had the chance to see what demon stalked him, the bedroom door flew open.

"What the fuck is going on here?"

The light from the hallway streamed into the room. Vincent's half-naked body remained silhouetted in the doorway. The screaming continued. Vincent's voice, loud, aggressive, reassuringly dominant.

"Fucking seagulls! If I had an air rifle, I swear to God I'd shoot every last one of them."

"Why seagulls want to attack doors and windows?" Stefan heard the shaking in his words and coughed several times to steady it.

"Seagulls will attack anything and everything if there's the slightest chance of getting their filthy beaks into food. Many a time I've been dive-bombed, while walking along eating a bag of chips. I'll bet you a fiver, some lazy git tossed the remains of his pizza or crap takeaway over the wall. One of us will have to get rid of the food source before we can get any more shut eye. And *you* have just been voted the best man for the job. Good night."

The door closed leaving a thin line of light beneath it, within seconds this was gone. Stefan turned to the window and could see, from the grey light bleeding around the edge of the blind, that morning was just about breaking. He pulled on the clothes he'd taken off just a few hours ago and headed for the back door, reaching for a long-handled broom as he passed through the kitchen.

Bolts top and bottom and a five-leaver-lock in between were released before Stefan could step out into the cold, grey dawn. A frenzy of fighting, feeding and flapping was everywhere and the screeching and screaming was deafening. He wanted to slam the door on the madness and crawl back into bed but what would that serve? Only his cowardice and memories he thought had been laid to rest. He forced his legs to move down the steps, holding the broom with both hands as he swung it above his head. But the determination of these large white birds was strong. In a taunting dance, they'd move easily to one side only to return as the broom arced away. He forced himself to concentrate on what Vincent had said, *get rid of the food source.* Throwing the broom to one side, he focussed his mind on what lay before him. Food was scattered everywhere. Not the remnants of cooked food. This was like someone had just thrown the contents of their fridge into the yard: meat, fish, bread, smashed eggs, salad and vegetables, all were being stabbed and prodded by sharp screeching beaks. Milk too had been poured over and amongst the food.

Stefan's eyes followed the trail of wanton waste and came to rest on a large plastic box, the type used for keeping food cold. It was on it's side and empty. He needed bin liners. On turning to return to the kitchen he saw something that made his blood run cold. Writing was scrawled on the back door. Letters formed from butter and cheese. Edible ink which the birds were eager to consume. Most of the words were broken and disjointed, whole sections having been pecked away and eaten. Stefan's disbelieving eyes wandered over to the nearby window. The window to his bedroom. Here also fragments of words. One word was complete. And Stefan understood it's meaning.

Hell

Vinny was vaguely aware of his bedroom door being opened. He hadn't yet slipped into proper sleep. But the screeching gulls had started to take on a softer tone allowing a blanket of twi-lighting to descend over him. But the rough shaking, and Stefan's voice hissing between clenched teeth, soon put paid to that.

"Vincent, you must come! Come quickly!"

"What the fuck is wrong with you, Stefan? And why are those fucking gulls still at it?"

Vinny tried to get his head around the blabber that was coming from a man who was normally calm, quiet and sensible. The blabber went on relentlessly as the bedclothes were whipped away and his clothes pressed into his hands. From what he could make out, it wasn't just a discarded takeaway tossed over the wall. Food had been scattered everywhere. "So fucking clear it up," he'd shouted when he could get a word in. "They're only birds, man, why are you so spooked?"

"I spooked because someone write message on door and window. You must come see before birds eat all words."

Within an hour a deafening silence had fallen over the respectable area of The Terrace. Vinny and Stefan sat hunched over the answering machine, playing, and then re-playing, just one message. At least they were now aware of how the food had come to be at Vinny's back door. But who was the mad bastard who had chucked it everywhere? They'd checked the cool-box, it's locking mechanism was sound. If it hadn't been for the graffiti Vinny would have put it all down to the ingenuity of gulls. But after seeing with his own eyes the words scrawled in food. Even the sections that were missing, grease had left its mark and it was unmistakable what the letters spelled out.

Linked in Hell   Thieving Liar   Revenge Time

"It had to be local yobs who else could it be? Go and make a brew, Stefan. Now we've got daylight, we'll go through your finds bag again, see if we missed anything that's worth a few bob."

Bovey Tracey

Isabelle awoke to a combination of Shaun's snoring and church bells calling the faithful to early service. A strange smell pervaded the bedroom. Her headache was gone but her nose was blocked on one side — and once it cleared, the smell would probably be even worse. Where on earth was it coming from? She cast her eyes around the floor looking for any sign that Shaun, in a drunken stupor and after having trodden in something nasty, forgot to remove his shoes before coming to bed. This had actually happened a few times, but not since they'd renewed the old carpet which was a mottled brown and masked a multitude of sins. She leaned across the bed and began sniffing her husband. His hair, his upper arm that poked out from the duvet and then his breath as it trembled in fits and starts from his half opened mouth. Nothing untoward, just the usual cocktail of warm body, stale beer and residue of aftershave. He wouldn't be awake for some time yet and that suited her. She needed to contact Mr Conway, preferably by email, and with the library shut her only chance was to borrow Robert's laptop.

Before stepping into her sheepskin slippers they were pressed against nostrils that were now fully functioning. Even her dressing gown was given the once over before it was allowed to drape her body. On opening the bedroom door, she realized at once that the stench, which could only be described as 'bad', was coming from down below. A wedge of light cut across the first three steps. Shaun had left the door at the bottom of the stairs open, allowing smells from the kitchen to rise up on a current of warm air from the stove. Something was definitely rotting down there.

Holding a tissue against her nose, she peered around the nooks and crannies of her kitchen, expecting to find some creature that had gained entry and died. The stench became stronger the closer she got to the stove.

Then she saw it. Almost stepped into it. Marks on the floor in the form of prints, leading to nowhere and coming from nowhere. A pair of prints made by heavy-soled shoes or boots. Boots that had trodden in something unspeakably foul. She rushed to the scullery, finding Shaun's casually discarded shoes on the mat. The soles were clean. Isabelle carried one over to the imprint of filth and found that Shaun's were approximately four sizes smaller than…Than whose? Robert's feet were smaller than his fathers and he'd never been allowed to bring friends home without her permission.

Almost gagging from the stench, she pushed aside the *who and why* from her mind and returned to the scullery. Waiting until the water ran hot, she shoved a bucket beneath the steaming gush, adding detergent, a quarter bottle of disinfectant and a large splash of bleach. Pulling on rubber gloves she set to work, obliterating the filth from her home. During this very unpleasant process, her curiosity turned to fascination as she probed, scraped and removed a mixture of cheese, fish, raw egg, and most unpleasant of all, shit. Yes, there was definitely faeces amongst the worst smelling mess.

Torquay

Vinny didn't say as much, but he was grateful that Stefan had suggested covering his desk with an old towel before tipping out the bum-bag of finds. The towel was now filthy with mud stains, deposits of green verdigris and lumps of lead in all shapes and sizes. What were regarded as 'finds' had been ceremoniously positioned in one corner, away from the rubbish, but in Vinny's opinion, it all looked the same. For a moment his disappointment overwhelmed him. Everything had suddenly turned to shit. And the warm glow of making some money, not just wages, but a bit of serious dough, was rapidly disappearing. Even the surveillance work wasn't going to pay much. Isabelle wanted proof that her husband was playing around. If what Shaun Thatcher was doing was grounds for divorce, then twenty-five percent of the male population over twenty-five should be watching their backs. A small glimmer of sunshine pierced through the gloom of his disappointment. He might not be able to sting Isabelle for her gold coins but he still had the copy of the ring which

Jimmy was itching to get his hands on. With a broadening smile he thought, *the price has just gone up by fifty percent.*

"Right Stefan, lets have a refill of coffee and see what we can learn about this site of ours. I've paid good money hiring that." Vinny nodded towards the upstanding machine and tapped the search coil with his foot, causing it to slide to the floor. "And it costs the same whether we have it for a weekend or the whole week. I know you have a thing about this place." Vinny had actually seen his friend making the sign of the cross as he left the field, bringing to mind some of the religious fanatics that played for one or two of the Spanish-speaking football teams. "Nevertheless, I feel certain that there's got to be more gold there somewhere."

"We find nothing if machine broken." Stefan reinstated the upright position of the detector and flicked the 'on' button. Vincent's small office was filled with loud 'beeping'.

"There you are. A good thrashing, or kicking, never hurts. It makes sure things work better next time. Now get your arse in gear, man, and stop moping around."

Stefan returned with fresh coffee and two bacon sarnies, a sure sign that normality was back. During the interim, Vinny had removed the obvious crap and the soiled towel, brushed off his desk and placed a sheet of A4 paper for the debatable, so-called finds. Five lead balls of approximately one centimeter diameter, were, in Stefan's opinion, the most telling finds. However, Vinny wasn't interested in 'telling finds', he wasn't an archeologist, he was a treasure hunter and he was only interested in hunting for gold — the only commodity in todays uncertain economic times that was worth having — and thanks to Isabelle, he'd been shown a way of getting his hands on some. And he intented to persist until he did.

"Look mate, I know you don't like the place but you're only here till next weekend and we can't search the field in daylight. So we work as planned during the day installing the security locks, then during the evenings we'll try different spots around the field. It's obvious that all sorts of things were going on there over the centuries," Vinny looked at Stefan for confirmation and received a grave nod. "Good, we'll head back there tonight. There'll be no evil doings on the Lord's Day, Stefan, but if it'll make you feel better, I picked up a bulb of Garlic amongst the crap out there. Even the seagulls couldn't bear to touch it. You can find a way to hang it round your neck before we go."

Bovey Tracey

Shaun Thatcher awoke with a raging thirst and a foul taste at the back of his throat. No good shouting for Izzy to bring him a mug of tea. Those little domestic pleasures went out the window ages ago, along with all the others. Women, he'd never understood how their minds worked. He'd thought Jules was different. She'd seemed genuinely interested in what he had to say and he swore to God she was giving him the 'come on'. Well, she'll be sorry, 'cause I for one won't be going anywhere near that pub for a while.

He dragged himself to the bathroom and whilst taking a long piss, scrutinised his face in the mirror of the cabinet. His life was going down the tubes and it showed. He was in debt, his marriage was on the point of collapsing and he hated his job. The increased smoking and drinking only added to the problems. If only Izzy would listen to reason. If only Izzy would listen, maybe…

The rattle of the bathroom door and his son's voice "That you in there, Dad?"

Shaun opened the door and greeted Robert with a slap on his shoulder. "Is your mum about? Can't hear any pots and pans rattling down below."

"She's sitting somewhere quiet with my laptop."

"What would *she* be needing with a lap top?"

"Wanted to check for an email, library's shut today." Robert pushed passed his father and started to close the bathroom door.

"Hang on, how long's she had an email address, and what's she need it for?"

"Dad, I'm bursting for the loo! Why don't you ask her yourself. Most people have at least one email address these days. It's cheaper than using the phone. Mum's probably doing her best to save money." The door closed and the locking mechanism slid home.

Shaun found his wife in the dining room. She was bent over Robert's laptop, her face locked in concentration as she slowly pressed the keys. The door had been closed, unusual because everyone agreed that the warmth from the Rayburn needed to reach all parts of this difficult-to-heat cottage. Even after opening it, her concentration had remained locked in place.

Shaun coughed and Izzy's eyes found his. Eyes that were full of fear, or full of embarrassment. She closed the lid and unplugged the lead without giving any explanation. It was only when she was back in the kitchen she spoke.

"Did you have a good evening, Shaun? I'm sure you're ready for a mug of tea by now."

Chapter 13

Sunday Afternoon—Lanzarote

Azure sky reflected in calm, transparent sea. Coconut palms arching gracefully over the pool and an air temperature that coaxed away all but the minimum of swimwear. This was paradise on earth and Lyn intended to make the most of the next six days in its glorious embrace. She was sitting at a shaded table on the terrace of their hotel where parrots flitted from tree to tree. James was in the pool and from time to time her eyes were drawn to his strong body, propelled in an overarm rhythm travelling the pool's length.

They'd eaten a late breakfast on arrival, over three hours ago, expecting this to keep hunger at bay until dinner at seven; but the self-imposed rule of no overindulgences, had already been broken. After unpacking they'd decided on a walk to shrug off the confinement of the four-hour flight and to take in the immediate surroundings of their hotel. Their walk had led them along the coastline and an intimate rocky cove named Playa Chica. A short stroll further along and the sound of music and the smell of food attracted them to a small market which had been set up in the vicinity of the harbour. Stalls selling everything from flowers, foodstuffs and jewellery were doing a brisk trade. But there was nothing they really needed. However, the lure and temptation to linger soon found them enjoying coffees and home baked pastries.

James was already shedding his intake of surplus calories. Lyn's intention was to keep off unwanted weight by walking. Walking for miles. This island fascinated her. The stark contrast of volcanic mountains, white flat-roofed buildings and colourful tropical foliage, encircled by deep blue ocean, was so charming, she couldn't wait to see more of it.

A copy of The Lanzarote Gazette, a colourful magazine printed in English, was handed to them by a couple leaving for their journey home. After briefly flicking through, Lyn realised this magazine could be very useful. Restaurants, markets, places of interest and even maps of the main tourist areas, were clearly indicated. They'd already decided on hiring a car later in the week, but for the first few days, Lyn intended to explore and see as much as possible on foot.

A sudden sprinkling of cool liquid. "Penny for them?" asked James as he rubbed the surplus water from his dripping hair and planted a kiss on the top of her head. "You look deep in thought, my darling." He carefully laid the yellow towel, supplied by the hotel, over the chair opposite Lyn, and sat down taking both her hands in his.

Lyn playfully brushed away droplets of water that raced down his nose. "I'm too relaxed to be deep in thought, how was the pool?"

"Gorgeous, like you. How about returning to our suite for an afternoon siesta. We didn't get much last night. I'm talking sleep, of course."

"Mm, I'm sure you are, Lyn said, as she pushed the magazine towards James, stretched and lazily got to her feet. "I'd like to shower first, I'm plastered in sun lotion."

"OK, I'll give you ten minutes then I'll be up."

Ignoring the magazine, James shifted his chair into full sun, sighing with pleasure as the heat of the rays evaporated the remaining moisture from his body. There'd be plenty of time for exploring once he'd hired a car. What both of them needed was time for relaxation, time just being together and sharing their feelings about what the future held. This lovely hotel was the perfect place for fulfilling those needs. This was going to be a week to remember. Two or three days to really unwind. Then they could start making plans for the wedding. He understood Lyn's predicament, and the reasons that lay behind most of her stress. All her family were in Australia and for one reason or another were unable to travel to England, which meant the wedding would be a small gathering of his family and a couple of her friends. As far as James was concerned, a quiet and private wedding on a small island paradise would suit him just fine. But he'd never hear the end of it from his mother or Helen. Still, might be worthwhile voicing the idea to Lyn. Save any more arguing about where to have the wedding.

One eye lifted at the sound of a mobile phone, a similar sound to his own. His was in the safe in their suite, placed there ceremoniously alongside Lyn's mobile after vowing that they'd only use them as and when it was absolutely necessary. Absentmindedly he raised his arm to check the time, remembering with a smile that his watch was also in the safe. Wrapping the towel around his waist and ignoring the lift, he bounded up the broad staircase two steps at a time.

He tapped lightly on the door of their suite. It opened immediately. Like him, Lyn was wrapped in a saffron-yellow towel, hair wet and body freshly showered. The door was kicked shut as both towels fell to the floor and two bodies merged. All thoughts and concerns were lost as touching, caressing, and deep searching kisses gave way to moans of pleasure. Moving as one, the king-sized bed was reached and fell upon. Hunger for satisfaction returned with breathless intensity, and with intertwined arms and legs they became lost in their lovemaking.

As the sun dipped lower in the sky, shifting the block of sunlight from the bed to the wall, James and Lyn still lay naked, sleeping in each others arms.

A loud clatter from below their open balcony door woke James with a start. Lyn remained lost. He gently released his body from her torpid embrace, slipped on a pair of shorts and stepped out onto the balcony. The area was small, barely large enough for the bistro-sized table and two chairs, but the view was stupendous.

A panorama of coastline, mountains and the Island of Fuerteventura, which appeared to be much closer than the remembered eighty-six kilometers. James felt sure this optical illusion was due to the flat-calm sea. Geography had been a favourite subject of his as a boy, losing himself in daydreams as his school master's cane pointed out the strange-sounding names on the huge atlas that was rolled out for each lesson. Back then, he'd had a strong urge to travel the world. But his father had gradually steered him away from such fanciful notions, instilling in James the need for sound education and the ability to earn respect, and a decent living, by entering an established profession.

More loud noises. Squeals of laughter as three children, each sporting a mop of ginger hair, splashed about in the pool. James looked back at the bed. Lyn, still lost in sleep. The splashing and the squealing became louder. He stepped back inside and closed the terrace door. Picking up the

Lanzarote Gazette, the sound of pages being turned, the hum of an air-conditioning-unit and the soft nasal breathing from the bed muffled the unwanted noise outside.

Chapter 14

Sunday Evening—Bovey Tracey

Rain had stopped and the biting wind had finally eased. In its place, an almost pleasant evening. Even Shaun was attempting pleasantness, putting Isabelle even more on edge. She'd arranged to meet Mr Conway in half an hours time, confident, when she'd made the arrangement, that Shaun would be, as usual, in the pub. But after hearing his whingeing about being broke and his intention to stay home and watch the telly, Isabelle had interrupted, asking if he was hinting for money.

"'Course I'm not hinting for money, Izzy; 'sides, I know you haven't got any. Things are probably tougher for you than me, what with food prices rocketing. No, I've made up my mind, I'm not wasting money in that pub anymore. Maybe pop in for an hour on Saturday nights. We could both go, do you good, a change of scenery."

Isabelle was stumped for words. She had a head full of responses. Responses clothed in choice expletives bursting to be released verbally. But she held her tongue, wise enough to know this wouldn't serve any purpose. Her eyes found the kitchen clock just as the second hand moved another minute closer to her eight o'clock appointment.

"Thanks for the offer, Shaun. We're a long way off Saturday night. Right now all I want is a walk in the fresh air. I'm sure that'll help me sleep better."

"I'll come with you, we used to do a lot of strolling, remember. Talk our way through lots of problems."

"Thanks for the offer, Shaun." She was repeating herself, such was the turmoil going on inside. She feigned a bout of coughing giving her time to think. Silence for a few seconds followed by a heavy sigh. "I've been really worried about this repeat smear test. They told me it's not unusual to need a second one and not to worry. Easy to say when it's not happening to you. Anyway, I'll have the results soon. I just feel like a gentle stroll, on my own, to get my mind sorted. I'll be back by eight-thirty. It'll be nice to have the kettle on the boil when I get back."

Without waiting for a response, Isabelle slipped into her winter boots, unhooked her warmest coat from the scullery rack and headed out towards the nearby bright lights of central Bovey Tracey.

Vinny stood at the bus stop outside Bovey Tracey's branch of Nat West Bank — the arranged meeting place. Arranged here because Vinny felt it less likely to arouse suspicion from the local nosey parkers. He'd been standing here for barely five minutes and already he'd had two people, both men, cast a strange glance his way. Glances that displayed a sneering hint of humour. Then an old biddy, head wrapped in a colourful scarf and bent over a three-wheeled walking-aid as she pushed up the gradient of Fore Street, stopped directly in front of him, pausing to catch her breath. Vinny was about to tell her to, clear-off, not wanting to attract attention by getting entangled in some mad discussion with one of the local loonies. But when she spoke her language was meticulous and her voice refined.

"Good evening, young man, I hope you're not waiting for a bus. If you are, I'm afraid your wait will be in vain. On Sunday evenings the final bus from here leaves at thirteen minutes past seven."

In spite of her age — which must have been anywhere between seventy-five and ninety — Vinny noticed eyes that were bright and cheeks that were rosy. He also noticed an unopened bottle of Jack Daniels perched horizontally within the bag of her walking aid. "Thanks for the info, darlin' but I'm just waiting here for a friend. You take care no one nicks that bottle of whiskey from you."

"Thank you for your advice, but I assure you that won't happen. Everyone in the town knows me and my daughter who happens to be a magistrate. Good bye." Off she toddled, head bent once again as she pushed on.

Moving a few feet away from the bus stop, Vinny passed a minute or two letting his eyes wander over the goods on display in the nearby shop. Suddenly he became aware of hurried footsteps. He turned and saw the figure of a woman heading his way. Yes, it was Isabelle, partially disguised by the hood of her coat. He looked about him. No one else in sight. Taking her by the arm he led her into the shop doorway, not completely private, but much less conspicuous than the bus stop.

"Isabelle, working on Sunday evenings only increases expenses for the client. Couldn't this have waited until during the week?"

"No…I mean, sorry, Mr Conway for dragging you out just to give me…to return my ring. You see I need it, I must have it back right away."

Vinny sensed fear behind the woman's plea. It's your husband, isn't it? He's threatening you, the bastard." He sensed her flinch at the use of his bad language, and tried to make amends. Sorry, Isabelle, it's just that I can't stand men who take out their frustrations on their wives."

"Please believe me, Mr Conway, Shaun hasn't laid a finger on me. Have you got my ring?"

Vinny reached into his inside pocket and brought out the small package and handed it over. He watched as the package was ripped open and the ring slipped onto her thumb, gripped with the other hand and pressed to her lips.

"So *who* is it you're scared of and why is it so important to have the ring back tonight?"

Isabelle, looked from the ring to Vinny's face and back again, as if leaving sight of it might make it disappear again. She answered the question with a question of her own. "Mr Conway, do you believe in reincarnation?"

Shaun Thatcher stepped back into deep shadow. His heart was thumping in his chest. Nothing he could do about that. But his breath, heavy and laboured a few minutes ago, was now stilled and silent. His wife walked by the narrow alley, completely unaware that her husband was barely two feet away. Several moments passed, then a gasp for air and the attempt to find reasons behind what he had just witnessed. Very slowly, poking his head out from concealment, Shaun could see his wife, a streetlight clearly showing she was in a hurry as she marched up the main street — the safest but longest way home. He, as did most people who lived in this area of town, would cut through the car park, even at night. It saved about eight minutes of time and a bit of shoe leather. Time, what should he do? The man she'd met was heading in the opposite direction. He too was marching, but where to? Shaun needed to know. But he also needed to get back home before Izzy. Needed to find out what this bloke had given her.

Turning back towards the car park he heard a sound from the alley. A sound like the soft rustling of leaves in the wind. But there was no wind. Then a horrible, cloying stench filled the air. The rustling came nearer and carried the stench with it. Shaun, highly alert now, felt fabric brush against him. A strong Instinct for self-preservation sent him running up the road. On reaching the car park he glanced back. A fleeting glance of a hooded shape was heading in the same direction as the man his wife had met.

Stefan was working steadily along the opposite side of the field from the night before. He was at the top of a slight hill and the soil was sparse and full of small stones, making it easier to walk on. His body relaxed, confident that the thick layer of cloud made him invisible from the road and the absence of any wind would make even the slightest noise through the headphones easier to hear. He felt content and lost in the rhythm of his task. Even the ground was quiet, very little chatter from the machine, very few indications of metal hiding within the dark earth beneath.

But he had found one coin — small, thin, and made from silver — the type of coin, in generations past, would be accepted around the whole of Europe and beyond. Coins of an age when the weight of it's silver content was its value, not the strange words and numbers stamped on base metal surfaces.

Unbidden, the memory of a happy event surfaced in Stefan's mind. He was in his fifteenth year, too old for childish things but, according to his father, not yet a man. Elena, his older sister, had just put spoons and coarse bread on the table. Mother wouldn't serve up the cabbage stew until Father arrived home. Father was late, very late. Stefan's younger brother continued to whine about hunger, but their mother wouldn't give in. *Without Bashta, we wouldn't be eating at all. We wait till he arrives.*

Soon, in a flurry of excitement, all thoughts of hunger were forgotten. Father staggered through the door carrying a large, broken jar encrusted with grime and mud. With a heave and a grunt he upended the jar on the freshly-scrubbed table, Elena quickly rescuing the spoons and bread. Eyes stared and mouths fell open but remained silent as a mountain of coins filled an area the size of Mother's large stew pot. A few spilled over onto the floor bouncing onto Stefan's shoes. Then father's eyes, beaming with happiness and his remembered words. *My beautiful family. No more going without.* Words spoken in his native tongue. Words that would return to haunt the rest of their lives.

Three flashes cut across the field interrupting and shutting down the memory. Stefan was relieved. Vincent was back from his meeting with Isabelle. He would wait, as arranged, for his friend to join him up here.

Vinny opened the back of his van and removed the wellington boots he'd bought earlier. No need to be concerned over the whereabouts of Shaun Thatcher, as predicted and then confirmed by his wife, 'lover boy' was staying clear of the Carpenters Arms and spending the night indoors. Vinny would join Stefan and each take turns, one using the metal detector while the other did the digging. It was a perfect evening for the work of a treasure hunter. He pressed the electronic-key-pad and two flashes from the van's sidelights indicated the locking mechanism was in place. But what was that? In the light of the second flash, a movement by the hedge. Soft rustling followed.

"For fuck sake, man, lighten up! It's an animal of the night, probably some fox or badger taking a dump and marking his territory; the vile stench in the air proves it." He'd voiced the thoughts, in the hope that whatever it was would scamper away in fright. He heard nothing. Vinny fixed his eyes ahead and began the steady walk towards his friend. In the pitch-black darkness, the occasional blink of light from Stefan's key fob torch, was the only guide to the area of search. The wellington boots, a size bigger than his shoes and needing a second pair of socks to aid comfort, slapped and flopped, intruding on the nights stillness as Vinny plodded slowly up the incline of the furrowed hill. Twice he stopped, relieved that the strange noise stopped too. He was determined not to look back even though he had a gut feeling that the creature in the hedge was watching his every move.

"Get a grip, man," he snarled through gritted teeth. "It's an animal, bound to be scared of us humans. Bound to be hiding and watching." Up ahead and another blink of light. In spite of the incline, the discomfort of the wellies and his laboured breathing, Vinny's legs had a mind of their own. They decided they should, and could, move much faster. With eyes trained on the last tiny blink of light, Vinny guessed it to be no more than twenty meters away. Panting, he arrived at the spot. No sign of Stefan! Just the stainless steel spade, upright with the business-end driven several inches into the ground. The metal detector, also upright, was resting against it. There was rustling nearby and the sound of something familiar. But Vinny's mind was in no fit state for analyzing. Where was his mate? He wanted to call out. Tried to call out but his vocal cords weren't as responsive as his legs. He looked down the field towards where his van was parked. Nothing. Just an endless black hole between him and any means of escape. Another rustle from behind. Then pressure on his right shoulder and words filled the dark silence of night. Vinny almost crapped himself!

"You get here very quick, Vincent. I just take a piss in bushes while I waiting. Is lovely evening, no?"

Vinny remained rooted to the spot allowing relief to wash away whatever it was that had momentarily gripped him. The firm hand on his shoulder was reassuring enough, but it was his own embarrassment that kept his eyes from looking into the face of his friend. "Any luck?" he asked, still staring at the black hole, desperate to sound, and feel, like his old self.

"The ground very quiet here. But I find one old coin and a button. I think, both lost naturally. You want to take turn with machine?"

Vinny shook his head. Never before had he wanted to be more in the light. Any light. "I'm ready for a bite to eat, he lied, how about you?"

"Sure. A pie and a pint, as you say in your fine country, will go down very nicely."

Staying close, they made rapid progress towards the ghostly shape of the white van. Vinny's key-pad was pressed several times before they were in range for it to engage the lock and bathe the area in a pulse of light. Nothing untoward. Without much care or ceremony, metal detector and spade were quickly loaded into the back. The door slammed after each occupant was seated and ready to go. It was only after a hasty reverse onto the road, a short drive and the welcoming light of a road sign that Vinny pulled over and removed his wellies.

I MARK THEIR HUNTING GROUND. I MARK THEIR HOME. I HEAR THEIR WORDS. I UNDERSTAND THEIR DESIRES. SOON, MY DESIRE TO INFLICT REVENGE, WILL BE FULFILLED.

Chapter 15

Monday—Lanzarote

Although it was less than twenty-four hours, it seemed to Lyn as if she'd been in the warm sunshine of Lanzarote for days. Gone was the familiarity of the daily routine. Gone was the acknowledgement of time and constant checking of it to make sure everything was on schedule. And, not quite gone but disappearing fast, the mental and physical tension which had been building over the last few months — the reasons for which she had always found difficult to fathom. Watches and phones had been locked in the safe to prevent intrusion into *their* week. A week where time didn't matter. What was most important was discovering each others needs in their forthcoming commitment. If the last twenty-four hours was anything to go by, satisfying their sexual needs seemed to have become the most dominant factor.

Sunday had been punctuated by four of these needy sessions: before and after waking from their siesta, after an early evening walk along the Avenida De Las Playas and later after returning from a delicious meal at one of the harbour restaurants. It seemed as though each time they returned to their suite, the urge to kiss, touch and discover greater heights of sexual pleasure, was so irresistible and the only thing that mattered. This morning, after waking from a deep, dreamless sleep, the urge again, waiting to be satisfied and James was only too eager to oblige.

As they'd languished in the afterglow, Lyn had reminded him of the phone call he'd need to make for hiring a car. They'd passed a car-hire place on their previous evenings walk, but it was closed. Bearing in mind that twenty-four hours notice was required, it was decided that James would phone after breakfast today for hiring the following day. They both wanted to see more of the island, but she was the keener. Accepting that for the first couple of days they were restricted to places in walking distance, it was fortuitous when a waiter in the harbour restaurant had recommended a cliff-top walk to Puerto Calero — a smart marina set in a beautiful cove less than an hours walk away. They'd been able to see the zig-zagging road leading to it from their table and were intrigued. Influenced by the waiters enthusiasm, it was decided they'd set out after breakfast while temperatures were moderate and use the water taxi to return in the heat of the afternoon — back in time for siesta, and probably more of the needy stuff.

Breakfast had arrived, a full English with all the trimmings and a pot of steaming coffee. They'd plumped for eating in their suite — as well as the luxury of complete privacy, maybe it was a subliminal test to show that other appetites could be satisfied within these four walls — and once their hunger for nourishment was sated and before any other urges began to develop, Lyn had reminded James of the car-hire booking.

Switching on his phone James found a text message. Just the one, and it was from his sister. Lyn saw the indecision on his face as his thumb wavered over the screen. Then it fell, a silent version of the auctioneer's hammer, the action irreversible. The message was blunt. *Phone me ASAP.*

They looked at each other and words weren't necessary. In spite of all the rhetoric and promises of not returning messages, they both knew this call would need to be made. They also knew that the making of the call would shatter the spell they were under and burst their magical bubble.

James walked out onto the terrace and was grateful that the immediate area was devoid of people. He was also grateful that Lyn hadn't followed him — eager to learn what lay behind Helen's hurried plea. His sister knew the importance of this holiday and appreciated its necessity for making their wedding plans. She wouldn't have wanted to interrupt them unless it was absolutely necessary.

He braced himself for bad news and tapped in her home number but it was answered by the machine, asking for a message. Without speaking, he tapped in her mobile number. After three rings Helen's voice, apologising profusely for disturbing their holiday. Pushing aside the unnecessaries, James asked, "What's happened?" He listened, without interrupting, as Helen explained how their mother had suffered a stroke during Sunday evening. Helen had popped in, as usual, on her way to work that morning. She'd found Mother on the floor by her favourite armchair, unable to speak or move. Helen then rambled on about curtains closed, lights on and the radio blaring out some God-awful song. James interrupted, recognising the building stress in his sister's voice. "Helen, how bad is she?"

"Sorry, James, my minds all over the place. It's too early to say how bad things are. I followed the ambulance to the hospital around seven-thirty, and I'm still here. Like I said, she can't talk and she has very little movement. I just hope… I know it's selfish, James, but I hope…"

"Helen, keep me informed of any changes, I'll arrange a flight back as soon as I can but I can't promise it'll be today. There's only one flight a week to Exeter from here so I'll need to phone around for other airports. Are you able to stay with her?"

"Yes. Yes of course I'll stay with her. Matt's doing his best to get her settled onto the right ward. At least I'm fortunate having a husband in the medical profession, believe me, James, it's bedlam here. There are people who have spent hours on trolleys, just waiting for attention. I'm so sorry to have spoilt your holiday. Apologise to Lyn for me."

Again he interrupted "Helen, this is not your fault. Try and get a little rest. Find somewhere quiet at the hospital and close your eyes. Leave it to the professionals now, you can't do anymore. I'll get to you as soon as I can." James ended the call but remained standing on the terrace, the beautiful panorama of Lanzarote's coastline before him. His eyes were closed, thoughts locked onto how his mother must have suffered. An independent soul trapped in a worn-out body. Unable to move. Unable to call for help.

Two years ago, he'd set up an account with, Care-line Personal Alarms. After weeks of badgering, Mother finally gave in to wearing a Pendant-Alarm which she wore when her children were around. Both knew that the gadget —which was what Mother had called it — mainly rested out of sight and out of mind. There was obviously no sign of it when Helen came upon the tragic scene.

He felt arms gently wrap around his waist from behind and the scent of Lyn filled the air.

"Is the holiday over?" she asked, voice muffled against his back.

He turned and they held each other in a tight, comforting

embrace. "I have to go back, sweetheart. Mother's had a stroke and I don't know if…"

Lyn kissed his mouth putting an end to words that no one wanted to say or hear. "It's alright, my love, we'll both go back."

"No! No, sweetheart. You wait here for my return. Once I know she's getting the best care possible, I'll be back. I need to give Helen some help and support first. I'm afraid the plans for our walk are out of the question. You go and relax by the pool, I might be some time making the necessary phone calls."

Forty minutes later and James had secured a seat on a flight to Bristol for the following day. The problem was, his car was parked at Exeter Airport and under the circumstances, it wouldn't be fair to expect Helen to make a three-hundred-mile round trip to pick him up. He skipped through 'contacts' on his phone, hovering over the name of his neighbour. One good turn deserves another, he thought as he tapped the number of Vincent Conway.

Lyn pushed the book aside, lay back and closed her eyes. Too many thoughts and too much emotion fighting for supremacy over a mediocre tale of two women fighting for the attention of one man — their manager. *Her* man, was obviously having trouble gaining the flight which would wrench them apart. She felt bereft at the thought of it, jealous of the sister who was desperate for his return and angry with the man she loved because he didn't want her to join him. Didn't need her to share his anguish, and quite possibly, console him in his grief. She should have insisted, should have made it clear to him that being here alone would be hell. (*For goodness sake, Lynda, get a grip on yourself!*)

An echo of Gran's voice, not experienced in ages, but usually eager to surface when Lyn felt at her most vulnerable. Gran had raised her from a baby, telling the teen-aged Lyn that her parents had died in a car accident. All lies. Lyn came to learn, only very recently, that her parents were in Australia, both renowned artists.

She sensed his approach. He leaned close and lightly pressed his lips to her forehead. Her eyes remained closed, feigning sleep, but she knew he wouldn't be fooled. With eyelids locked in place, she felt the draft from the towel as his wrists flicked, sending it into a semi-levitated position before settling and covering the sun bed, perfectly. She heard creaking as his near-naked form surrendered its weight to wood and canvas. She was aware of his sigh of pleasure when the sun, lover to everyone, kissed every inch of his body — except the area that only she was allowed to kiss. Unable to resist any longer, she opened her eyes and turned to him. He was waiting for her to say something, looking into her face, their sunglasses a barrier to reading the truth. Determined not to speak first, offer some meaningless platitude just for the sake it, she turned her head back to the sky and waited for Gran's reproach. But it was James' voice that filled her head.

"I managed to get a flight, sweetheart, I need to be at the airport by one-thirty tomorrow. So lets make the most of today. What shall we do? You choose."

She knew what she wanted to do. She wanted to scream and shout at the unfairness of it all. Turn the clock back an hour and without his knowledge, take his phone and fling it into the depths of the ocean. Drown out Helen's need to take him from her. She wanted to be back inside the magical bubble; even if it were for just one more day.

(*Lynda!*)
For Christ sake Gran, leave me be!

Afraid that she'd voiced this mental plea, Lyn looked at James, embarrassed, then relieved, he was calmly waiting for her response. "Well, as I'll be making *all* the choices for the next few days, I think it only fair that *you* choose what we do today."

James understood the disappointment that Lyn was feeling. This holiday had been her gift to him. The gift of a whole week to discuss and make plans for their future together. A week without interruptions from either of their businesses. But *this* interruption was different. *This* interruption needed his full attention.

His mother was coming to the end of her life, a life in the main that had been sacrificed for the benefit of her children. James' parents had denied themselves, in order to obtain a first-class, public-school education for their offspring, and as a result, both had secure, well-paid professions and a decent quality of life. At Mother's insistence, Helen had been landed with the lion's share of her care during the last few months. Maybe if Father hadn't died first, things would have been different. *Maybes and ifs* were a time wasting indulgence that James never courted. He needed to put aside his own future plans, temporarily, and take responsibility for his share of the burden and before it was too late, he needed to show his mother how much he loved her.

The sun, warm and inviting yesterday, was hot and uncomfortable, and the thought of a walk in it's searing heat was the last thing he wanted.

"Under the circumstances, sweetheart, I'd just as soon relax in the shade." Shall we move to a table under the pergola and order coffees?"

Lyn frowned and made no attempt to move. She answered his question with an enquiry of her own. "How will you get from Bristol to Exeter to pick up your car.?"

"Vincent has agreed to meet me at the airport."

"That's very decent of him." Lyn had responded without thinking, her words, although innocuous, sounded sour."

"It *was* decent of him, especially at such short notice."

Silence fell as each retreated into their own thoughts. James' thoughts returned to Vincent and the unexpected rendezvous. Each had something to gain from it. James brought back to mind the gist of their telephone conversation after the initial request for a lift to Exeter. Vincent had told him that his lady-client had decided to sell her gold ring. But it isn't cheap! (His words.) He'd then given James all the elaborations of a salesman's pitch: the rising price of gold, the vast age and condition of the ring in question, its provenance and attribution to maker. All unnecessary. James wanted the ring and Vincent knew this, so a high price was expected. But when the price was finally extracted from the man, James coughed a little and fell silent. In those few seconds of silence, he thought of Lyn and how much he wanted to make her his own. This ring, with it's engraved, ancient poem, conveyed his feelings perfectly. The silence had obviously caused concern. Vincent had become the salesman again, telling James there was another interested party. James had ended the call by telling Vincent that he'd have the ring, at the price just quoted but, he had no intention of entering into an auction-style free-for-all.

Monday—Torquay

Vinny slipped the phone back into his breast pocket, pursed his lips and whistled a cheerful rendition of Here Comes the Bride while he continued to remove the cheap, crappy lock from the cheap, crappy door which was the main entrance to a cheap, crappy flat. Old tenants had moved out — more than likely thrown out for default — and new tenants would be moving in by the end of the week. He did a fair amount of work for this particular landlord, Jack Lovell, a guy who was obsessed with the notion that every tenant acquired spare keys so that they were able to return and rob the next tenant.

The phone call from Jimmy was a ray of sunshine in the gloom. A gloom which had been present since, if he was to be completely honest, he'd stepped onto the dark, ploughed field the night before. What was it about the place that seemed to be spooking everyone, including Stefan, the most grounded bloke he'd ever met. Isabelle was well and truly freaked out by something. Her head was filled with stuff and nonsense about the previous owner of the gold ring being back from the dead; 'reincarnated' was her actual word, she even claimed he was emailing her. Vinny had told her that someone was just having a laugh and not to take it seriously. At this point she'd become really indignant. The woman was definitely bonkers! Shame really. After their first meeting, there was a point when he actually thought, with hubby off the scene and her having the house to herself — a house all paid for — she would still need a part-time job just to help pass the time. Vinny could've supplied that need by making her his secretary. You never know where it might have led. He was even prepared to control his swearing for her. Well, you can fucking well forget that now, mate. Having a raving lunatic in his line of business was just fucking financial suicide.

"I finish locks on number 12. You ready for coffee, Vincent?"

"Bloody-hell, Stefan, give us a break." Vinny spun round to face the Bulgarian, screwdriver held high, before realising he'd just created a pun. "Ah! There I go again, cracking jokes nonstop. Just call me Mr Happy and just remember this, Stefan, the only reason you have finished before me, is because *I* have been on the phone negotiating a profitable, financial deal." A cheeky wink accompanied a face-cracking grin.

"I hear you say, you sell gold ring to Mr Fairbank. How so, when you already give ring back to Isabelle?"

"Mind your own fucking business! Go and get the flask from the van."

Bovey Tracey

Shaun Thatcher reached for the flask which was part of his packed lunch. The sandwiches and bag of crisps were long gone, eaten not in an urge to satisfy hunger, but more to quell the gnawing sensation in the pit of his stomach. It was gone nine-thirty and although he'd left for work at the usual time, seven-fifty, he hadn't yet set foot on his employer's premises. He'd parked a safe distance from the house and sat with his eyes glued to the front gate, waiting. Waiting for what? He wasn't sure. The only thing he was sure of, something was going on between Izzy and another bloke and he intended to get to the bottom of it.

At their brief meeting the night before, he definitely saw

the bloke give her something. And he definitely saw Izzy pleading with him. He couldn't hear what was said, but he could read her like a book, she'd done enough pleading in his direction over the years. He'd wanted to have it out with her when she'd come back but she'd looked so… so fragile, so vulnerable, he hadn't the heart to start a row. But after a night spent tossing and turning he'd made up his mind to get to the bottom of what was going on and he'd do it *his* way. He'd bloody well follow her everywhere she went until he could piece together what the hell was going on.

He'd been bored, frustrated and worried. Yes, he was bloody worried. Who wouldn't be? Sitting in the car waiting gave him plenty of time for thinking. Plenty of time to wonder where all this would end. A little way into that thinking, Robert had dashed through the gate looking like he'd just crawled from his bed at twenty to nine. He'd watched his son balancing his rucksack as he shoved arms into jacket with toast between his teeth, turning the opposite direction to where Shaun sat like some bloody peeping Tom. Shaun loved his son, wanted something better for him but there weren't the opportunities round here. Not wanting to pursue that line of thought any longer, he had turned on the radio. Some bloke had been banging on about the worsening employment figures, as if it wasn't common knowledge to the whole bloody nation. What did *he* know about the struggle to make ends meet on a minimum wage? He wouldn't have any concerns about money, not with the high salaries they earned. Shaun had snapped off his superior-sounding voice and returned to the silence and the comfort of eating what remained of his lunch.

Izzy had finally emerged at almost ten o'clock. She'd looked all about her, causing Shaun to slink down in his seat even though he knew he couldn't be seen. Then pulling her coat tightly about her, she bowed her head and marched in the direction of the car park, turning right into it.

Shaun scrambled from his seat, feeling the stiffness of having sat too long, and loped along the road to where his wife had turned off. He caught a glimpse of her head at the bottom of the sloping row of cars, disappearing from view. He hurried to catch up. Within minutes realizing where she was heading. The library doors, which open at ten, were inviting a mixed bag of pensioners, unemployed wastrels and Izzy. Why was she there? Who was she contacting on the bloody computer?

Luckily, Isabelle managed to secure a computer straight away. The majority of the other visitors were here to read free newspapers and magazines within the warmth and peace of the library. What *she* sought above all else was privacy. Privacy to communicate with, with what? An entity? A figment of her own imagination? A real live person who knew her? And if this, this, Nicholas, was a normal human being, how could he know about the ring? She'd kept her secret from everyone, except Mr Conway. Now, desperate to share her fears and concerns, she'd confided in him again. He'd tried humouring her, but she'd recognised that look in his eyes. No doubt about it, Mr Conway thought she was unhinged. Maybe she was. She was caught up in something she didn't understand. Frightening yet compelling.

Pulling herself together she concentrated on why she was in the library. Checking that no one was around, she logged on. It seemed to take forever but at last her eyes were focusing on the screen. Reading again the email she'd found yesterday before Shaun had interrupted her. Remembering only the last few words. She now read the whole message over and over again.

HELLO BELLA, MY BEAUTIFUL BELLA. SOON WE WILL BE TOGETHER AGAIN FOR ALL TIME. TAKE BACK THE RING AND KEEP IT SAFE. IT HAS AN IMPORTANT TASK TO FULFILL. YOUR BELOVED NICHOLAS.

Without realising what she was doing, Isabelle brought her thumb to her lips and pressed them against the ring. Closing her eyes she tried to imagine her beloved Nicholas. She wanted to see him. She needed to feel him to make sure he was real.

A hand, touching her shoulder, freaked her out. Isabelle turned to find an unfamiliar librarian looking concerned.

"Are you alright, madam? Do you need help logging off? I'm afraid your time is up and there are others waiting."

"Sorry, just give me a minute to shut down." A part of Isabelle wanted to respond to the email, but she couldn't bring herself to do it. It would be admitting to…no she couldn't do that. Besides, what could she say. He had the advantage. She was just a poor wretch who appeared to be losing her mind.

Chapter 16

Monday Evening—Lanzarote

Lyn watched the sun gradually sink from view, leaving behind a sky streaked with broken crimson clouds and an air temperature suddenly several degrees cooler. It was time to leave. They'd finished eating ages ago. Several tapas-portions of local fish delicacies had been ordered and served with a chilled bottle of Lanzarote wine. The food looked delicious but the main ingredient for full enjoyment — hunger — was missing in both of them. Each dish had been picked at and then pushed aside, leaving the concerned-looking waiter wondering why we had bothered taking up space on the terrace of his popular restaurant. Even the wine, normally guaranteed to lift the spirits, failed to play its role and perversely exaggerated their melancholy mood.

It had been at Lyn's insistence that they take the walk to Puerto Calero. She'd been tired of sitting around doing nothing. Tired of just 'chilling out' on a sun bed by the pool while inside her emotions flared with a mixture of jealousy, resentment and uncertainty. In spite of the rising temperatures, James had acquiesced. What else could he do?

They'd set out with hats, sun cream, and a bottle of water.

And, *his* bloody mobile phone. Within fifteen minutes they were on high cliff tops wishing they'd brought along the binoculars that sat forgotten in the hotel safe. A school of dolphins, seemingly, escorting a passenger boat, mimicked the waves as they leapt high in the water then fell from view. It had been delightful to watch, and as it turned out, the pinnacle of their afternoon. All too soon they had disappeared to wherever dolphins go, leaving two lost souls scanning the ocean in the hope of catching another glimpse of their playful antics. But the influence of their appearance did leave behind a little magic, albeit temporary. The walk was continued, hand-in-hand. Silence gave way to chit chat about how beautiful the sea looked and how quaint the nearing buildings and boats of the place they were heading.

Before reaching Puerto Calero, Lyn's attention had wandered to the mountains and the intriguing lava fields that lay around them. She'd admitted her intention to explore some of the countryside whilst waiting for James to return. He'd halted, abandoned the hold on her hand and took hold of both her shoulders. For a brief moment, she thought he was about to shake the living daylight from her but his hands remained still, it was his words that shook her to the core.

"Promise me, Lyn, you will not venture into that barren wilderness alone."

He saw at once shock and confusion on her face. He'd pulled her close, and as their bodies had pressed into one, she'd felt the strong, rapid beat of his heart. A heart driven by feelings that were hard to understand.

James unwound his jacket from the back of the chair slipping his arms through its sleeves. It didn't offer much by way of warmth, the temperature had plummeted with the setting sun, making him even more anxious to get back to the hotel. Walking was out of the question and the promise of a return journey by water-taxi had been scuppered. The last one returning to Puerto Del Carmen had left ages ago. Nothing for it, he would have to arrange a taxi. A taxi making a circuitous route on roads and tracks through, what he regarded as, a lunar landscape.

His strong commitment of the previous day — mastering a once-familiar language that had become very rusty over the years from lack of use — had deserted him. Left him in favour of the easy route of letting others struggle through scant communications. He picked up the bill for the meal and carried it up to the bar. Here, it was simple enough to indicate that he needed a taxi. In return, and probably helped by the generous tip, the waiter obliged and soon made it perfectly clear where they should wait for the ordered car.

Having found the allotted place of pick-up, they stood for several minutes in the fast-fading light, looking about them. Lyn's attention, he could see, was focussed on the exotic array of palm trees and foliage, jagged shapes silhouetted against a darkening sky which surrounded them on three sides. The ocean, a crystal of aquamarine two hours before, was now a dark, moving mass of unfathomable mystery.

He pulled her close, half wrapping his own open jacket about her. "Taxi shouldn't be long, darling, are you warm enough?"

"Yes, I'm fine." She slipped out of his protecting embrace, turned to face him and zipped up his jacket. "There, that makes more sense than having it flapping open. Besides, my jacket is much warmer than yours."

Lyn suddenly crossed over the road to inspect a shrub in full bloom, its true colour hard to ascertain through lack of daylight. She called out, "This is absolutely gorgeous!"

James resisted the attempt to be drawn over. Obviously, her interest in flora was part and parcel of her work and it was natural for her to seek out and enjoy the discovery of alien plants. Completely understandable, that she'd want to photograph them and share that pleasure of discovery with her business partner, Jill. However, venturing out to uninhabited parts of a foreign land just to take photographs of plants that could be found in books or 'on the net' seemed to him, a pointless waste of time. And when he voiced this, sounding churlish and immature, he deserved the backlash that sprang from it. He should have been honest. He should have explained his fears for her safety. He'd lost count of the news reports of women going missing while visiting foreign countries. The loved ones who suffered the pain of what might have happened to them. James hadn't mentioned any of this to Lyn, they were his fears not hers, but her constant overtures relating to walking in the 'real' Lanzarote, away from the tourist spots, filled him with dread. She had mentioned there were several walking groups that advertised in the local magazines, along with information about times and places to meet.

His thoughts came to an abrupt end as a taxi pulled alongside and in a strong Spanish accent asked.

"Mr James, you order taxi?"

Monday Evening—Bovey Tracey

Shaun Thatcher wasn't the kind of guy who could just sit quietly in front of the telly whilst the news was on. He regarded it as a debating platform. The poor sod who happened to be reading the latest happenings, was sworn at, argued with, and, as a rule, even verbally abused in regard to his personal appearance — especially if he was imparting further increases in tax or further decreases in benefits to the hard-pressed-working-man. But, from the time Shaun had plunged his empty dinner plate into the sink of soapy suds and settled his tired body into a chair, barely a meter away from the screen, he hadn't said a single word of derision. In fact he hadn't said a word about anything. Not to Izzy. Not even to Robert.

With a concerned look from Robert, "You OK Dad?"

"What? Sorry mate, I was miles away."

"Somewhere sunny, I'll bet. It's peeing down again out there."

"What, no, no I was just thinking that's all. Were you needing a lift, son?"

"No, I'm staying in tonight. Got a bundle of homework to get through. You sure you're OK?"

No, he wasn't bloody OK, but he wasn't about to pile that on his son's shoulders. So he produced a smile and what he hoped was a reassuring nod. Poor kid, working his socks off to gain a better chance in life but he'd find out soon enough. For now, Shaun needed to find out what was going on between his wife and this bloke.

He'd gone into work three hours late. The excuse of visiting his doctor, with a complaint too personal to relay to his immediate boss, hadn't gained him any sympathy. What it had gained him, was a warning. A warning that if he took any more time off that had not been prearranged, or unless it was a dire emergency like his wife had just dropped dead, he would be sacked on the spot! No 'ifs or buts', just thrown on the scrapheap of the unemployed.

Suddenly, the cause behind that dire warning was at his

elbow. She was offering a mug of tea and asking him if he'd had a bad day. He turned to her on the brink of transferring his frustration, but held back. She looked drawn and pale. Purple smudges under eyes that had lost their sparkle. She couldn't be having an affair? Who would fancy her in the state she was in? "Maybe I should be asking you the same thing, you look terrible, Izzy."

"I told you, I'm not sleeping well. In fact I'm hardly sleeping at all. Suppose I've got too much on my mind."

"You wanna tell me what it is that's on your mind?" Shaun waited, eyes remaining on her face while he sipped the hot brew. She opened her mouth and then closed it immediately. He sensed she wanted to unload some burden but she remained silent, squirming under his gaze.

Averting his eyes she said, "I'm just worried about my health, that's all. I'll be fine if I get the all-clear on the smear-test."

Shaun suspected this was a load of bollocks and she was lying through her teeth, but why? Sod it, he needed a walk. He needed a drink.

The back door slammed shut. The noise from the television was shut off and the deafening silence that followed caused Isabelle to hold her breath. The silence pervaded every inch of the old, thatched cottage. Then a soft thud from above her head made her flinch, relaxing as she remembered that Robert was just a few feet away. She also remembered that she needed to contact Mr Conway straight away, to let him know that Shaun had gone out, he'd insisted from the start that this was her part to play. She could hear the rain pelting down, imagined it soaking through her, chilling her body and bringing on a fever.

She grabbed the phone and looked about her. She moved quickly to the dining room and closing the door quietly crouched in it's furthest corner. After the fifth ring Mr Conway's voice.

"Yep, Conway, here."

In a low voice she said, "Sorry to disturb you in the evening, Mr Conway, but Shaun has just gone out."

"Shit! Sorry Isabelle, do you know where he's gone?"

Impatient to be off the phone before Robert had a chance to overhear, she lowered her voice even more and through gritted teeth said. "I presume, he's gone where he always goes, to the pub."

"I didn't catch that, Isabelle, is everything alright?"

She slowly repeated what she'd said, cutting the connection immediately after Mr Conway told her to leave it to him.

Torquay

Vinny tapped the pen against his teeth, all was not well with his lady-client. That bastard of a husband must be knocking her about. There was no evidence of cuts and bruises but something or someone was definitely getting to her. He heard the rain slashing against the window. He was aware of his full stomach after eating one of Stefan's strange but delicious concoctions and all he wanted to do, was sit down and watch a bit of telly. And once this fucking paperwork was out of the way, that's exactly what he'd intended to do. But, business was business. He closed his book of accounts and stuck the pen in the pot.

"Stefan?" Vinny shouted. No answer. Without leaving his seat he shouted again, louder this time. Still no answer. A stream of under-the-breath expletives before dragging his body from his office chair — the arms hugging his broad hips as if begging him to stay. A hefty pull and he was free.

Bedroom, bathroom and kitchen were all devoid of Stefan's presence but not of his attention to tidiness. Even the kitchen, where several pots and pans had been used to cook the hearty meal, was clean and tidy with everything back in place.

The back door swung open and Stefan stepped onto the doormat, bending to unlace his boots. Vinny's voice stopped him before his hands had a chance to reach the sodden laces.

"What you doing out there in the rain, checking for ghosts? I've been shouting myself hoarse for half an hour."

Stefan straightened his back. "I hear you perfectly well, two times in a few seconds."

"So why didn't you fucking answer?"

"I answering now. I leave what I'm doing and come to listen. Only fools shout their words and everyone hear what they say."

Vinny bristled but didn't respond. Two raindrops fell from Stefan's angular jaw and trickled down the bare section of his neck, exposed due to buttons undone, but his eyes remained riveted on Vinny. This man was tough, very tough, and Vinny wouldn't want to get on the wrong side of him.

"Well, I'm happy to see you're ready for the great outdoors, Stefan. I've had a phone call. I'm on surveillance duty and *you* can continue searching a different part of the ploughed field. Ask me nicely, and I might loan you my wellington boots."

"I need two plastic bags without holes in them."

"Why? You prefer them on your feet to my wellies."

Stefan's face remained serious. "I need to keep rain off top of searching-machine. If rain get inside, it goes kaput. Other plastic bag for things I find. There will be much mud everywhere."

Bovey Tracey

Shaun Thatcher sat at the bar hugging his pint with both hands. He'd been sitting there for some time, appearing to be looking deep into the amber nectar that was still filling half of his glass. In reality, his thoughts were anywhere but. The Carpenters was very quiet, which was usual for a Monday. What was unusual, was that Jules wasn't around and according to Danny, she wouldn't be around for the rest of the week. This was welcome news and a relief, no more feeling obliged into buying drinks he couldn't afford, for a barmaid who, in his opinion, didn't deserve them. Besides, he'd already decided not to do it anymore. Tonight, he'd just stick with the one pint then get off home, maybe have an early night.

He casually asked Danny if Jules was unwell? After all the partying and boozing on Saturday night, it wouldn't have surprised him. Danny shook his head, looked over to the only occupied table where two old boys sat engrossed in a game of dominoes, and lowered his voice.

"She's up in London for the week," he said. "Apparently there's a land-auction, parcels of land for sale in the home counties and Jules is hoping to secure one with planning permission. It's cheaper for her to stay with family in London than keep travelling back and forth."

"Where would Jules get that kind of cash? asked Shaun, "She only works evenings."

"I believe she's managed to sell one of the properties she owns in Exeter."

"One of the properties. Bloody hell, how many has she got?"

Danny took a large gulp of his orange squash. A few seconds to reflect on the rights and wrongs of idle gossip. He concluded that Jules would soon be leaving anyway. Onwards and upwards was one of her favourite sayings. While on the other hand, Shaun Thatcher would still be propping up this bar, long after Danny was pushing up daisies. "She's got a few, rents 'em out, that's her main trade. Working here gave her extra savings. She's been trying for a while to sell off her biggest property as a going concern, a big house split into studio-flats with the ground floor apartment for the landlord, a ready made income for someone with the cash to invest. Actually, I believe it's someone local who bought it."

Everything suddenly fell into place. Jules had been flaunting herself. Working on him to sell up in Bovey and buy a place in Exeter. *Her* place. What she had said about moving to Exeter had all made sense. Unbeknown to Jules, the three-bed-thatched cottage that he'd boasted about, wasn't his to sell. Izzy's name was on the deeds and Izzy wasn't about to part with it. "So, you'll be in for a quiet week then?"

"Tis true, Jules does enhance the trade. Won't be too long afore she moves on though and I'll be looking out for another lass."

All heads turned as the pub door opened and a stocky man walked in, looked around, and without saying a word, headed for the Gents. Shaun couldn't believe his luck. This was the second revelation of the evening. The mystery-man that Izzy had met the evening before had just walked straight into his hands. He looked at Danny and doing his best to remain nonchalant, asked "Who's he, someone off the street desperate for a slash?"

Keeping one eye on the door to the toilet, Danny imparted the knowledge he'd gained on Saturday night, adding that in his view, he was a snoop, plain-clothes cop or someone of that ilk.

Shaun drank his remaining beer in one long gulp, thanked the landlord for the interesting information and headed for the door. The two old men smiled and nodded sagely.

Hiding in a pub toilet wasn't the best situation to plan your next move but Vinny had been cornered in worse places. He hadn't reckoned on the bar being so empty. Hadn't reckoned on four pairs of eyes taking notice of the stranger in their midst, an outsider who would definitely not be welcome. Ordering himself to calm down, he considered his options. The two old guys looked to be getting on for ninety, probably only saw him as a blur and even if they did see well enough, at that age, their powers of recollection would be shot to pieces. Danny, the landlord, would remember him — he had served him drink, along with an enquiring little chat, on Saturday night, — so Vinny would have to bear that in mind. Shaun Thatcher was the dilemma. Once you've been clocked, it was Vinny's opinion that it was almost impossible to continue trailing the clocker. But then again, maybe Thatcher being here, right under his nose, was a blessing in disguise. Yes, he thought, brazen it out. Get as much information as he could from this wife-beating-bastard. Shaun Thatcher liked his beer. Time to oil the wheels and maybe loosen his tongue. If all went to plan, he wouldn't need to do any more surveillance on him.

Feeling pleased with his decision, as Vinny swaggered into the bar, three pairs of eyes locked on him. There was no sign of Shaun Thatcher. Without thinking, he looked back toward the Gents. Fuck, he thought. What now? He could hardly make a dash for the door.

"How'd the funeral go?" This was Danny with a friendly smile, waiting for an order and knowing he'd caught the man off guard.

"Oh yeah, well, you know how funerals are, a bit of God-bothering and a lot of boozing." Vinny was in a quandary, and before he shot his bolt by ordering a drink, he thought he'd chance his luck. "That chap that was at the bar when I came in, Shaun…Shaun…no, I can't think of his surname, I was hoping to buy him a drink, do you know where he's gone?"

"Home, I expect," said Danny, taking a clean cloth from a place below the counter.

"No, not the Shaun I know. He likes to get a few down his neck, and I do believe the last time we had a drink together, we parted on the understanding it was my round next time we met."

Danny started to wipe down the already scrupulously clean bar. "All's I can suggest," he said, as the cloth swiped in rhythm to his words. There're half a dozen other drinking places in these parts. You're welcome to check each one out, but I knows for a fact that Shaun only drinks in 'ere." The barman turned his back, and continued his cleaning as freshly washed glasses were subjected to brisk polishing from his cloth. Conversation over.

For a second, Vinny wondered if it was worth pumping the two old geezers. But thought better of it when one started having a coughing fit that lasted until he stepped into the street and the door slammed behind him. Raucous laughter filled the void where the coughing had been.

There was a damp chill in the air but at least the rain had eased off. Accepting defeat, Vinny turned up his collar, thrust both hands in his coat pocket and headed for the van — the only vehicle in the parking bay alongside Nat West bank.

He looked about him in all directions. Not a soul in sight. But as the lights flashed from unlocking the van, Vinny caught sight of someone's large, booted feet. A figure, pressing himself back in the shadow of the banks doorway. The observed, turned observer. Not only did Shaun Thatcher know he was being watched. He'd seen his watcher and the vehicle he drove. And with very little effort, he would soon have Vinny's name, address and occupation. Not only had the evening turned to shit, but it put an end to any more surveillance of Isabelle's husband. *Lets hope Stefan's having more luck than me,* thought Vinny, as he revved the engine and sped away, leaving a cloud of foul-smelling exhaust fumes suspended in the damp air of Bovey Tracey's main street.

The lower quarter of the ploughed field, furthest away from the entrance, was different from the rest of it. Different in two ways. Here it was level and there were signs of daytime activity. Activity from earth movers preparing to lay pipes or foundations for buildings. Is true, Stefan thought, if he were to return to this place in a few years time, the field would be gone. Buried and lost forever beneath tons of concrete. It was happening everywhere. More people in the world, so more houses were needed.

The rain had stopped but the soil was wet. Each of his boots the weight of a bag of potatoes, as he slowly moved towards a mound of earth that had been taken from it's rightful place. He switched on his keyring-torch, keeping it aimed at the ground. Good timing. Half a meter ahead the earth had been dug away leaving a deep trench at least four meters wide. The torch beam, aimed low and moving slowly in a wide arc, stopped at a stack of new pipes, confirming Stefan's foresight.

Steering clear of the trench, he worked slowly towards the mound of earth and was rewarded by a sharp 'beep'. There was no need to remove the protecting bag from the machines indicator, the sound alone was enough. This small object, laying just on the surface, was made of silver. Careful fingers slipped it into a cushioning pocket before continuing. The mound was almost upon him and so were many more 'beeps'! The ground was covered with them. So many signals fighting for his attention, Stefan soon found himself kneeling on the ground, scooping up soil and moving his hand across the search coil. If a positive signal rang out he his fingers filtered through the soil, checking the signal then placing the small amount of mud into the spare plastic bag. The spade had become unnecessary. His hands, thick with mud, retrieved more and more of what he was now sure, were coins. Coins of a similar size and age. His pockets were filled with them, and the plastic bag was becoming heavy with them and the protective layers of damp soil.

Vincent would be very pleased. As pleased and excited as he and his family when his father had found the coin hoard in Bulgaria. But Stefan would not make the same mistake again. He wouldn't speak of it to anyone. Only he and Vincent would know of their good fortune.

The loud honking of a horn froze his movements. In the entrance to the field, Vincent stood in the headlights of the van, arms beckoning him to come. Stefan had been so engrossed, he'd missed the warning flash. Such a pity, he thought, as he turned off the machine, cradled the plastic bag and dragged his mud-encrusted boots across the field. Others would be here tomorrow. Hopefully, they will remain unaware of the treasure which lay just beneath their feet.

Chapter 17

Tuesday morning—Lanzarote

Lyn checked her watch, hardly believing the time showing on the hotel's computer she was using. In less than five minutes her time would be up, and she was determined not to pay for more.

She'd had seven unread emails waiting for her attention. Six were ignored, business contacts selling their wares and services, she was on holiday, they could wait. The seventh was from Jill, wishing her and James a wonderful holiday in their fabulous location. She'd replied with a few words of acknowledgement, thanks, and an impression that all was sweetness and light, then sent it before she had chance to change her mind. She'd hated deceiving her friend but was in no frame of mind for sharing her feelings. Feelings of obsessional jealousy towards Helen. Feelings of resentment towards the man she was supposed to be in love with. Feelings of something dark and powerful erupting from the depths of her being. How could she share what she didn't understand? She'd closed her mail box and clicked on google, exploring sites for Lanzarote Walks. She'd jotting down dates, times and meeting places for areas that sounded interesting —

determined to see more of the island, even if it meant walking with a bunch of strangers.

After breakfast and In between two phones calls to Helen, James had made it quite clear that Lyn wasn't to go off walking alone, especially to the quieter, less-populated areas of the island. Her response, had been a look that was meant to convey, *do you think I'm stupid?* His response to that look, was a more elaborate replay of what he'd already said. To avoid the expletives that were gathering inside her head from escaping through her tight-pressed lips, Lyn had simply turned and walked away. Walked away from the conflict that was raging in them both. And this hotel, with its air of refined elegance, was not the place to let rip. James had called after her, asked where she was going. She'd wanted to scream out, *mind your own bloody business,* but instead, she'd turned and told him, in a forced calm and civilised manner, that she was going to find a computer to check her emails.

Not yet ready to return to the suite, she wandered into the hotel gardens finding a seat alongside a trio of date palms, her back turned to the bustling activities of others and in front of her, the broad expanse of clear blue ocean. A soft breeze rustled the fronds overhead and dappled shade moved in a merry dance across everything that lay in the sun's path. The whole scene was beautiful. Achingly beautiful! Soon the turmoil that raged within gradually began to lose its hold. She retrieved the notes from her purse, shorthand scribbles easily defined by the scribbler, but the names of routes, villages and meeting places were all unfamiliar. She made a mental note that buying a detailed map of Lanzarote would be the first thing she'd do after James left for the airport.

James plugged his phone into the charger he'd borrowed from reception. The battery was low and he didn't want to risk losing contact with Helen at such a worrying time. Neither of them had brought phone-chargers, they'd expected the top-up-charge before leaving to be sufficient for any eventuality — especially as they'd agreed to use the phones only in emergencies. He should have known better. The small space taken up with a charger compared to the peace of mind it offered was just plain common sense. It had been Lyn's mantra of 'travelling light' that had influenced his better judgement, and set in motion an embarrassing situation where a member of the hotel staff felt obliged to track down a compatible charger from a fellow guest. Obviously, he wasn't about to mention this to Lyn, she wasn't in the best frame of mind, but he felt confident that once she'd settled into the hotel routine and the lovely weather began to take effect of mind and body, she'd relax and realize it had been the right thing to do. It was pointless them both returning. Sitting for hours on end in a hospital, on edge and waiting for news of his mother's condition. In his opinion, it would have been unfair to Lyn. After all, this was a family crisis. He wanted to shield her from the anguish that he and Helen were experiencing. Lyn needed this break and she'd paid good money to have it. And if his mother was found to be in no immediate danger, he would return as soon as possible. The news so far was, no change, but Helen had been warned that Mother's condition could deteriorate drastically, especially if she suffered another stroke.

He checked his watch. Ninety minutes for topping up his phone, ninety minutes before a taxi would drive him to the airport. Everything was packed and he was ready, mentally prepared for what lay ahead back home. He locked the door and went in search of Lyn, wondering if ninety minutes was enough time to make things right between them.

Torquay

With a grunt that translated as thanks, Vinny accepted the mug of coffee from Stefan. He was sitting at his office desk, unwashed and still wearing the clothes he'd slept in — a pair of faded boxer shorts and an oversized tee shirt. — items he kept handy for cold nights and last night was especially cold. As usual, Stefan was looking fresh as a daisy in a clean shirt and his best jeans. No evidence of the mud that had caked him from head to toe the evening before. Not the slightest hint that he'd taken offense nor was he smarting from Vinny's constant verbal attacks from the time he'd arrived back at the van and climbed aboard with his sodden bag of filth. The bag revealing very little of what lay within apart from several kilos of soil. According to Vinny's recollection, Stefan had only spoken two sentences on the whole journey back.

Firstly, in answer to Vinny's "Is there anything worth having in that bag of stinking soil?" Stefan had answered "Is just pieces of metal till I wash clean and see." Later into the homeward journey when Vinny had unloaded his frustration and finally run out of words, Stefan had taken advantage of the silence and asked Vinny if he'd seen Isabelle's husband?

That simple little question had set Vinny off again. Through swearing, hollering and beating his fist against the steering wheel, he'd given Stefan a run down on how the evening had gone and how this marked the end of the surveillance of Shaun Thatcher, which also meant the end of increasing Isabelle's bill. Stefan hadn't responded, except for one of his silent knowing nods that really pissed Vinny off.

They'd arrived back and the silence between them continued except for Vinny's parting words. "I'm off to bed. Make sure the van is clean of all that shit by ten tomorrow. We've got more locks to fit and in the afternoon I've got to pick his lordship up at Bristol Airport. Wouldn't want him complaining about mud on his holiday sandals, would we?"

Vinny closed the account book with a loud slap. He'd been updating it and it had taken him best part of an hour. He checked again for any emails that Isabelle might have sent. Relieved, he found none. "Right, I'd better get myself together, Stefan. Is the van fit for purpose?" He didn't wait for the affirmative. This guy was the most reliable bloke he'd ever met. He'd risen very early, washing and scrubbing under a running tap for what seemed like hours. God knows how much the next water bill will be.

The tips of Stefan's fingers still bore wrinkles from too much water, too much brushing and too much ingrained mud which then needed scrubbing away. But he was happy. He'd been right. He'd come upon a hoard of hammered silver coins approximately two centimeters across. He'd counted thirty-eight in total, but guessed there were many more just waiting to be gathered up Their condition looked good, confirming that they'd lain in the ground undisturbed for centuries until the JCB showed them the light of day. As to the exact age and how valuable they were, Stefan didn't have a clue.

The excitement of the night before was short-lived and that was good. He was a man now, able to keep his feelings under control and his mouth shut. Not like before when one little coin out of many hundred had cost his father his life, robbed his family of the chance to escape poverty, and stripped Elena, his sister, of innocence and any future opportunity to have children. But worst of all, that one little coin, which had spilled off the freshly-scrubbed table and landed in the ragged turn up of a fifteen-year-old's worn trousers, had cost him years of guilt. Guilt that would weigh heavy for the rest of his days.

But in some way he would try to make amends. For this he needed to get back to the field, rescue as many coins as possible before heavy machinery crushed and pressed them back into earth littered with stones and grit. Maybe the wet conditions will keep the workmen off the field. If not, he would have to become invisible and move amongst them.

Bovey Tracey

After the dismal weather of the day before, the sky had begun to lighten and a slash of autumn sun briefly put in an appearance for those interested enough to take notice. But unlike most housewives — cheated from having God's fresh air to dry their weekly wash on Monday, and pondering whether today would be a safer bet — Isabelle hadn't noticed this brief spectacle of sunshine. Isabelle wasn't noticing anything right now. Getting to grips with her overspilling laundry basket, was way down her list of priorities.

She was sitting at the kitchen table, her second cup of coffee of the morning steaming in front of her. The steam was mesmerising, a brief comforting interlude from the burdens that plagued her mind. She was smart enough to realise that lack of quality sleep was the main reason behind how she felt and how she looked. After catching a passing glimpse of her face in the bathroom mirror — nearly jumping out of her skin at the stranger invading her space — she'd looked closer and the truth was laid bare. The thirty-five year old, healthy and vital just a few days ago, looked at least ten years older, and felt much older than that. She took a tentative sip of the hot, strong brew knowing that this was the only means of keeping her alert enough to follow through what needed to be done. To compensate for the false hyper-activity, she would try and grab an afternoon nap. Try her hardest to be the devoted mother and the dutiful wife when her husband and son returned home. Try to get her life back to some kind of normality.

Her eyes glanced at the clock. Five minutes had passed since she last looked. Determination gripped as she forced herself to remain seated for ten minutes more. After that ten minutes she would return to the library. A computer, booked especially to her, would then be available. She would move to it and keep her head down. No pacing up and down. No embarrassing interludes where acquaintances stopped and stared, then blatantly asked if she was alright. Of course she wasn't alright! Any bloody fool could see that! But she wasn't about to satisfy their curiosity with her business and then have it spread like wild-fire around the whole town. Perhaps Shaun was right. Perhaps moving to Exeter wouldn't be such a bad idea.

Not wanting to expand on what Shaun thought and what she knew he suspected, she picked up the coffee and downed two large gulps, half emptying the mug. It was still quite hot and she felt sweat break out on her forehead and neck — pin pricks of moisture desperate to escape. She needed this liquid inside her, she needed to feel that familiar buzz in her head that would give her the energy to get motivated. Placing the mug to her lips, she closed her eyes and tilted her head back allowing every drop of the remaining dark liquid to slip down her throat.

Checking her purse, Isabelle found the folded scrap of paper hidden in the small compartment where she kept stamps. With shaky hands she opened the folds and stared at the email address. A line of letters and symbols that opened up a communication route to…to what? The reincarnation of a man who had lived and died over three hundred years ago?

The side-loading fork-lift truck juddered to a halt as Shaun Thatcher realised he'd taken the wrong turning. Swearing under his breath, he reversed back the way he'd come. It would have been much easier, continuing forward to the top of Aisle 4, turning right and right again on reaching Aisle 6. But this would involve passing the foreman's glass-fronted office which was located at the top of Aisle 5.

Shaun had been taken off his usual position of warehouse-operative and given a lesser role as the warehouse general dog's-body. It's just for a couple of days, the foreman had said. An extra pair of hands for the large order that had come in whilst Shaun was 'indisposed' the day before. 'Swinging-the-lead', is what the foreman would liked to have said but in these days of litigation, he was just playing it safe. Oh aye, the foreman was definitely on side with the management. On many an occasion Shaun had heard him rant on about feckless workers using any excuse to squeeze money out of the hard-pressed factory owners who were struggling to keep their workforce in gainful employment. No doubt about it, the foreman was a malicious old git and Shaun tried to keep out of his way. How he would love to tell him, to 'stick his job up his arse!

On reaching the intended location, Shaun ran his index

finger down the checklist which was clamped to the board in front of him and set to work removing thirty-six boxes of 33cm x 25cm tiles, Ref. 6470/MB. After loading only four of the boxes. A bell rang out, signaling it was time for a break.

Relieved that the weather was a bit brighter, Shaun moved out into fresh air and lit up a fag. He was in no mood for listening to the chit chat of the others. Most of them were kids, killing time until something better turned up. He'd been like that once, killing time for a while until the *right* job fell into his lap. He'd been waiting for that particular miracle to happen for eighteen years. Jules had told him to think laterally, become self-employed and independent. "And do what?" he'd asked, thinking of his mounting debts. Cashing in your assets to start on a new way forward had been her response. To be fair she had inspired him and given him hope that something better could come of his life if only he could find out what he wanted to do and just go for it. He wasn't sure what he really wanted to do for a living but he was sure of two things; he wanted to leave this job and he wanted to move from the thatched cottage.

As always, when his mind turned to moving, Izzy was the stumbling block. Something even more disturbing was now occupying his mind. Who was this guy she had met up with. Shaun had tried to gain some information before setting out to work but as always, she'd clammed up, acted as though he'd never even spoken to her. For a second, frustration had taken hold and he'd wanted to shake a response from her but he knew in his heart that wasn't the answer. Her eyes seemed blank she was lost in a world of her own. She hadn't yet got the results of the second smear test. If she hadn't heard by tomorrow he would visit the Surgery himself and he had no intention of mincing his words. Then he'd let the foreman do his worst!

Newton Abbot

Fortunately, the traffic along the Newton Abbot road was light when Vinny and Stefan made their way to a gated-community of twelve apartments — all requiring upgraded security locks on doors and windows. Vinny was leading the way, frustrated that the van, desperately in need of a service, was finding it hard to keep up with his Ford Kuga. It had been Stefan's idea to take both vehicles, pointing out that it would give Vinny more flexibility regarding driving to the airport. Vinny had argued against the idea at first, the unnecessary use of a second vehicle with the horrendous rise in the cost of petrol would be cutting his profit margins to the bone. He'd reconsidered when Stefan — Mr Perfect who never put a foot wrong — owned up to leaving Jimmy's stainless steel spade on the field the night before. But what really clinched it for Vinny, was Stefan agreeing to fill up the tank of the van out of his own pocket. So, the man in the van would be working his nuts off and using his lunch break to drive to the field for the spade — which might well have been nicked — whilst *he,* travelling in comfort, could pick up the ring from Taffy and then speed up the motorway to meet Jimmy. Sorted!

With just the slightest hint of guilt, Vinny realized that Stefan must be feeling pretty sheepish. He hadn't mentioned anything about the bits of metal he'd brought back in the filthy bag of soil. It was obviously a load of metallic crud, otherwise he'd be crowing about it by now. No, hiring that metal detector had been a complete waste of time and money. The quicker it was returned to the thieving-bastard at the hire place, the happier he'd be.

The thoughts ranting through Vinny's head stalled as he glanced in his rear-view mirror. No sign of the van. "Fuck!"

Stefan must have got himself caught up at the last set of lights. Heaving a sigh Vinny pulled into the kerb, blocking the entrance to a guesthouse. With eyes locked on the rear-view mirror and fingers drumming on the steering wheel he waited. And waited. Suddenly, he caught sight of the van's roof, just visible behind several other vehicles. Vinny pulled clear, easing the nose of the Kuga into a tight gap between a car and a small pickup lorry, the type you find spewing clouds of black filth into the air. The pickup braked hard and the gap widened. Vinny accelerated and moved in. The pickup's driver pressed down on his horn, filling the air with loud noise and foul language. Vinny's response was quiet — one finger in the air and a smile on his face. At least it wouldn't be *him* trapped behind the shit-on-wheels, breathing in its noxious fumes.

The tall, wrought-iron gate, which afforded a sense of security to the small community of retirees, had been left open, enabling Vinny and Stefan to drive straight in and park in close proximity to the apartments. Curtains twitched and eyes peered, eager to catch a glimpse of the invading workmen. Vinny unfolded himself from the car, stretched and looked about him. Nice quality buildings, with well tended gardens and decent cars were in the allotted parking bays. You definitely needed a few bob behind you, or a very respectable pension, to join this select community.

The door of No 1 — a two-storey house that stood alone — opened, and a straight-backed, silver haired man marched down the path that dissected a garden that was obsessively neat. He offered his right hand in greeting, the other remaining hidden behind his back.

"Good morning, Mr Conway, Brett Robson, I'm the new head of The Management Committee."

Reaching out his hand, which was firmly shaken, Vinny asked, "What happened to the old one?"

"I beg your pardon?"

"You said you were new; what happened to the old head?" Vinny's face almost creased into a grin at the possibility of a humorous pun, but thought better of it when, straight-back, straightened even more.

"I'm afraid he's no longer with us."

Assuming this was, straight back's, respectful way of saying the previous head had popped his clogs, Vinny changed the subject. "Right, better crack on with the job, I'll be leaving for a business meeting in…" He made a point of looking at his watch. "…Just over an hour. My assistant is extremely competent and the work should be finished, as promised, by the end of the day."

"Just so long as we are absolutely clear, Conway, until all the work *is* complete, *and* to my satisfaction, there will be no money forthcoming."

Arrogant bastard! Vinny thought as the silver-haired git turned and marched back to his spick and span structure.

With a broad smile and a nod that was meant to show appreciation, Stefan accepted the coffee and cake from the old lady. This was his second apartment and also his second offering of refreshment. *Tis good*, he thought, *my belly will be full by midday, no need to waste time and money.* His plan was to use a system that was used by the building contractor he worked for in London. When doing multiples of a similar job, you could practically halve the time spent if you followed certain rules. On other occasions he'd mentioned these certain rules to Vincent but he didn't like the idea. He'd said, if the job is done too quickly, the customer won't like what he charges. However, Stefan would soon be left alone and he could choose his own system of working.

Suddenly, he heard Vincent's voice calling his name and then finding him drinking coffee. "Bloody-hell, Stefan, you taking a break already? You've got a lot to get through here, mate, I haven't factored in a second trip and *I* need to get going now, OK?"

"Don't worry, Vincent, I no leave till work finished."

Vincent lowered his voice. "Make sure Robson settles up before you leave. Here's the paperwork, he's already approved the quote so don't let him bamboozle you into accepting any less than that figure. Before an invoice was shoved under Stefan's nose and a chubby finger tapped on an amount that was underlined and boldly typed in red, Stefan was asked if he understood the word, bamboozle. He'd never heard the word before, but it was clear what it meant. Vincent tucked the paperwork in Stefan's back pocket and continued talking in a lowered voice. "Remember what I told you, Stefan, old folk are very suspicious of foreigners. Two of these apartments have been robbed in the last month, that's why they're upgrading all the locks. They'll naturally assume the robbing was done by Gypsies or Eastern Europeans, so keep your trap shut and your head down. I'll give you a bell once I've dropped Jimmy at Exeter Airport."

"Say to Mr Fairbank, I sorry for his mother."

"Yeah, whatever." Then Vincent was gone, spitting up gravel as his car sped down the drive and through the gate.

They had arrived at ten-thirty, spending the first hour or so removing some of the old locks from the doors and checking that they'd brought along enough for the windows — both anxious to avoid having to drive to the nearest builder's supplies — but they had plenty because as it turned out, most of the window locks didn't need replacing. Stefan worked out that if he was lucky, he could have half the new door locks on by one o'clock, drive to the field, recover the spade, spend a little time searching for more coins, and still have plenty of time to finish here by six.

He was working on apartment no 4, concentrating hard on making sure the strong, lever-handle-lock fitted perfectly and opened smoothly. A voice from behind interrupted his concentration.

"Sorry, lad, didn't mean to break your flow, wondered if you'd like a brew?"

Stefan turned to find an old man, in good shape except for the wooden stick he was leaning on. This was the old man's apartment. A dust-free, framed photograph, where he appeared young and virile as he linked arms with his bride, stood on a well polished cabinet. The thatch of black hair, seen in the photo was now white, a strange contrast to the light brown eyes that peered through folds of deeply-furrowed, weathered skin. "Thank you, but I don't need drink right now." Stefan caught the shadow of disappointment that passed over the old mans face, reminding him of his own grandfather, who, even in retirement, still needed to feel useful. "Maybe I have brew in half an hour, OK. You have nice home, you stay here with me if you like."

The old man moved closer and lowered himself into an armchair situated at an angle where Stefan could be seen through the open door of the sitting room. "I'd like to stay," he said, looking Stefan straight in the eye. "Not because I think you might rob me and not because I don't trust you to do a good job. I can see from your method of working, you know what you're doing. Has to be said though, there are a lot of cowboy-tradesmen around these days. By the way, I'm

Joe." Joe reached forward and offered his right hand. Stefan obliged, introducing himself while taking hold of the aged hand, surprised by its strong grip.

An easy conversation developed between the two men. Joe discovering where Stefan was from and how long he'd been in England. Stefan learning how Joe, a Londoner, had served his apprenticeship as a joiner back in the early 1960's and how he would probably still be employed had it not been for his accident. An accident that happened over twelve years ago whilst Joe was working at a Canary Wharf development site. A badly-stacked pile of concrete blocks had fallen on him from two floors up, pulverising his right leg — which eventually had to be amputated — and putting an end to his working life in the building trade. He also learned that it was years, far too many years before he received the compensation that his solicitor promised would set him up for the rest of his life. Eventually, he was able to move out of London, buy this nice apartment without a mortgage and have a little money invested to top up his meager state-pension. What the money hadn't compensated for, Joe revealed with bitterness, was the stress and strain of the years spent pursuing the claim. So much stress that Doris, his wife, became sick and died before she had the chance of sharing what was theirs by right.

Joe returned from the kitchen pushing a trolley ahead of him. On the trolley sat two plates, each holding a hot sausage roll, a custard tart and a clean, white-linen napkin. Alongside the plates, a steaming coffeepot, milk, sugar and two china mugs. Stefan lay down his chisel and moved to help.

"It's alright, lad, I'm used to moving this around. Haven't spilled a drop of anything in since I moved in here. I might have a false leg," Joe whacked his stick against the right side of his trousers and a hollow sound rang out, "But there's nothing wrong with the rest of me. I offered to fit all these locks myself, save the community the labour costs, but Robson wouldn't hear of it. He said it was the rules of the community that they have outside firms doing all the maintenance work. Bloody stupid if you ask me. Still, keeps you younger ones employed. I got no beef with that."

"I sorry, I understand how necessary to do something useful."

"Aye, lad, you and me both but the Robson's of this world understand one thing only, the power to spend other people's hard-earned cash. He'll be off playing golf all afternoon, same as most of the husbands in this tight little community — retired civil servants on inflation-proof pensions, enjoying their early retirement at the tax-payers expense."

Stefan wondered why Joe had moved here in the first place. "Maybe is better for you to live somewhere else, Joe."

"I bought this apartment off-plan, two years before it was actually built, sold a lot of personal stuff, including a valuable coin collection, to fund the deposit. Me and the Mrs wanted to move closer to our daughter and grandchildren, but like I said, she fell ill and died before everything was settled. She made me promise that I'd still move here. She'd wanted to make sure I had family close by. I know I'm a square peg in a round hole, but no, for the sake of the wife, I'll stay put."

Stefan swept the curls of chiseled wood into a dustpan, explaining to Joe that he needed to make a short trip during lunch time and would be back as soon as possible. "Is very good of you to feed me, Joe, but I must leave now. I still have much work when I get back."

"Take your time lad, it's important to have a proper break. You needn't worry about the locks for no's 5 and 6, the husbands are playing golf and the wives will be out at the gym. I'll install their locks while you're doing your other business."

Chapter 18

Tuesday Afternoon—Lanzarote

Lyn couldn't help herself. The wardrobe, and each of the drawers where James' clothes had been previously neatly placed, were opened and searched. Searched for anything that might have been left behind, but there was nothing. Due to the rigorous housekeeping of the hotel, even the sheets and towels were devoid of any scent of him. There was absolutely nothing to indicate that they'd shared this suite. A sense of total abandonment washed over her and loneliness followed in its wake. Reasoning that it had been the logical thing for him to do because if his mother deteriorated he wouldn't be returning and Lyn would then be left with extra luggage to carry home, didn't alter her depressed state.

Their last hour together had been strained. Strained because it had seemed impossible to agree on anything. When eventually James had made it plain there was no need for her to accompany him to the airport — said it made more sense for her to continue to enjoy the facilities of the hotel rather than waste holiday-time sitting in an airport — she hadn't even bothered to argue the point. Now, all she wanted to do, was curl into a ball on the freshly-made bed and slip into oblivion.

Footsteps and then laughter followed by the sound of lighthearted banter outside the hotel door, seeping through the mental crust of Lyn's self-pity. Remembering, the encouraging words from Gran had already tried to break through. Those silent words had been easy to ignore but now these voices outside her door were real. Attached to flesh and blood. Words from people who were still alive. People who were enjoying themselves. The sounds grew faint and disappeared. Silence returned and she retreated back into her self-imposed shell.

Lyn opened her eyes and was surprised to find herself facing the glass terrace doors. A scattering of clouds had formed, the largest covering the sun. Her mind registered this, aware of how refreshing a simple change can be. Since their arrival, the days had been hot and cloudless. She checked her watch, hardly believing what it was telling her — she'd been dead to the world for over an hour. What now? She did have choices, she told herself, we all have choices. The trick is, to exercise those choices. She clung to a rising force of determination. Uncurling her body, she rolled off the bed. Frantic, that the determination might weaken at any moment, she grabbed her rucksack and began stuffing it with the items she had put to one side. Items carefully considered earlier in the day when her mind was more stable. Satisfied that she had everything, she headed for the door.

Bovey Tracey

Isabelle was see-sawing between determination and fearfulness. This was her third trip to the library, and she was trying hard not to allow the strange look from the librarian to affect her.

On her second trip, an hour later than the first, she had found a response to the brief email she had sent to Nicholas. She had simply asked if he was 'real' and not just a figment of her imagination. And his response had been just as simple.

I am real. Meet me and you will see.

With heart pounding and hands shaking, she had made several attempts to respond, deleted them all and finally settled on.

I'd like that. When and where do you suggest?

The moment she'd sent it, she was filled with regret. What the hell was she thinking? She felt nauseous from the fear that churned in her stomach and she knew without a shadow of doubt, she'd be back here. Back soon to capture his words and to do his bidding.

And here she was, wringing her hands and pacing the small area of the library, again. Again, waiting to grab the next available computer. The woman on No.2 would be finished in five minutes, the librarian had informed her, without being asked. The same librarian that had tried her best to find out what was going on in Isabelle's life. Soothing talk that offered help and understanding. Nosey Cow! Isabelle hadn't been fooled.

Yes…Yes. No 2 had finished. The computer screen was back to the library's logo but the bloody woman was still sitting there. Still writing something down. Isabelle took two large steps towards her, was about to physically evict her from the chair when a mobile phone rang out and No 2 fumbled in her bag to answer it. Librarian to the rescue, No 2 was approached and within seconds was shoving her belongings into her bag and moving off.

Isabelle closed her eyes and took a deep breath, several more followed as she logged onto her mail. There was one message. It was from him. Sent almost immediately after hers. She wasn't sure if that was a good sign or not. Wasn't sure if he'd be angry at her delay. At least she'd had time to think. Time to worry about what to do if he'd wanted to meet after dark. Two more deep breaths which wavered on exhalation. Then she clicked on the message and it was revealed.

We'll meet where the ring was found. 2.00pm today.

Isabelle felt relief flood through every fibre of her body. *Ghosts don't come out in daylight.* Then, how should she reply? Was it even necessary to reply?

Yes, no need to let manners slip just because she was scared. After a short period of indecision and realising how little time she had, she settled on.

I'll be there.

Exeter

Vinny cut the engine of the Ford Kuga as he parked to the right of Taffy's workshop. Stefan, having just entered the field-gate of the Bovey Tracey field, performed the same unconscious act — turning off the engine to the van. But neither would ever be aware of this simple act of perfect synchronisation. As far as

Vinny was concerned, Stefan was working his nuts off to get all the locks done by the end of the day.

The black and silver, Mini Cooper S, a special hand-built job, parked directly in front of Taffy's workshop, indicated that the jeweller had a client with him. No matter, Vinny had arrived early and sitting here mentally accessing the profit he'll have made by the end of the day was pleasurable enough.

Halfway through eating a bar of chocolate, Taffy's door opened and a tall, heavily built, middle age guy emerged and opened up the smart, sporty-looking car. "Fucking Poser", croaked Vinny as a lump of chocolate caught in his throat. "This should be entertaining."

But instead of the expected difficulty climbing into the driver's seat, due to the guys size and age, the client opened the boot, removed what looked like a makeup bag and pulled free a couple of wet-wipes, using them to give his hands a good scrubbing. After finishing his little ritual, he swiped a brush through his shoulder-length white hair, slid easily into his seat, gunned the engine and performed a perfect three-point-turn before roaring away. "Bent as a fucking cork-screw," Vinny snarled as he slunk lower in his seat, anxious not to be seen as the guy sped by.

The last square of chocolate followed the rest as the Kuga's door swung open and Vinny took a deep breath, tasting the Mini's exhaust fumes. He squeezed out of his seat and strode over to Taffy's door. Two raps from his knuckles and three words filled the air. "Taffy? It's Vinny." No good trying to just walk in. Taffy's security-minded-ways wouldn't allow for that.

The jeweller was very economical with information relating to the guy who had just left his premises. "Would you want me discussing your business with all and sundry", he responded to Vinny's curiosity.

"OK, OK, don't get your knickers in a twist. He looked a bit of a poser, that's all. Long hair, driving a Mini, what's all that about? He's an old geezer".

"So? He's getting on in years, does that mean you have to stop living the life you enjoy. That Mini is just one from a collection of over twenty Classic cars and he likes to turn the engine on all of them whenever a situation presents itself. Do I detect a hint of jealousy?"

Growing impatient with the 'ticking off' Vinny sat on the edge of Taffy's workbench and held up his hands in a gesture of reconciliation. "I understand what you're saying, Taffy, but what did the old geezer want with you? Is he looking for a new boyfriend or what?"

"Hah!" The single word that exploded from Taffy sounded like the loud slap from a book being closed aggressively. "You think you can use a dirty trick like that to squeeze information from me? And I think you were unwise to sit on my bench without asking me first."

"Don't be such a fucking old woman! Get me the ring and I'll be on my way."

There was a small ante room off the workshop, about the size of a walk-in wardrobe, it's door fabricated from steel, Taffy disappeared inside and returned within seconds, holding a tiny box. He handed it to Vinny along with a scrap of paper with the amount of money owed. Vinny released a low whistle on inspecting both. From his jacket he pulled out a wad of £50 notes and slowly counted out the exact amount. He knew from past experience, it was pointless haggling with this man.

"It's a good job, Taffy, thanks. I'd better be off."

Taffy nodded, accepting the words and money as satisfaction. "It's as promised. A perfect replica. And before you leave, if I were you, I'd wipe your backside. I'm sure you wouldn't want to mess up the seat in that smart car of yours."

Vinny stood and turned. He'd plonked his arse onto something that had spread across the left cheek area of his best chinos. "Shit!"

A chuckle from Taffy. "No, not shit, just a small spillage of releasing oil that the old geezer accidentally knocked over."

Bovey Tracey

On arriving at the field, Stefan couldn't believe his luck. The wet, sticky mud of the evening before had changed to damp soil which crumbled to the touch. This was thanks to no rain since yesterday and a brisk, drying wind. Also, he had the field to himself. No sign of any workmen. No sign of anyone. Even so, he'd pushed his arms through the bright green, fluorescent waistcoat that Vincent kept hanging over the seat in the van. If anyone did turn up, at least he looked like a workman. He had intended to find what he could using only his eyes. This would be time-consuming and he was in a hurry. So he'd uncovered the detector from the safety of where he'd placed it in the van earlier that morning, and with long marching strides, headed straight to the find spot of the night before.

He'd been working the same area around the mound of earth and his pockets were already heavy with coins, silver coins that were blackened by age. But now it had changed. Even when he slowly moved the detector to left and right of the area, the ground was silent. From this, he worked out that the hidden stash had been disturbed by the huge bucket of the JCB. He pictured in his mind's eye, it lifting and dropping the treasure on the growing mountain of earth. Saw the spillage of coins trickling down to ground level where he was standing. If the driver had been more alert, more observant, Stefan wouldn't be here today. But if he wanted more of the coins, he would have to disturb the mound. Disturbing the mound, trampling his heavy boot marks all over it, could lead to trouble and Stefan was very wary of inviting trouble.

Suddenly, he realised he wasn't alone. A tall figure, dressed in the way of a gentlemen in the city — smart trousers, light coat that reached his knees and an expensive-looking hat pulled low hiding most of his face — stood against the trunk of a half-dead tree. How long had he been there? wondered Stefan. How long had he been watching him? He looked at his watch and was amazed to see it was already five minutes passed two. Five minutes later than he'd planned to leave. He switched off the detector, scraped the surplus soil from the spade, and turned to give the tall figure one last glance. But he'd vanished! Halfway back to the van, Stefan halted. A woman was coming toward him, waving her arms in the air. Stefan was happy to be leaving this place.

Forgetting that she was wearing her best shoes, Isabelle staggered across the furrows of soil as she tried to catch the attention of the only person around. "It must be Nicholas. It must be Nicholas," she gasped, feeling a sense of relief overlay the fear as the targeted person began to walk towards her.

She'd been five minutes early, at least five minutes. She'd stood, arms wrapped around her chilling body as the stiff breeze had mocked her attempt at a neat hairdo. No matter which way she'd turned, she'd felt its cold, biting touch around her head, encouraging tears to stream down her face, diluting the freshly-applied mascara. She'd suffered that way for almost ten minutes. Wondering, frightened, but increasingly disappointed that Nicholas had let her down. And still she was afraid to leave the place. The place where she'd found the ring. The ring which even now was clasped tightly by her right hand, clasping the thumb on her left which had become its home. Its throne.

Then she'd seen him. A man in the distance holding something in each hand. A man wearing a green workman's jacket, luminous against the stark black of the field. Nicholas wanted to meet where she'd found the ring but how could he know the exact place? She was certain that she was the only one on the field that day. A glimmer of hope surrounded this thought and gave her courage. Her stiffened legs bolted forward, towards the man in the bright green jacket.

Each was now aware of the other The gap between them closing like a slow-motion scene in a film when lovers come together at last. Barely five feet apart and they stopped. He looked so normal, so young. Twice she tried to speak, but her breath was ragged from the effort of reaching him. Searching his face she saw confusion. Confusion and concern but he remained silent. A deeper breath, a choking cough, and then Isabelle managed to ask. "Nicholas? Is it really you, Nicholas?"

"I sorry. Who are you?"

"Bella. Your beautiful Bella."

Shaun Thatcher was worried sick and his pacing around the kitchen wasn't helping; but the very act of moving seemed to keep at bay the full ramifications of his dire situation. He'd been sacked! Dismissed. Given his cards and shown the door. Whichever way you said it, it meant the same. He no longer had a job and there would be no money coming in. He forced his body to sit down. Perched on the edge of the kitchen chair, one hand holding a glass of water, the other holding his head, his mind ran through again, how, out of the blue, his life had been made disastrously worse than it was.

He'd left for work at the usual time but an accident on the main road leading out of Bovey to Heathfield had caused a long tailback. No big deal, Shaun knew all the roads in this area like the back of his hand and was soon on a quiet, single-track road that was slightly longer in miles, but would be quicker in time. That was before he'd come up behind a tractor laden with bales of straw. A tractor that couldn't, or wouldn't move faster than twenty miles an hour. After five minutes of this frustratingly slow progress, Shaun had tooted and hollered to the driver to pull over — they had passed several field gates — but the only response, was the tractor's speed dropping to ten miles per hour.

He'd been fifteen minutes late for work. Again, no big deal, unlike the shift workers, *he* didn't need to clock-in. However, his foreman had clocked him, made a point of letting him know he'd been seen. It was several hours later that Shaun was to learn that those fifteen bloody minutes, had been the deciding factor for his dismissal.

He'd decided to take his morning break in the canteen, there was a cold wind blowing outside and he was out of fags anyway because he was trying his hardest to give them up. Shaun had sat next to a bloke he'd known since school and they got into the usual gripe about all that had gone wrong with the country, Benny was worse than him when it came to rubbishing the politicians. Then an interesting conversation had developed and Shaun remembered every word.

Benny had lowered his voice and leaned closer. "I tell you, mate, I'm seriously thinking of moving to Australia. My brother's got the final OK and he'll be out of this bloody country by Christmas."

"What's your brother doing these days? It ain't that easy to get into Oz."

"He's a plasterer by trade but with the housing market on the floor, he'd been forced to change direction. Bought into a franchise, steam-cleaning ovens for restaurants. Then thought he'd do even better aiming for the domestic market. He's got a fully equipped van and a list of clients who use him regular as clockwork. Sometimes as often as every three months, others every six months or even once a year, depending on how much messy oven cooking they do. It's profitable enough. Takes two to three hours to bring the cooker and hob back to as-new condition. And the clients are so impressed, the majority of them book the next appointment there and then."

"So why's he off to Oz if this business venture is doing so well?" Shaun had asked.

"Lifestyle, mate."

"What do you mean, lifestyle?" If he's his own boss and earning a good wedge, surely that's all the lifestyle you need."

"They've got three kids and Jackie, that's the wife, whose parents already live in Sydney, reckons they'll get a much better start in life out there. Besides the fact that free-childcare will be on tap, so to speak, will allow her to get a job."

"So what's he gonna do with this thriving oven-cleaning business, just let it go?"

"No way! Even when he went into it, he knew it'd be temporary. But you know our Dave, always had a good head on his shoulders, always one jump ahead of the average Joe in the street. He knew if he built up a business that provided a nice little earner with minimum outlay he'd have no problem selling it on. Why, you interested?"

"I might be. How much he asking?"

"Twenty grand."

Shaun had let out a long, low whistle, which turned several heads in the canteen. "Twenty bloody grand."

"I know it sounds a lot, but he told me that's less than the original outlay, and I believe him. It includes everything, van, equipment, a list of booked clients well into next year, and, he's happy to show any interested party the ropes. Take em out with him on a few calls. He was hoping to sell for more than that, but to tell you the truth, Shaun, now he's got the final papers come through, he's shitting himself he won't be able to get rid in time."

"So if it's such a fantastic opportunity, why don't you go for it? It's gotta be better than working in this dead-end place."

Before Benny had had time to answer, the bell rang out for the end of break. All around him chairs scraped across the floor and bodies moved in unison back to their work stations. Shaun had lingered a while, reflecting on what Benny had told him.

On his return to the warehouse. The foreman was waiting. Hands on hips and a grin cutting across his stupid face. "You're out on your ear, Thatcher. You can collect your cards tomorrow. No need to work the obligatory week's notice, we're pleased to see the back of you."

Stunned into silence for a few seconds, then breaking into a half laugh, convinced the bastard was having a joke at his expense, Shaun had asked, "What do you mean, *we're* pleased."

"This is coming from the boss himself. I've been reporting to him, about all your liberty-taking, Thatcher, and this morning was the last straw."

It suddenly sunk in that the bastard was serious. "You can't fucking fire me, just like that."

"Can and have. Several people overheard you in the canteen, boasting about how you're just killing time here till you find something better. Your heart's not in it, Thatcher, never has been. Apart from collecting what's due tomorrow, you're not to set foot in the place again!"

Shaun had grabbed his belongings and marched out to the car park, dazed from shock. He was in such a state he didn't trust himself to drive. After a while he'd pulled himself together, took out his mobile and phoned home. Better to soften the blow first. Tell Izzy there'd been radical cutbacks in the workforce and he was one of the unlucky ones. The phone had just kept ringing. Izzy wasn't there.

Shaun tipped back the rest of the water and placed the glass in the sink which was already filled with dirty dishes. God almighty, what he'd do for a fag right now. Unsure what to do next he wandered from room to room. "Izzy, where the hell are you?" He climbed the stairs and checked their bedroom. And froze. The bed was still a tussled mess from the night before and on the dressing table makeup spilled out of it's bag onto the surface. Lipsticks with tops left off, various shades of eye shadow smudged on tissues and the air heavy with perfume. What the hell was going on? Shaun suddenly understood what it must be like to suffer a nervous breakdown.

Lanzarote

The bus stop to Tias had been easy enough to find. As Lyn approached the bench that helped to mark it, there was no one waiting apart from two young Spanish women totally absorbed in a conversation that sounded like the rapid fire of artillery. The hours sleep, although therapeutic, had cost her dear. As well as lost time, it had cost her the chance of meeting up with a small, English-speaking group who had planned a short walk around a place called Tegoyo. A place where the Tias bus conveniently dropped you almost at the start of that walk. After studying the time table, framed on a post by the bench, and comparing it with her scribbled notes, she realised that she'd missed them by just forty minutes.

With twenty minutes to kill before the next bus was due, she decided to spend that time running through her English-to-Spanish dictionary to help communicate to the driver where she wanted to go and to make sure where the stop was for returning. She perched on the edge of the bench and tried her best to concentrate. But the close proximity of the rapid fire of artillery made this impossible. Behind her, a broad rise of steps leading to an upper level of shops, would be, she thought, a better bet. Climbing to the top step and positioning her back against the wall she flicked through the dictionary for the appropriate words.

Twenty-two minutes later the bus hissed to a stop. The two Spanish women climbed aboard, lay down coins and gathered up change without breaking the rhythm of their rapid conversation or without even taking breath, or so it seemed. Fortunately the bus was almost empty, and thankfully, they wandered through to the far end of it. Lyn, having already forgotten the alien words she needed, gave the driver a helpless smile, pointed to Tegoyo on her map and offered him a palmful of the foreign coinage to cover the cost of travelling to it. He took what was needed and rolled out a ticket. After attempting a bold, "mucho gracias", but making a pig's ear of it, she sat right at the front of the bus, hoping the driver would give her the nod when she was at the appropriate stop.

The interior of the bus was warm but it could have been worse. The scattered clouds of earlier had now coalesced, forming a much broader expanse of protection from the searing sun, and as the bus had no air-conditioning, or if it had, it hadn't been switched on, travelling on it during the afternoon under cloudless skies would be like hell on wheels. As if reading her thoughts, the driver suddenly flicked a switch and a cold blast of air began to circulate, catching the back of Lyn's neck as it moved around the bus. For a while she ignored the discomfort, then thought again about choices and exercising those choices. She rooted in her rucksack, pulled out her light-weight, long-sleeved top and wrapped it twice around her neck, half expecting the driver to take notice and oblige by turning the air-con off. He didn't.

For such a small island, the condition of the roads was good. In fact they were excellent. Probably due to the small amount of traffic using them. In no time at all the bus trundled its way through the outskirts of Tias, a small town north of Puerto Del Carmen. Villas, apartment blocks, shops and business premises, all with flat roofs and all painted white, passed at a steady pace before her eyes. Two stops into this shifting scene of white-painted buildings, a bell rang indicating that the two Spanish women had reached their destination. They moved as one to the exit, still rapt in conversation. The doors opened and they stepped out. The door closed, and blessed peace descended.

After several more stops, buildings became sparse and the mountainous backdrop more apparent. Lyn was the only passenger left on the bus, and now on high alert for any sign from the driver that she'd reached her dropping off place to

Tegoyo. Again she rooted in her rucksack to locate the dictionary, torn between concentrating on any road signs that may hold a clue, or trying to get through to a driver who had probably forgotten she even existed.

In the midst of her rooting, he suddenly pulled up sharp, so sharp she almost exited the bus through the front window. "Lo siento! Sorry! Terminar, finish! Back now to Tias." He was genuinely embarrassed, probably mainly due to his mixture of languages. Lyn didn't need the dictionary to interpret, she knew she would need to backtrack, on foot. Fortunately because her powers of observation had been on such high alert, she remembered the last couple of turns.

Stepping down from the bus she looked around. Several small clusters of white buildings were scattered here and there across the rocky, barren landscape. James had argued about calling it countryside; his description was more in line with 'one huge slag heap'. But there was a beauty and a majesty that belied that notion. You needed to be here to see it for yourself, to feel it and experience it.

After backtracking for a while she came upon the all-important bus stop, missed, by her and the driver, and sure enough, here was clear indication of which way to go for Tegoyo. Being on slightly higher ground she could see quite far into the distance. Before starting out, she removed her binoculars and phone from the rucksack. The binoculars were slipped over her head, the phone pushed safely into her jeans pocket. She took a large gulp from the bottle of water then shoved this, wrapped in her jacket to keep it cool, back in the main compartment. The air here was much cooler than in the sheltered bay of the hotel; and for this she was grateful.

She moved at a steady pace, leaving behind the scattering of homesteads. All was quiet, deathly quiet. It suddenly dawned on her that it was siesta time. The near-empty bus, the almost deserted roads. The homesteads and shops, closed and devoid of life. It was mid-afternoon and the local population were resting. Even back at the hotel, the calmest and most relaxing time of the day was during the afternoon. Pretty obvious really, it was the hottest. But not today. Today was beautifully overcast with a refreshing breeze. Perfect conditions for walking.

The dirt track Lyn had been walking along forked about ten meters ahead. She lifted the binoculars and scanned the horizon in a slow arc of 180 degrees. About a third of the way through the right angle she stopped. "You clever girl!" she said with a growing smile, removing her sunglasses and looking again through the 10x magnification of the binoculars. She locked on to the image that had caught her attention. Five ant-like creatures walking in single file up the gradient of a hill. Five creatures carrying bags on their backs. "Yes, it's got to be them." Convinced that these were the walkers who took the earlier bus, and reckoning, with a bit of luck, she should be able to catch up within the hour, Lyn looked at her paper of scribblings, which had a mobile number at the bottom, and hoped it belonged to one of the walkers up ahead. She pulled out her mobile and checked for a signal. Nothing. Just a warning EMERGENCY CALLS ONLY. Nothing for it, she thought, as she put on a spurt, took the right-hand fork and marched in the direction of the anthill.

From time to time the sun had peeped through gashes in the thinning cloud. And during these brief interludes of intense warmth, several lizards had been spotted sunning themselves. But even if Lyn had had the time to stop and try to capture them on camera, she knew they would have scurried away as soon as she moved closer. Even so, they were a delight, and the sight of them had bolstered her mood even more. She'd also come across plant life. Unusual varieties of well known species, visible in shaded pockets of the lava rock. She'd seen photographs of vast swathes of flowers on Lanzarote but you needed to be here in the short rainy season between January and March, to experience them. In spite of everything, she was really enjoying this little adventure, and was looking forward to sharing the adventure with the other five walkers.

Her legs registered the gradual accent of the hill. It was pointless checking the other walker's progress until she reached higher ground, the hill was blocking the view but she couldn't help herself, besides a minutes breather wouldn't hurt. Once again she scanned an 180 degrees arc, most of it dark and dense with the hill in front of her. Suddenly she caught a movement, a movement of something low to the ground. She removed her sun glasses and checked more carefully. Sure enough, a couple of hundred meters away, a dog crouched low and watching. Thankfully it was tethered. She could just make out a thick rope leading from its neck. Unnerved she looked about her, there were no buildings or homesteads around to show who it belonged to. In spite of her complaining legs, she increased her speed and continued up the incline of the hill.

The ground gradually leveled out and Lyn was ready for rest and a drink of water but before taking either she removed her sunglasses and lifted the binoculars. She swept the area where the dog had been. No sign of it. Maybe it lived in an underground hole and it popped out of that hole from time to time. But what did it live on? Where where was it's water source? And why was the dog tethered out here? "Oh my God!" Without the aid of binoculars, the final question had an answer. The dog wasn't tethered. How could it be? It was now closer than the last time she'd looked, and Lyn could clearly see the rope, about three meters of it falling over the rocks, ragged on the end where it had snapped, or been bitten. A stupid thought jumped into her head —an attempt to remain calm — *I wonder if the dog's friendly?* Then panic took over and before she realized it, she was running. Running as fast as her tired legs could manage. Gran's words, frank and unemotional, surfaced above the pounding of her heart and the gasping of her breath. *(Never turn your back on a vicious dog, Lynda. Basically dogs are cowards. But if they smell your fear or if you turn and run, they'll have you!)*

Chapter 19

Tuesday Mid-Afternoon—Bovey Tracey

For the third time the hot tap was turned on, topping up the bath to just a few inches from the overflow. Isabelle knew she was being extravagant but she didn't care. And nor did Shaun. In fact it was his idea that she take a hot bath in the first place. The warmth of the water was calming her down, soothing away the torment that circulated round and round in her head. Sweet Jesus, if only she could turn the clock back a few days. Undo the lying that was now out of control.

She'd arrived home shivering, tears streaming down her face. and even now, in a calmer state, she wasn't clear why she'd been crying. Didn't understand why it had been so important to meet this… this phantom of a man. She remembered running towards someone in workman's clothes, he was the only soul around, so she assumed it was Nicholas. But in her heart she knew. She sensed it before she was anywhere near him, this man was too ordinary. Poor chap, he looked so shocked, so embarrassed.

Her shock, *her* embarrassment, had been finding Shaun sitting at the kitchen table as she'd stumbled through the door, looking pale and vulnerable. He'd jumped up and asked her where she'd been, said he'd been worried sick. How could she even begin to tell him all that had happened. And was still happening. How could she explain what she didn't understand? So she'd taken the easy way out. She'd lied again. Said she'd been down the doctors to get her results. She hadn't said any more, she didn't need to. Shaun assumed the worst. He'd taken her in his arms and held her tight. Held her for ages repeating over and over how sorry he was and that they needed to talk but first she was to run a hot bath and wash the smudged make off my face. She'd done what he suggested, relieved not to continue the lying. Relieved not to look into his eyes and see the misery that she'd caused.

Whilst the bath had been filling, she'd wiped the face cloth across the steamed-up mirror, taking a step back in horror at the image that stared back. Bright green eye-shadow, filled the whole of her eyelids and part of her eyebrows. Spiky, black caked lashes which had streaked down either side of her pale, sunken cheeks. Her mouth, a gaudy red slash of lipstick that had smeared her teeth. Sickened, she'd looked away, plunged the facecloth into the bathwater and scrubbed at the ghastly mask. Rubbed and scrubbed until every trace of the unnatural was gone. Then she'd lowered her shivering body into the warm scented embrace of water that reached up to her chin.

Stefan had left the field but he was still in Bovey Tracey. He'd stopped at a public toilet on the edge of town. Not to relieve himself but to wash the mud from his hands and clean up his boots; he was returning to furnished homes, not a building site. He'd stayed longer at the field than intended. Why? Because he'd been seen, watched very closely by a smartly-dressed man, and instinct told him this was probably the last chance he'd get to recover more of the coins. But he was content. In the locked toilet cubicle, he'd lowered the seat cover and emptied his pockets onto it, counted out twenty-seven coins of similar size to the others. All but one were scooped into a strong plastic bag which he intended to hide in the van. The singled out coin was carefully washed, patted dry, wrapped in a piece of toilet tissue and placed in his jeans pocket.

Thankful for light traffic, he made his way back to Newton Abbot, mindful of how late it was and also mindful of the guilt this brought. An image of the woman on the field flashed into his mind. What had happened to her? Had she been abused? Had she managed to escape her attacker and was looking for help. No, she hadn't wanted his help, she just wanted Stefan to be Nicholas. Maybe Nicholas was the smartly-dressed man who had suddenly disappeared. Stefan had asked her name and for a moment she'd looked confused. He could sense her mind grappling with what he'd asked. Then with widening eyes and a manic smile, a smile that revealed teeth red with lip-paint reminding him of the time his little sister had eaten too many strawberries, she'd walked right up to him, prodded his chest with one finger and told him her name was Bella, who else would she be?"

A touch on the horn from the car behind and Stefan realised the traffic lights were green. With a wave of his hand he moved forward. He was now only a few minutes drive from the apartments.

The gates had been left open, allowing Stefan to drive straight to the same parking bay as before. He slid the van door open and standing directly in front of him, feet astride and both hands behind his back, was the white-haired man who Vincent had spoken to when they first arrived.

"And where the hell do you think you've been?"

Stefan was a little taken aback, but he stood firm. The man was much shorter and looking him straight in the eye was difficult, so he did the next best thing. He ignored him. Took what he needed from the van and walked straight past him without saying a word.

Brett Robson followed shouting "Hey, do you understand English? I've already warned your boss, don't expect a single penny from my community, until every lock is fitted and every screw is tightened to my satisfaction. You got that, matey?"

One of the windows opened and Joe leaned out. "Bloody-hell, Robson, stop playing the sergeant major, you're just an old retiree like the rest of us. Besides, the lad was doing *me* a favour, picked up something for me."

"Picked up what?"

"None of your bloody business. Get back to your golfing and give us all a bit of peace!" Joe watched as Brett Robson marched to his car, left the confines of the community and the gates closed silently behind him.

A black car, with the sort of dark windows that concealed the occupants, was parked opposite the gate. But Brett Robson was too lost in his own thoughts to notice.

INTERESTING. VERY INTERESTING. I FOLLOW THIS MAN, EXPECTING HIM TO RETURN TO THE PLACE NEAR THE SEA. TO THE PLACE MARKED FOR REVENGE. THIS MAN IS STRONG IN WAYS THAT THE OTHERS ARE NOT. SHOULD I BE WARY? I THINK NOT. AFTER WATCHING HIM CLOSELY, I SEE THAT HE TOO HAS HIS WEAKNESSES.

Stefan was soon to learn that Joe had fitted locks on three of the apartments, he didn't need to check the work, the man had years of experience. And still Joe wanted to do more, saying it was nice to know he was still up-to-the-job and thanking Stefan for trusting him. Stefan offered to pay, but Joe refused. Saying Stefan's company was payment enough.

Both men fell into a companionable rhythm of working, later, during a break where tea and more sausage rolls were offered, Stefan thanked Joe for lying on his behalf. "I sorry, Joe, for being longer than I say. I sorry for making you lie for me."

"You didn't make me lie, lad. You're not the sort of person to swing-the-lead, if you get my meaning?" Stefan smiled and nodded, in the building trade these words were used many times. "Which means you were late back for good reason."

Silence hung between them, an empty page of a book crying out to be written upon. Stefan thought of the coin hidden in his jeans pocket. Thought about when he was a boy of fifteen, holding the coin from the hoard his father had found. Thought about how he'd shown that coin to a friend, boasted to him about how rich his family had become. And how, by breaking his promise of silence, he had not only caused his father's death, but he'd brought shame and ruin to his whole family.

Both men picked up their mugs and gulped greedily at the lukewarm tea. Joe seemed calm, relaxed in his own environment. Stefan's mind was still active, comparing and weighing this situation to the one that happened in a country rife with criminals. He drank the remainder of the tea, reached into his jeans pocket and liberated the hidden package. "You say you collected coins, Joe. Can you tell me anything about this one?"

The older man carefully opened the tissue wrapping, and after lowering his glasses from the top of his head onto his nose, scrutinised both sides of the coin. "Mm, what you have here, lad, Is a Charles the first half groat. In near mint condition, which usually means, if it's fresh from it's resting place, there could be more of 'em."

Lanzarote

Lyn crouched amongst a cluster of rocks that offered shade from a bout of searing sun, privacy to empty her bladder — though privacy was hardly necessary, there wasn't a soul in sight — and most importantly, a safe vantage point where she could keep a look-out for the four-legged stalker. Common sense told her she couldn't stay here for long, but she needed to rest up and gather her forces.

She'd stumbled twice during the initial panic to close the gap between her and the five walkers (and lengthen it between her and the dog) and her mad dash seemed to have worked, at least as far as the dog was concerned. On coming upon the rocks, she'd collapsed into its shade, caught her breath and peered through the binoculars. Peered until her eyes watered and the lenses began to mist. Thankfully, there had been no sign of it but sadly, no matter which way she angled, no matter how much she peered — even after cleaning the lenses and peering again — she couldn't see the walkers. She felt sure they couldn't be far away. The problem was, the landscape undulated all around her and they could have turned in any direction at any point and be hidden in a dip or behind a rise. She'd been tempted to call out, shout for help, but the thought of rousing that dog had kept her silent.

After cleaning the grazes on her knees with spit and tissue, trying her phone again, to no avail, she decided it was time to leave her temporary sanctuary and keep moving in a direction that would hopefully lead her back towards Tias. The binoculars had shown her small pockets of buildings here and there, but she'd come to learn that not all were habitable and those that were, usually had a dog that barked it's head off until you were out of ear shot. No, she'd seen enough of the isolation, now she wanted roads, shops and people. After studying the map, she felt confident she could achieve that goal without the aid of the other walkers. As soon as the tip of the next bank of clouds moved across the sun, she threaded her arms through the straps of her rucksack and headed in a north-easterly direction.

She'd been walking for about twenty minutes, checking regularly through the binoculars for any sign of the walkers, when a sound from behind froze her to the spot. The sound was unmistakable, a dislodged piece of rock rolling over another. She turned and saw nothing. Without lowering her head she fumbled for the binoculars, cursing under her breath because they'd become twisted and she was making the twist worse. When finally free they were pressed to her eyes and kept there whilst she surveyed the whole area around her. She saw nothing. There was no movement anywhere, no sound of anything. She realised she was holding her breath, and a strange notion crossed her mind. Was the ability to unconsciously stop breathing, a primeval instinct that kicks in during a critical point in hunting? Or, being hunted? Because she was now convinced the creature was still stalking her. Sensed it with every fibre of her being. What should she do? Running wasn't an option, she'd left behind the dirt tracks ages ago, and lava rock was uneven, sharp and riddled with air pockets. Again the binoculars were yanked into position. A few hundred yards in the opposite direction to were she'd been heading, an isolated building filled the focal area of the lenses, window a blank hole, door missing but walls strong and sound. Again she checked the phone. Still no signal. A flare of hope. Maybe she could text the walkers. Does texting still work in no signal areas? But even if it did, she'd need time and concentration to explain her predicament. She didn't have the skills to text with one eye whilst using the other looking out for a stalking dog.

Taking a deep breath she gauged the distance she'd have to cover and looked for an easy route towards the building — a worn pathway up to the unmaintained drive just visible to the right of the missing front door — but from where she stood there was nothing but uneven tons of rock. She had no choice. Packing away the phone and binoculars, picking up a smooth, palm-sized rock she maneuvered her way through the chunks of hardened lava.

The gap between her and the building had closed by at least fifty percent before she heard evidence that the dog was still following. This time, the giveaway sound was far more menacing. She turned, rock at the ready and saw the brute crouched barely ten meters away, a snarling growl dominating the air. As she turned and faced her stalker the growl abruptly stopped. Fear and frustration erupted. "Fuck off and leave me alone you vicious bastard!" The shouting carried, bouncing off the hills around. The dog didn't move, apart from showing a healthy set of teeth through a slavering snarl. Instinct commanded that she stand firm. She felt the weight of the rock in her hand and threw it. It missed by a mile but the snarling lessened. She reached down and scoured around for another loose rock, keeping one eye on the dog. She felt one, locked her hand around it and stood tall, this time aiming. It just missed the target. Maybe Gran had been right. The dog hadn't advanced while she was facing it. Could she pick her way to the building backwards? Absolutely not! Another rock was found, smaller but still weighty and another rumbling growl building towards a snarl. A silent prayer, a steady aim and an overarm throw. Yelping! "Yes!" The rock had sailed over its head and landed on its back. More startled than hurt, but it still didn't advance.

Taking a huge gamble — a gamble that needed to be made if she was to break this standoff and reach the building — she ran a few steps forward, stopped, turned to face her adversary, grabbed another rock and flung it. She repeated this three times, gaining ground, but the dog wasn't stupid. It could see where she was heading. Instead of closing the gap between them, it started to circle round to the building itself and very soon, she realized with dread, it would soon be standing directly between her and sanctuary. Her eyes caste about for any sign of the walkers. Nothing. She checked her phone. Still no signal except for emergencies. But how long would it take for her to explain? And how long before anyone could reach her? Panic rose and adrenalin pumped through her body. Gripping on to her phone she looked at the gaping hole of the building, imagined herself running through it, then bounded over the rocks. She was almost there. Had reached level ground to the right of the door that was no-door. Suddenly the beast, snapping and snarling cut across her path. She swung her rucksack hitting it across the shoulder, it yelped and fell sideways, unbalanced by the force behind the hit. It righted itself easily and stood guard of the only entrance to safety, panting and slavering on the threshold.

Lyn hooked her rucksack over one shoulder, backed off slowly for several steps, then ran, full pelt, round to the back of the building. There was no other way in. A plank of wood lay a few feet away. She bent to grab it as a snarl to her left followed by the dog leaping to attack, caught her off-guard. With full force she swung the plank upwards, stepping back in a deep hollow and wrenching her ankle, causing her phone to fly from her grip and land with a sickening crash somewhere in the back of beyond. But the plank had hit its target. The end of it had caught the dog in the chest, leaving it winded and whining in a heap. The end of the coarse rope that had once tethered the monster was inches from her fingers. She grabbed it, wrapping it several times around a nearby concrete post that stood at a drunken angle in the ground. Her ankle was throbbing with pain but realizing that her survival depended on it, she grabbed her rucksack and hobbled around the remaining circuit of the building, disappearing within its dark, gaping mouth.

On entering, she realized why the front door was missing. She was standing on it. But it wasn't really a door — that must have been recycled years ago — what she stood on was four planks of wood held together by two cross bars, fixed to an inside frame. Desperate to gain access someone had bashed at it long enough until the makeshift door had simply fallen inwards. All around was gloom and foul smells. She dragged off her sunglasses and peered around for another door. For more protection. There wasn't any. Just two empty doorways, one with a filthy piece of material hanging from two nails.

Outside she could hear the dog frantically trying to free itself. it was only a matter of time. Harnessing every ounce of strength, she lifted the flattened planked board and tried to push it into the gap. Twice it slid from her grip at the point of tipping it into place. Third time she managed to tip it but there was a gap at one end and an overlap at the other. Suddenly, there was a change in the animals noisy frustration to free itself. All that she'd managed for protection, was to close the gap to a about three inches, put her back against the door, form a brace with her body by positioning her good foot in a dip in the floor, and pray to God that it was enough to save her from the beast.

Bristol Airport

A resounding thud as the wheels on the undercarriage touched down. Brakes applied, and everyone inside the plane felt their bodies react to the force. A shared sense of relief when the craft finally came to a halt instigating a wave of clapping that became infectious. With a sigh of relief, James removed his phone from his jacket pocket and turned it on. Thankfully there'd been no messages from Helen. The plane had landed on time — in fact it had landed ten minutes ahead of schedule — but the gain was soon to be lost by having to queue.

James had been allocated a seat in the centre of the plane and as he'd been one of the first to board, was seated and settled quickly. However, disembarking was far more frustrating, even though he'd been on his feet the second the seatbelt light cut out. Although the doors at the front and rear of the plane were opened, whichever way he went, he was trapped by slow-moving, disorganised passengers. By the time he'd finally made it into the airport, he was delayed once again behind a whole line of the same people waiting to have their passports checked.

The carousel spewed up his suitcase, but before moving into 'arrivals', hoping Vincent had made it on time, he decided to phone Lyn to reassure her that he'd arrived safely, but he couldn't get through, nor could he leave a message.

Disappointed, he phoned Helen confirming his arrival and told her he'd head straight to the hospital once he'd picked up his car. The call was brief, still no change in Mother.

Vincent was sitting at a small table chomping his way through a beef burger with a steaming mug of coffee at his elbow. He caught sight of James, held up his hand, and released a loud whistle that turned more heads than was intended. James walked over to join him, the smell of the food and coffee setting his stomach rumbling. He hadn't eaten since breakfast because he never consumed refreshments on planes — not since a nasty bout of food poisoning eighteen years ago — and the only chance now to buy ready-cooked food would probably be in the hospital's cafe. He shuddered at the thought.

After shuffling behind another queue, James returned to the small table, large coffee in one hand, beef burger and chips in the other.

"I'm sure Lyn wouldn't approve of what you're eating, Jimmy. *Now* I understand why you've left her behind. You need all the little flings you can get, mate, before you get hitched because once she's got you under this," Vinny displayed an upside-down thumb, "It'll be wholemeal bread, salads, fish and copious amounts of water to wash it down." Vincent shoved the last chunk of burger into his mouth and took a large swig of coffee.

James let Vincent's playful jibes wash over his head. He was hungry and in the habit of keeping talking to a minimum when he ate his food. "As I explained, Vincent, my mother's in hospital. That's why I'm here."

"Sorry, mate, just trying to lighten the situation. I'm nipping to the Gents to wash my hands, wouldn't want to transfer burger-grease onto your lovely, gold wedding ring, would we? And, give you a chance to finish your grub in peace."

Vincent was gone a while and by the time he returned, James had finished eating and was half way down his coffee. He stood to leave, taking the takeaway coffee with him but Vincent intervened.

"No point in rushing, Jimmy. I've just been talking to a cab driver who reckons the M5 is chock-a-block on the southbound section between Bristol and Taunton due to an accident earlier this afternoon. The good news is, the road should be cleared of debris very soon. Give it half an hour and by the time we get there, traffic should be flowing again."

The solicitor sat down again, making a mental note of the time wasted on queueing, but Vincent's broad grin, as he placed the tiny package on the table, stole his attention. Donning his reading glasses, James carefully revealed the ring from its several layers of white tissue paper. Once again he felt its satisfying weight in the palm of his hand. He brought it up to within an inch or two of his right eye and turned it slowly, reading silently the poetic line.

Suddenly his phone rang. He lay the ring back inside the tissue and placed it in his pocket, moving away from the table as he answered Helen's call.

"Just thought I'd warn you, James, there's a holdup on the M5. Should be clearing soon but it might be a good chance for you to grab a meal, unless you want to eat in the hospital cafe."

"Thanks for the tip, Helen. I'll phone you as soon as I've picked up my car."

James turned back to the table and without sitting down, finished the remains of his coffee. "Thank you for securing the ring for me, Vincent. I can write you a cheque now, or, if you prefer, I'll get the cash as soon as I'm back home, but I'll probably be in Exeter for at least twenty-four hours."

"If it's all the same to you, Jimmy, I prefer the cash. It's not linked to my business and I don't want the taxman sniffing around, besides, I'm sure my client would prefer cash. Right, now that's settled, lets hit the road and hopefully, burn some rubber!"

Bovey Tracey—Late Afternoon

Isabelle awoke with a start. She'd been on the field. Only this time things were different. Nicholas was waiting for *her*. Even though in the dream she knew she was late, she'd just slowly strolled onto the field which erroneously was lush, green grass. He'd stood patiently waiting, not in the area where she'd found the ring, but much further away. Almost as far away as the workman had been. In spite of the distance they recognised each other, closing the gap as they moved towards each other in slow motion — just like in the films — arms stretched out, eager to touch, eager to kiss. The sun had been in her eyes, blindingly bright. Nicholas, a black silhouette, a sharply defined shape without feature or detail, suddenly stopped. There was knocking and talking. And Nicholas melted away.

"Mum? Mum? Me and Dad have rustled up some supper. Nothing fancy, hot soup and crumpets." Isabelle saw the knob on the bedroom door slowly turn and then the door opened a few inches. Robert's face peered through, the concern on it squeezing her heart.

"I'll be down in a few minutes, love." Her voice sounded strange, thick and clumpy, almost alien. From her dream, which had now dissipated, one factor remained. She'd been aware of feeling happy, lighthearted, felt as though she could do anything, change everything. Without speaking a single word in the dream, she knew her voice would have reflected that confidence, that self-awareness. She needed to communicate with Nicholas. Too late now. She'd go down to the library first thing in the morning.

Stairs creaking followed by a rattling door latch was Shaun Thatcher's cue to ladle out the soup and butter crumpets that had been kept warm in the Rayburn. Izzy walked into the kitchen, a shadow of her former self, her face wan in spite of the effort to smile and appear as though everything was normal. Nothing was normal any more and as far as Shaun was concerned, nothing gets back to normal until you've thrashed out what's gone wrong and then talked, even argued, if that's what it takes, to put things right again.

"Come on Izzy…love, sit yourself down." Although he'd meant the endearment, it sounded strange, false to his ears. It had been so long since they'd exchanged such words. His wife didn't seem to notice anyway. She did as she was asked and sat at the table, lifted her spoon and swirled it around in the thick liquid, tasted the broth and made the right noises in order to please. But they knew he and Robert, that she wasn't…*all there.* It was the only way he could describe it. They'd been here before. It had happened a couple a times in the past, although not as bad as this. Post Natal Depression, were the fancy words they gave it after Robert was born and Izzy hadn't coped well with the extra responsibility. Then when he was nine years old, he was knocked off his bike by a learner driver — broke his collar bone and suffered from concussion — sent Izzy into a state that lasted for weeks. But at least they'd communicated then, talked things through, which helped a lot more than the bloody tablets the doctors kept prescribing.

Robert dragged his chair closer to his mother, reached out his hand and stroked her shoulder. "Sorry about the test results, Mum, God only knows how much you must be worrying, Dad and I just want you to know…" Robert stopped, faltered when his mother turned to him and wildly shook her head.

Isabelle dropped the spoon with a clatter, hitting the bowl and flicking spots of food onto the table. She looked at her son as if seeing him for the first time. Saw the anguish as tears filled his eyes, felt his pain, just as she had when he was small and she couldn't find the strength to do anything about it. Again she shook her head and cried out, "It's lies! It's all bloody lies!" Then she ran from the kitchen and up the stairs.

"Well that was bloody clever wasn't it? Didn't I tell you not to mention the tests, she's obviously in denial, and she'll hate it that I told you. Well, I intend to go visit her doctor tomorrow morning. Get it from the horse's mouth just how bad things are and give him a piece of my mind about the stress she's been under, waiting for them to get their arses into gear. In the meantime, Robert, just be loving and supportive. I know your hurting, son. We both are but now's not the time to mention certain things. Last thing we want is to tip her over the edge and for Christ's sake, don't mention that I've been made redundant!"

Lanzarote

Using a minimum amount of the water, Lyn swallowed two tablets and leaned against the cool wall, giving her a chance to calm down and take stock of her situation. In front of her were the tipped out contents of her rucksack: waterproof jacket, binoculars, map, tissues, packet of nuts and a half empty bottle of water. It was only when she'd rifled through the zipped pocket inside her rucksack that she'd come upon a grip-top polythene bag with contents that were worth their weight in gold.

She hadn't used the rucksack since her trip to Australia, and the bag of precious items, hidden and forgotten about, were packed for emergencies. But they were never needed, until now. A blister-pack of ten Aspirin — two had been used on the outward journey for keeping the blood thin during the long-haul flight, she hadn't remembered to take any on the flight home — a tube of antiseptic cream, to administer to mosquito-bites that were particularly nasty in Australia, a small box containing fabric-strip plaster and a tiny pair of round-ended scissors. It was the scissors that gave the most delight, not because she would be able to cut to size the plasters she needed. Oh no! Her mind was contemplating uses far more vicious than that. But in order to help her vicious plan to succeed, she needed to find a way to sharpen the ends of the scissors.

She shuddered as she recalled the first minutes of her entry into what had now become part sanctuary, part prison. She'd thought she'd be safe once she'd braced her back against the door. Thought the animal would lose interest and wander off, giving her a chance to secure the boarding with something other than her body. But within seconds, the brute had rammed it's solid body against the makeshift door. The shock and the impact had almost thrown her off balance. If there hadn't been the chiseled out dip for her foot, she'd have been done for. After the impact she'd peered through the three inch gap, hoping that the dog would now give up. She'd watched as it's muscular, black body walked several paces away from the door. She'd held her breath, daring to hope that this was the end of the nightmare. Then the creature had turned, glared at the target and lowered its head. Knowing what was about to happen she wedged both her feet in the crevice, ignoring the bolt of pain that shot through the injured foot, and closed her eyes. The impact had her hands scrabbling for purchase on the rough walls. More bleeding, more sweating and more panic. She was worried that the hound, sensing her fear, would renew it's attack.

There were two planks of wood laying against the far interior wall and several others strewn about the place. But none within reach, none that could be grabbed without leaving the safety of her bracing position. She had a three inch gap to poke something through and stab at the dog when it came close enough, but after she'd feverishly looked about her she'd realised there was nothing she could reach without moving. If she moved her weight from the door, the dog would only have to sneeze and it would have fallen inwards. Even her rucksack was out of arms reach. Something she'd berated herself for several times.

In desperation she'd shoved her hands into her jeans pockets thinking she might be holding a key, anything sharp enough to poke the bastard's eye out if she got the chance. But all she'd gained from this act of desperation, had been more bleeding when her fingers had been caught on the buckle of her belt. Her pockets had been empty, except for a tissue. This she'd wrapped around the painful, bleeding finger whilst cursing the belt buckle. She then had an idea, followed by a glimmer of hope. She'd unfastened her belt, a hefty type made from strong leather and a cast brass buckle formed in the shape of a curled dragon. She'd twisted to look through the gap and saw the dog was still visible and it still was panting from the last strike. Gripping the belt so that the heavy buckle dangled free, she'd caste it in the direction of her rucksack aiming to hook one of the straps and drag it closer. Her first attempt failed and she had tried again but the buckle snagged at the strap. Slowly dragging it towards her, periodically checking that the dog was still resting, until finally the bag was in her arms. She cuddled it like a babe before rummaging for the opened packet of chocolate biscuits that James had insisted on bringing from home. With one hand, her thumb nail counted just four biscuits left in the wrapper which was enough to keep the dog busy for a while. She then squeezed her hand through the gap to throw the biscuits out towards the panting dog, and waited.

She didn't have to wait long. The animal was obviously starving. While it was preoccupied, tearing through the paper to get to the food, Lyn hobbled across and grabbed the two planks of wood that stood against the opposite wall. As she'd expected, they fitted perfectly between floor crevice and the upper crossbar. She had closed the gap to barely an inch, and the makeshift door was now secure, allowing her the freedom to move around.

Now that she had a treasure trove of goodies to dress her open wounds, in addition to nulling the pain of her sprained ankle, all she really needed was a miracle. A walker strolling by, or better still someone in a car. Someone who could help her find her phone, and find it in working order. Lyn slumped in the corner of the smelly space and wiped her tears on the sleeve of her top. All she wanted was to be rescued from the hound that was waiting just a few feet away.

Chapter 20

Tuesday Evening—Newton Abbott

It had gone six-thirty and Stefan had expected to be on his way back to Torquay with payment for the completed work. However, although everything was done to satisfaction, and Brett Robson, after very carefully inspecting each lock, grudgingly admitted it was, he wouldn't hand over the cash to Stefan. He was insisting it be given, in person, to the man whom he'd contracted to do the job. Or, if that wasn't possible, he could have payment in the form of a cheque made out to Mr Conway. Stefan understood the implication he was making. Robson didn't trust foreigners, believing they all spent their time thieving and lying. Stefan phoned Vincent, who was still on the motorway heading towards Exeter with James Fairbank, so Vincent hadn't said much, just to sit tight and he'd be with him as soon as he could.

Sitting tight suited Stefan very much. He was in Joe's comfortable apartment, setting up two places and looking forward to sharing the dish named Shepherd's Pie that Joe's daughter had brought in earlier. Stefan didn't have many friends, well, what *he* regarded as friends. In fact, he made a point of not making friends. His best friend from childhood had turned into his worst enemy when Stefan was fifteen. After the pain and anguish of that time, he'd become wary. But it was different with Joe. Friendship had just happened. Neither man had been looking for anything from the other, things had just moved easily between them, without the effort of having to think twice about invisible price-tags or favours owed.

When Stefan had shown him the full extent of his find on the field that day, Joe had shown no envy or curiosity about where it was found. He showed only pleasure at Stefan's good fortune, sharing in the excitement of how the coins had come to light and been missed by the inattentive JCB driver. He did warn Stefan, however, about keeping quiet and not mentioning the find spot to anyone. Not even him. Stefan had pushed five of the coins towards Joe, saying simply, for you Joe. The older man had hesitated for a while, searching Stefan's face, wondering about the motive behind the generous gift and calculating what effect a refusal to accept them would have on their friendship. Then, content with what he saw and felt, he'd scooped them into the palm of his hand saying the gift was much appreciated.

During the meal, Stefan listened as Joe told him how his passion for coin collecting had started back in the 1970's. "As a builder in London," Joe began. "It was commonplace to find stuff that'd been lost or buried over the centuries. I lost count of the tasty bits and pieces that had fallen through floorboards in the summer when boards shrink back, lying there undiscovered for generations until the floor was replaced. Lofts and fireplaces were favoured hiding places for all sorts of family treasures. Treasures that became forgotten about or the concealers had suddenly died. They were perks of the trade and with no way of knowing who the original owners were, it was a case of 'finders keepers'. Money was tight at the time, so me and the lads would sell the finds we made. Took them to this Polish dealer, who'd buy our stuff for cash, no questions asked. Mind you, being a dealer, I believe what we got was only a fraction of the true worth. But as life improved for me and the wife, I got to thinking about the gold and silver coins we'd let go for a song and began to read magazines on coin-collecting, coins earlier than the nineteenth century. I don't mind admitting that I became that fascinated I vowed never to sell another coin that pleased me."

Noticing that their glasses of beer were low Joe stood, excused himself and disappeared into the kitchen. When he returned he was clutching what looked like a photograph-album under his arm and a bottle of beer in each hand. Stefan knew better than to jump to his aid. After topping up the glasses, Joe pushed the album across the table. "There's photographs of the best coins I used to own", said Joe, adding that he'd never shown them to anyone else, not even his wife. "If she'd got an inkling of their value, she'd have been pestering for holidays abroad and such."

Stefan took a long gulp of the topped-up beer before entering this interesting conversation. "Must have broke your heart to sell them, Joe. Will you start collecting again?"

"No! What's the point? In fact if I had my time over, I wouldn't have kept anything from the wife. And if she had wanted a treat like a holiday, I would have taken her. She was a good woman and sharing time with her whilst enjoying a few holidays on foreign beaches would have been riches enough."

Joe sensed there was more to the question before it was asked. "So you'll sell the five coins I gave you. Do you mind giving me a contact where I'll get a fair price for mine?"

Joe smiled, congratulating himself on reading the lad right. "I've got a couple of coin magazines you can have, Stefan. There's several reputable dealers advertise in them. But if you don't mind me suggesting it, do a bit of reading up yourself, and anything you particularly want to know, I'm here at the end of the phone." In a neat hand, Joe wrote his name and telephone number on the back of one of the magazines. "But I'll not be selling the coins you gave me. They'll be passed on to the grandchildren eventually, and until then, they'll be a reminder of a friend. A friend who gave me back a sense of purpose."

A ruckus outside interrupted the easy flow of questions and answers. Stefan could hear Vincent's strong words of frustration aimed at Brett Robson. It was time to part company with Joe.

The driver's door of the Kuga was slammed shut with unnecessary force as Vinny left the confines of the neat community. Stefan followed in the van, sending a friendly salute to Joe who stood watching the scene on his balcony before turning and stepping back into the warmth and security of his flat. Brett Robson had retreated back into his own personal fortress as soon as the cash had been handed over to the tradesmen he'd vowed never to use again.

As the well-oiled community gates slowly and majestically swung to meet, no one noticed the dark-clad figure slip through the diminishing opening, temporarily halting its slow progress.

The Kuga sped along the Newton Abbot road towards Torquay. Vinny was lost in his own thoughts, not checking, or caring if Stefan was keeping pace behind. The afternoon had turned to shit and he was mentally cursing the bastards that had caused it.

The decline in his good fortune had begun halfway between Bristol and Exeter. His passenger, understandably on edge and eager to reach his own car, was bored with the stop-starting of the slow-moving motorway traffic. Jimmy had been constantly checking his phone for messages, relaxing a little, then a few minutes later checking again. In order to take the guy's mind off his sick mother, Vinny had asked if he and Lyn had decided on a date for getting hitched? His answer of, "there hadn't been time to decide anything," had cut short any attempt of further conversation on the subject.

Next thing, Vinny notices Jimmy with the gold ring in his hand, giving it the once over, again. Suddenly the solicitor pulls out his reading glasses and starts scrutinising every millimeter of the inside. Then as calm as you like, tells Vinny that this isn't the ring he'd negotiated to buy, wrapped it back in the tissue and plonked it on the dashboard directly in front of Vinny's eyes. Shocked, Vinny had turned to the solicitor, mouth gaping, and had almost run into the lorry in front of him. After regaining his composure, Vinny laughed, Fairbank was joking, had to be, the ring was identical to the original, right down to weight and colour. But he could tell from the serious look on Jimmy's face, he wasn't happy.

They'd progressed at least a full mile of creeping along before the traffic halted again. With gear shift in neutral and handbrake on, Vinny had turned to the solicitor and asked him pointedly what the fuck was wrong with the ring.

And just as pointedly, Fairbank had told him. 'The ring I agreed to buy was made by Nicholas Payne of Exeter. This ring, has a stamp mark showing 'R', are you aware of what that means?'

Vinny didn't have a fucking clue, the only words racing round his head were, refused, rejected and recompense from the Welsh git who had dropped him in the shit, but he knew the solicitor was about to enlighten him on its true meaning. Suddenly a sharp blast of a horn from behind, and forgetting that he was in neutral with handbrake on, he'd leaped forward, stalling the engine and causing the ring to disappear into the footwell, where it remained because the traffic was moving again.

Jimmy's lips were also moving, as he learned that usually, if a replica was made of an older, more valuable piece, it was often stamped with the letter 'R' so as not to confuse it with the original. So whoever had made the copy, the solicitor had continued in that know-all way that always put Vinny's back up, he or she had enough integrity to mark it as a replica.

Vinny had been silent for a while, cursing Taffy to hell and back, when an idea had suddenly floated into his head. For effect, he'd slapped his hand down hard on the steering wheel, giving out a loud 'ah' as if he'd just been touched by some divine power. Then he'd told Jimmy a cock and bull story of how Isabelle, his client and owner of the said ring, mentioned that she was having a copy made so as to keep a record of it for her descendants. Emphasising the final words of the story he'd stated that his client, an honourable person, had obviously mistakenly handed over the wrong ring.

Another halt in the traffic found him groveling in the footwell and placing the package back on the dashboard, where it quivered with every movement of the car, seemingly mocking Vinny's effort to rescue the deal, causing his head to ache with thoughts on how the hell was he going to get the original off Isabelle? He'd grabbed it and shoved it in his pocket, promising that by the end of the week James would have the original. He'd then put the matter out of his mind.

Stefan's phone call had helped. It arrived hot on the given

promise. But the call had contained more grief. Vinny hadn't been pleased. In fact Vinny had been livid that after dropping off Fairbank, he'd have to make a detour to Newton Abbot. Brett Robson's intimidating and uncompromising ways were the last straw. And he was the perfect candidate to receive all of Vinny's pent-up frustration of the last few hours.

Bovey Tracey

Isabelle grabbed her warmest coat and before leaving the confines of the cottage reassured her husband and son that she was alright, that she just needed some air and a short walk to clear her head. "There's no need to follow me, Shaun, I promise I won't be more than half an hour, then we'll sit down and talk. Talk properly as a family." She hadn't a clue what she would or could disclose about the bizarre happenings that seemed to be dominating every facet of her life. But what she was clear and determined about, was putting an end to the lying.

Although chilly, the evening air felt refreshingly pleasant as she headed once more to the library. Tuesday was late opening and as she reached the library door found there was still fifteen minutes to closing time. Fifteen minutes to keep her resolve and confront the demons within and communicate with the demon without.

Thankfully, the only library assistant on duty was a young man she'd never seen before, men weren't as observant as women, or as nosey. Her favourite computer, tucked away in the corner, was available and she promptly set about logging into her mail. She located the last short message from Nicholas and pressed 'Reply'.

Hi Nicholas

Sorry you couldn't make the arranged meeting. I'm not annoyed, honestly, we're only human and things do crop up to alter our plans. I'm about to make some changes in my life which means this will be the last time I'll be contacting you. Hope life brings you everything you want.

Bella

She read it through, editing one word only. She had finished the message with her proper name, Isabelle, thinking it added more gravitas, but Nicholas had only ever called her, Bella. She pressed 'Send' and moved on. She had five minutes left. Time enough to send a brief message to Mr Conway, telling him she'd no longer be needing his services.

Lanzarote

Lyn stood before the huge open gap in the larger section of the derelict building, its only blessing being that It was too high off the ground to allow mad dogs to jump through. The sun had disappeared leaving behind a dusky sky partially covered in cloud. But within the breaks there was no sign of a moon. It was only a matter of time, a very short time, before she'd be plunged into complete darkness. The air temperature was falling rapidly, and in spite of the waterproof jacket fastened up to the neck, the only part of her body that registered warmth, was her injured ankle which burned and throbbed. The pills had helped, dulling the pain to manageable levels, allowing her to explore the interior of her prison, but the moving around hadn't helped and it was too soon to risk taking more. She looked about her. The whole of this space would soon be affected by the chilling breeze coming directly through the opening, bouncing off the wall opposite and circulating around the rest of the large inner room. Even hardened squatters would stay clear of this area, unless it was a really warm night.

She dragged her weary body back to the front door area, realizing as she flicked aside the tattered curtain — someone's feeble attempt to stop the draught — that unless she was rescued soon, cold would be a fiercer enemy than the hound.

Settling back and positioning herself again in such a way that she was able to look out through the floor to ceiling gap of the door, reality slowly dawned. After hours of patiently keeping watch. Hours of telling herself that on an island as small as this, where homesteads and roadways criss-crossed it from end to end, someone was bound to come within earshot. But she'd seen no one. Not a single flicker of life. Except for the hound that every so often paced the perimeter and sniffed at the opening, emitted a low growl before wandering back to its place of waiting — somewhere out of Lyn's line of vision.

She'd lost hope in sharpening the points of the little scissors and ramming them into the monster's eyes. For a start, the scissors were hardened steel, and after vigorously grinding the tips against the densest rock she could find, all she'd achieved was a sore hand. Another obvious setback to this half-baked plan was apparent after the dogs first sniffing visit to the gap. Although the hound was flat-nosed, like a bull dog, she'd realized at once the impossibility of reaching the eyes. Besides, even if she managed to slash it's throat and witness it's dying breath, where would she go in the pitch black of the night, even if she could walk. (*Come on, Lynda, don't waste time, get yourself as comfy as possible while you've got the light.*)

For once, Lyn welcomed the echo of Gran's voice. An echo that had usually irritated more than helped. (*Get your arse in gear, my girl, and stop feeling sorry for yourself. You were warned about coming out in the wilds alone and as usual, you have to have it your own way. You've got a long night ahead so use your brain.*)

There was only one corner in the abandoned building that was free of drafts. The corner that was filled with rags. Rags that might have been covering something that had died — the stench there was strong enough — and the thought of this had kept Lyn away. With gritted teeth against pain on the outside and fear on the inside she hobbled over to a stray plank of wood, easing it into her hand. Slowly she moved closer to the stinking mound of cloth, aimed the plank, closed her eyes and gingerly prodded. Feeling braver, she opened one eye and with breath held, carefully began lifting and shifting using the crude extension to her arm. Relief washed over her taught body as the words "thank God" involuntarily escaped her lips.

Beneath what was once a colourful blanket and a striped sheet so faded it was hard to define any colour differences, lay a large pillow, its only covering, a map of stains. The thought of tramps or drug addicts using the bedding turned her stomach and she abandoned any thought of using it. The plank of wood was discarded as she hobbled back to her place by the door. The chill of the encroaching night air stung her face and tears began to form.

In her heart she knew. Knew there'd come a time when she'd have to make use of the stinking mound if she was to survive the coming night. And that time was approaching fast. She let the tears roll as she thought of those she loved and who might never be seen again. A vision of Martin, her beautiful little grandson, filled her head.

Exeter Hospital

With a heavy sigh James switched off his phone. The battery was almost flat and he had no way of recharging it until he was back in Torquay. It was the third time he'd tried to reach Lyn. To put her mind at rest that he'd arrived safely and to pass on the news that his mother was neither better nor worse than when she'd first been admitted to hospital. 'No change' seemed to be a mantra that was used throughout the hospital. At least he'd been able to sit at her bedside, holding her hand and trying his best to convey how sorry he was that this had happened. She'd been awake part of the time, but still unable to speak, or smile, and this was the most distressing thing for all concerned. The panic and frustration in her eyes were easy to read.

A tap on the door to the small, private room, and Helen entered carrying two takeaway coffees on a makeshift tray of cardboard.

"Did you get through to Lyn?" she asked in a normal volume voice, not thinking to check if Mother was asleep or not. James checked. She appeared to be sleeping but appearances weren't solid fact at this point in time. Without answering, he relieved his sister of one of the coffees and indicated that they move outside into the corridor where a row of three seats were usually vacant Once seated he said, "No, her phone is still out of action. Probably turned off and in the safe."

"I wouldn't put Lyn down as a person who showed lack of consideration in a situation like this. In fact, I'm amazed she didn't return with you."

James took a tentative sip of the dark, dubious-looking liquid, grimacing before responding. "She wanted to return with me, it was I who insisted she didn't."

"Why on earth did you do that?"

"She needs this break, Helen, she's been so wound up lately. Don't you agree that relaxing at a luxury hotel in beautiful weather is far better than sitting here for hours on end, interspersed with…with this awful brown sludge?"

"Of course I agree, if that's what Lyn wants. But you said she wanted to return with you, that it was *you* insisted she stay. What was her reaction to your insistence, James?"

"Helen, *I* didn't want this to happen any more than *you*. If Mother's condition doesn't deteriorate further, I'll be returning to Lanzarote as soon as possible." He turned to his sister, eyes pleading for her to understand. "It just seemed to make more sense to come back alone and allow Lyn the luxury of some quality time to herself."

"So you don't think her not answering the phone has got anything to do with your insistence that she stay there, alone?"

James didn't answer. He did what he thought was best. There was no more to be said.

Bovey Tracey

Twice Shaun Thatcher had been on the point of leaving the cottage to look for Izzy and twice his son had stopped him, insisting it only fair to give his mother her half hour of peaceful walking. However, the minute the half hour was up, so was Shaun, shrugging into his coat and pulling on his boots. But halfway through tying the laces, the door had swung open and Izzy had stepped in. Both of them remaining silent as they removed their outer garments.

Father and son had tried to keep busy in the half hour that

the woman of the house was out walking. The Rayburn was well stoked, the filled kettle singing as it progressed to boiling and a plate of ham sandwiches were cobbled together by uninitiated but willing hands, before placing them in the centre of the table.

On taking this in, Isabelle was filled with shame, her voice shaky as she said, "I'm so sorry for all the trouble I've caused. Please…please forgive me."

Both males expected an outpouring of tears and then a dash for the door to the upstairs. Thankfully neither happened. Shaun said, "Come and sit down, love." he pulled out the chair nearest to the warm stove and as Isabelle lowered herself into it, he rested both his hands gently on her shoulders. "There's a lot that needs talking about, from each one of us, we're a family and it's not right to keep things from each other. But before the talking starts lets have a nice fresh brew and polish off these sandwiches that look like they were made by a cow with a crutch!"

Newton Abbot

Joe felt uneasy, not scared, just uneasy. He'd experienced too much in his life to allow a stranger to scare him, even when that stranger's intention was to intimidate and frighten. But when his ten-year-old grandson, George, arrived twenty minutes later — a usual visit on a Tuesday evening while his parents played badminton — the same stranger had collared the lad. Watched him as he punched in the code for opening the gates. Then, according to George, the bloke, who spoke in a very deep scratchy voice, had asked his name, which school he went to, and what he was doing in a private gated community for the retired? The lad had been brought up to be wary of strangers, especially men, but when a bloke in a suit introduces himself as a detective, a detective investigating recent robberies on the same community he'd just entered, the lad felt obliged to answer all his questions. Including the last one, the full name and relationship of the man he was visiting.

Joe knew it must be the same bloke he'd twice caught sight of hanging around outside. A bloke in a suit he'd assumed to be one of Brett Robson's cronies. George's description fitted perfectly. When the suit had buzzed Joe's apartment earlier, demanding in his coarse, gravelly voice, to be let in because he had questions concerning two men that had just left in separate vehicles, Joe had told him he could ask what he liked, but he couldn't promise that he'd answer, and he certainly wouldn't be letting him in. The suit hadn't been expecting that and his voice took on an even more intimidating tone. He claimed to be a detective with reason to believe Joe was involved in receiving stolen goods and if necessary, he could obtain a warrant to search his premises. Joe had asked for his name and rank and told him he'd be down directly he'd checked his credentials with the local Police.

He hadn't had to wait long. His last sighting of the man was from the back, as he'd headed towards the gates and Joe had assumed he'd seen the last of this particular con artist. It was the safety of his grandson that now played on his mind. His daughter would be collecting George in just over an hour. In the meantime he'd consider contacting Stefan, with just a friendly warning to watch his back.

Bovey Tracey

For Isabelle, the last hour had been so pleasant and so normal. Just like old times. Sitting in the warm kitchen, sharing food, exchanging niceties, both of the males in her life smiling as though nothing in the world was wrong. It was Robert who had finally broken the spell. Checking his watch and announcing that he'd be late for work if he didn't leave now. His 'work', was earning a pittance-for stacking shelves at the local supermarket, the only way he could obtain things that his friends took for granted because their parents had more disposable income. He'd dropped a kiss on the top of Isabelle's head and rushed out the door, leaving behind an atmosphere loaded with uncertainty.

She began gathering the used plates but was halted by Shaun's hand.

"Leave it Izzy, I'll wash up later. It's time for talking. Time for trying to put right what's gone wrong."

She returned to her chair remembering her promise. Remembering how certain she'd felt that it was the right thing to do — allowing all the poisonous lies to rise to the surface, confess to them, then feel cleansed and renewed — but now she wasn't so sure. Where would she start? She'd told so many lies. She took a deep breath. "It's hard to know where to start, Shaun."

"I know love. I know it's always been hard for you to discuss things, especially when it involves having to make changes. I understand that this is the way you are. But Izzy, there are times when we need to be stronger. I'm asking you to be stronger now because there's something I need to get off my chest."

Shaun briefly cradled his head in his hands. Then he sat

upright, and after swallowing deeply looked her straight in the eye and said, "I've got the sack, Izzy and I told Robbie I'd been made redundant, but the truth is I was dismissed. Kicked out because my heart's not in the job, never has been. From the first day I started, that job was just a means for paying bills." A sneer and a shake of the head. "And it hasn't done that for ages."

His head fell back into his hands. Isabelle wondered if he was crying and reached out her arms, but before they could take hold he sat upright again, appearing to be smiling.

"You know Izzy, when we first got wed and we moved in here, I was so happy, so full of hope for our future. I thought moving into this cottage was a signpost to our future. I had high hopes of picking up where my own grandfather had left off, thatching for a living like his father and his father before him. All enjoying their craft and earning a decent living. We're in the heart of Devon where there's still a fair few cottages with roofs to be maintained.I felt confident of getting the training." It seemed that now Shaun had Izzy's attention he couldn't stop talking. "Maybe you don't remember, but it really stuck in my throat that after trying week after week, even almost begging at once stage, offering to work for nothing as an apprentice until I learned the trade, but I couldn't find a single thatcher who was prepared to give me a chance. So I had to return to a shitty job that held no satisfaction, until something better presented itself. But if it's one thing I've learned, Izzy, nothing just presents itself. You have to make it happen. You know we could've sold this place, started up a little business together, been less reliant on the big boys whose only interest is profit."

Shaun suddenly appeared to run out of steam. His body slumped and his face took on a weariness that tore at her heart. "Now you've fallen sick and I…I'm not sure which way to turn Izzy. What should I do? What can I do?"

Isabelle caught hold of Shaun's fist as he bit down on fingers to stem the tremour in his voice. "I'm not sick, Shaun, I mean I don't think I am. One lie was to cover another, then everything just got out of control. I promise to do everything I can to help us get over this. I'm going to try and explain how the first lie came about. But before I do will you promise me one thing?"

Shaun looked confused as he tried to take on board what Izzy had just said. "Of course I will, just say what it is."

"I don't like being called Izzy. If you must shorten my name, I prefer to be called Bella."

Chapter 21

Tuesday Late Evening—Lanzarote

Darkness had fallen suddenly, absolutely. Within minutes of positioning her meager essentials within arms reach, Lyn could barely see any of them. From left to right she'd placed, in order of importance, four items and memorised their position by using the first letter of each word. P,W,F,W — pills, water, food, weapons — sticks and stones and a miniature pair of round-ended scissors. From where she now sat, on the pile of old bedding in the draft-free corner, the gap that ran down the length of the makeshift door appeared as a lighter shade of pitch-black. No stars were visible. The assumption that cloud must now totally cover the heavens gave a modicum of comfort — cloudy nights were always warmer than clear ones. The wind too had dropped, leaving behind an eerie silence. A silence that opened doors to thoughts of doom, inviting the imagination to dwell on what lay beyond the few short years of a human life.

Tired and weary but not the least bit sleepy, she pulled her mind back to the present, wondering what the time was. Pushing up the sleeve of her jacket, a sudden thrill. The Swatch she was wearing had hands that glowed bright green in darkness. The thrill soon evaporated, little time had passed since last checking in the fading daylight. There was still fifty minutes before any more pain-killing tablets could be taken. At one particular low point she had considered taking the whole lot, such was the pain and the depth of her despair, but on realizing she didn't have enough tablets to do the job properly, she put her efforts into working out a time scale for keeping the worst of the pain at bay until daylight. The swelling to her ankle had increased, forcing the painful removal of both shoe and sock and raising her leg by resting it on her rucksack. This helped, but the heat and the throbbing pain, although diminished, were constant.

Silence persisted. The soft tick of the Swatch and its eerie green glow, the only thing indicating movement. Even the dog had ceased making its rounds of sniffing and growling, had the monster quit it's prowling, returning to the place it had escaped from? She doubted it. Besides, what difference would it make? She was trapped until daylight in this God-forsaken-hole. Bored, she reached for the half empty pack of nuts, then thought better of it. There was approximately two inches of water left in the bottle — an inch for each pair of tablets left. Ironically, she had deliberately chosen salted nuts because in hot climates you lose salt from the body more rapidly because of sweating but the more salt you consume, the more water you crave.

Without thinking, or caring, she shifted and settled into the stained pillow, tucking the smelly blanket behind her head and shoulders. Her eyes closed, trapping the forming tears that she couldn't afford to lose, and she forced her mind to concentrate on the future. To face up to how a life shared with James, as his wife, would change things. Comparisons with her first husband, Martin, who'd died in a climbing accident years ago, were inevitable. Martin had been her first love and

Sarah was born within a year of their marriage. And now Sarah was married with a son of her own — a beautiful blond-haired boy who had helped to make Lyn realize just how important family was. But sadly, all *her* family were thousands of miles away in Australia.

Years ago when Sarah was a toddler. Martin had wanted to emigrate to Australia. He'd spent months talking about it, trying to persuade Lyn how living in such a young country with vast opportunities would be the making of them. It was *his* dream. For Lyn, the dream sounded too good to be true. Gran had put an end to his dream and in a way had sealed both their fates. If Martin had been allowed to follow that dream, he would never have taken up such an adventurous sport as mountain climbing. If Lyn hadn't allowed Gran to dominate their lives, she might well have been captivated by his dream; which may even have led her to finding her estranged parents when they were middle-aged and healthy, instead of coming upon them only a year ago when dementia had robbed her of getting to know her father.

And to cap it all, she wouldn't be marooned here in a nightmare situation, wondering if she would ever wake up from it.

Torquay

The phone was ringing. Vinny almost dropped his fish and chips as he struggled to open his front door. Shoving the hot, vinegar-smelling package into Stefan's hand, he darted through the doorway and grabbed the handset.

"Yes?" A long pause and a deep frown.

"Who? Listen mate, this is well out of business hours. I'll

see if I can find him." Vinny placed his hand over the receiver and scowled at Stefan. "Some bloke named Joe, says he needs to speak to you urgently. Hope there's no fucking problem with any of the locks you fitted." He handed over the phone, settled into the chair opposite and began eating his supper.

Knowing privacy was out of the question and turning his back on Vincent would look suspicious, Stefan fixed a smile as he said, "Joe, thank you again for your kindness, I have your number, I ring later and we have little chat, no?" Stefan then fell silent, hearing the urgency as well as the reason behind Joe's call. Joe was warning him about an unwelcome visitor. A well-dressed bloke who'd apparently been watching Stefan and his boss. Joe just wanted to warn Stefan to watch his back.

"Thank you, Joe, I speak later using my mobile, you then have number for contact me." With a preoccupied look Stefan replaced the receiver.

"So?" asked Vincent, holding a fistful of battered fish that was about to follow the handful of chips he'd crammed into his mouth.

"Joe is kind old man. He remind me of my grandfather. He give to me many refreshments, and we talk a lot. Joe is lonely for friend, that's all."

"Oh, please, Stefan. I'm a private investigator. And that's the biggest load of bullshit I've heard in weeks." Vincent's face was turning pink and bits of food sprayed from his mouth as his frustration rose. "I'll say this once only. You are no good to me unless you speak the truth. You are no good to me if you fraternise with clients behind my back. I can see from your blank look you don't know the meaning of the word fraternise so let me make it clear. Do not cosy-up and make friends with clients. And lastly, all calls that come through this office are my business and I want to know every single word from every single call. Even if it's your best mate or the Queen of England. Got it?"

The smile had left Stefan's face and what was left was unreadable. "I make coffee then we talk." He moved towards the door.

Vinny shoved the last of the fish into his mouth and screwed the paper into a tight ball, aimed it at the waste basket and missed, bending to retrieve it just as a blast from the air purifier filled the air, dispelling the smell of vinegary grease. "Forget the coffee, Stefan," he called out. "There's a pack of four beers at the back of the fridge. Kept 'em there for a little celebration tonight. Bring 'em in 'ere, we'll pretend we're on the beach. With fish and chips, chilled beer, blasts of ocean smells; what more could a guy ask for?"

Stefan realized he couldn't keep his fears to himself. From Joe's brief description, he felt certain the man in the suit had followed him from the field.

"Why you celebrate?" Stefan asked as they tapped bottles and both took a long swallow of the chilled beer.

"That's not important now, I want to hear what's going on between you and your new friend, Joe?"

Between sips of beer, Stefan relayed his fears about the suited man who had seen him on the field and for some unknown reason had followed him back to the apartments in Newton Abbot.

Vincent knew there was more, and kept quiet until more was forthcoming.

Stefan continued telling him of the suited man threatening Joe, saying he was a detective and could obtain a warrant to search Joe's apartment for stolen goods. Implying that we had sold him these stolen goods.

Vinny tipped the remainder of the beer down his throat, released a loud belch and asked. "Was there anyone else on the field beside this bloke in a suit? And whereabouts was he standing? Think carefully, Stefan, this is important."

Stefan took a deep breath and closed his eyes — there were things he had to leave out and he knew the deception might show. "I walk over field to area I leave spade. I walk back and forth a few times looking for spade, I see no one. Then I find spade and turn to come back to van and see the man in hedge, watching me. I see no one else at field." Stefan's body suddenly changed. "Yes, I sorry, there was woman. She come running to me thinking I someone named Nicholas."

"A woman? What sort of woman? I mean what was she like?"

"She strange. She look cold and sick. She have too much make-up on face, smeared making her look like clown. I think she been crying. She told to me her name is Bella."

"You sure she didn't say Isabelle?"

"I sure. She say Bella, I'm your beautiful Bella. Maybe she your client, Vincent and man in suit is husband keeping eyes on where she go?"

"Shaun Thatcher in a suit. No way! Boots, jeans, checked shirt and anorak is more his style. I'll bet you a fiver if he does own a suit, which I very much doubt, it wouldn't have seen daylight since he got married, unless there'd been a funeral in the family."

Before starting on the second beer Vinny scooted his chair over to the computer and checked for emails. There were four, three of which were junk and were immediately deleted, the remaining one was a curt line from Isabelle, telling him she no longer needed his services. No surprise there. Problem was, he still held her coins, one of which was extremely valuable and she still owed him money for the work he had carried out. Today he'd been on a losing streak but tomorrow was another day, another chance to gain the upper hand.

"That magazine I saw you holding as you got out the van, Stefan, the one about coin-collecting and values, do you mind if I look through it? Here's a tenner, nip down to Tesco and get another pack of beers. Then when you get back I'll tell you what we're celebrating."

WELL WELL, THE OLD MAN IN THE APARTMENT HAS SPIRIT. I LIKE THAT. IT'S ALWAYS MORE INTERESTING, MORE SATISFYING, TO REEK HAVOC BEFORE SNUFFING OUT A LIFE THAT DESPERATELY CLINGS TO ITS OWN MORTALITY.

THE TEMPO OF THIS GAME IS RISING. BELLA HAS HAD ENOUGH AND WANTS TO LEAVE. WANTS TO LEAVE ME BEFORE SHE'S EVEN SET SIGHT OF MY FACE, BEFORE SHE'S EVEN FELT THE CHILL OF MY LIPS. POOR BELLA DOESN'T UNDERSTAND THE RULES. DOESN'T UNDERSTAND THAT I AM THE ONE WHO DECIDES. THE ONLY PLAYERS IN MY GAME TO LEAVE, ARE THE ONES WHO DIE.

Exeter

James felt a ripple of fear grip his insides. It was getting on for ten o'clock and there was still no answer from Lyn. He'd tried three times to contact her by phone, each time getting the same response — unable to connect and unable to leave a message. Finally, in desperation he'd phoned the hotel, asking to be put through to the suite, only to be told no one was answering.

Helen saw the concern on her brothers face. "James I'm sure Lyn's probably out enjoying herself. She's on holiday, remember. I know if I were there on my own, I certainly wouldn't be twiddling my thumbs in a hotel room on the off chance that someone might phone.

"I'm hardly just someone, Helen, I told her I'd phone and keep her posted on what was happening at this end."

"Well maybe she's not that interested in what's happening this end and why should she be? You made it pretty obvious you didn't want her here with you. You can't have it both ways, James. Relax, she's probably paying you back for your gross insensitivity."

James wondered if he would ever come to understand the workings of the female mind. He thanked his sister for her offer of staying overnight. Mother didn't appear to be in any immediate danger and he needed his own bed. Helen was probably right, the time for worrying would be if he couldn't connect to Lyn in the morning. "Goodnight," he said planting a brief kiss on the side of her cheek, "I'll drive to the hospital first thing in the morning and spend the whole day with Mother, giving you a chance to catch up on your own things."

Midnight—Lanzarote

All senses were thrown into high alert as Lyn struggled to free her arms from the blanket-cum-straitjacket. A foul stench emanated from the cloth as she twisted in panic. The very touch of it — stickiness that had dried and hardened — bombarded her brain with images of the blanket's history. The rancid taste that permeated every pore in her mouth had her wondering, no, not wondering, had her remembering that the corner of the stinking material had been stuffed in her

221

mouth to stop the escape of a scream. There was light, even with her eyes closed the impression was there, a single bright stripe from the edge of the makeshift door, leaking its illuminating properties around the rest of the shit hole. But most disturbing of all was the noise. The sound of men's voices, loud and incessant, hollering foreign words — Perro Diablo! Perro Diablo! And those repeated words setting off the howling and barking of her number one enemy. This was reality! This was no dream!

She *had* been dreaming. Dreaming she was in James's home searching for a way out to her own place next door but all the familiar routes, doors and windows, had disappeared. No matter how hard she had searched, there was no way out. She could still recollect her emotions, every nuance of how she'd felt. Then dream and reality mingled. Where James's door should have been, the wall shook with the savage clawing of an animal. The barking and howling that followed dragged Lyn into full wakefulness, pumping the adrenalin to make ready for flight. But the sound of a vehicle, it's headlights pointing towards her only means of escape, caused her to use the closest thing to hand to plug her mouth and keep her silent.

Another vehicle and more headlights criss-crossing the first. Lyn had crawled on all fours and was peering through the gap. She saw a well-built man emerge from the second truck to join the others. He was wearing a cap and carrying what looked like a stick. No! Not a stick. A rifle! The howling stopped suddenly and the hound ran towards the newcomer. Lyn watched, wide-eyed, as the rope from the dog's neck was seized, yanking the animal closer to him. Shouting was followed by a dull thud, as the rifle was used to land a blow across the brutes hind quarter. A sickening yelp was heard as the creature was lifted and tossed into the back of the open truck. Both vehicles moved easily away and as Lyn watched the red tail lights gradually disappearing from view, she realised how close she was to a single track road.

Darkness and silence returned. Tears stung her eyes as she crawled back to her corner, misjudging her route in the darkness and grazing her bad foot against a chunk of concrete. Pain flared and expletives fired. No fear of being overheard. She was now completely and utterly alone but, God willing, at first light she'd be able to crawl out of this hell-hole.

Chapter 22

Wednesday Morning—Torquay

The sound of sirens dragged James from a wine-induced sleep. Rubbing eyes that wanted to remain closed he squinted at the bedside clock. Six thirty-five. Far too early, complained his thoughts, for such a racket. The screaming increased to a deafening level before stopping abruptly outside, flashes of blue light bleeding through gaps in the haphazardly pulled curtains. The solicitor leapt from his bed and peered out the window. Two fire-engines were parked askew about fifty yards away to his right, hoses gushing on one of his neighbour's properties. Parked alongside James's car and blocking the road, the latest arrivals, a police car and ambulance.

He pulled on clothes he'd taken off the night before and ran down to the front door. On opening it, the stench of acrid smoke hung in the damp, chilly air, catching at his throat and seeping into the lightweight material of his cotton slacks and polo shirt. He scanned the chaotic scene from his porch, but couldn't see whose property was burning. Vincent, dressed only in dressing gown and trainers, was already on the scene talking to two of the fire officers. He headed towards them and to his horror saw the jets of water aimed into two open windows on the ground floor of Peter Radcliffe's property. He was suddenly reminded of the strange occurrence of the night before.

He'd arrived home from Helen's at around eleven fifteen, physically exhausted but mentally alert — too alert to sleep. After opening up and finding the place cold and uninviting, he'd quickly adjusted the boiler, pulled on a warm overcoat and set off for a stroll around the harbour hoping to quell the mixed bag of concerns and emotions that filled his head.

In spite of the bright lights and the pleasantness of the late evening, very few people were about and after one slow circuit, via the millennium bridge, he was ready for the steep walk back, and a couple of glasses of wine before sleep. As he'd turned to enter his premises he'd caught sight of a figure outside Peter Radcliffe's front door. Old age and illness had forced Peter to keep early hours so James assumed it to be his son-in law. (Peter's daughter and her family had moved back from South Africa almost a year ago and were living at The Terrace until they found a place of their own). Not wanting to snub the man, James had called out a few pleasantries then bid him good night. No pleasantries were returned and on looking again, the figure had gone.

Not wanting to interrupt Vincent's conversation with the fire officers, James wandered down to the only other person he recognised. "What's going on here, Stefan? Is anyone hurt?"

"Good morning, Mr Fairbank. Your mother, is she…?" Stefan struggled to find the right words.

"She's stable at the moment. Thank you for asking." James pointed to the stricken building where flames licked greedily at the wooden frames of the sash-windows on the ground floor. "Have they managed to rescue all the occupants?"

"Firemen talk with man in basement apartment, he tell to them Peter Radcliffe on holidays with family. No one inside. Is good fortune, no?"

"But they have searched the premises haven't they? I saw a man at Peter's front door late last night. And I feel sure he entered. It must be Peter's son-in-law. I'd better have a word…"

Stefan caught hold of James's arm. "Firemen have searched every room. There's no one in there. They say fire was started by vandals. This man you see, What he wearing?" Stefan's hands pointing at his own clothes and head. "Suit, coat and hat?"

Although James hadn't thought about it at the time, a part of his mind couldn't help wondering why Peter's son-in-law, who had reared cattle in South Africa and had found a temporary position as farmhand here, would be dressed in such a formal way. "Yes, he was dressed like a business-man. It was dark, I couldn't see his features, the hat pulled low over his brow. He was tall, and a little bent to one side as though he had back trouble. Yes, come to think of it," said James, almost as though he were thinking aloud, his profile wasn't the slightest bit like the man I thought it was. "Stefan nodded but showed concern. "Who was he, Stefan?"

"One day soon I know, then I tell to you his name."

In the distance a phone was ringing. James recognised the ring. "That's my phone, Stefan, we'll speak later." It was his mobile. He sprinted back to his door, leapt up the stairs following the sound, groaning aloud when it suddenly stopped. "It's got to be Lyn. Where the hell is my phone?" he called out. A moment of calm thinking and he remembered the overcoat, the phone began to ring again, confirming he was right. He saw at once it wasn't Lyn. Helen was the caller, and at this early hour he braced himself for bad news.

"Sorry I didn't pick up when you first rang, Helen, I was outside. Peter Radcliffe's property is going up in flames."

"Bad start to the day for both of us, then. Mother had another stroke half an hour ago. Too big for her body to cope with. She died ten minutes later! The hospital have only just let me know. I'm on my way there now, will you meet me there? Please!"

"I'll leave right away."

The fire had been brought under control quickly but hoses still played on the smoke-filled, ground floor sitting room to safeguard against any further ignition. Vinny had learned that the fire had started in Radcliffe's inner-porch and had rapidly spread to his sitting room — probably a petrol-soaked rag pushed through the letterbox — and more than probably carried out by vandals. Fortunately, due to doors off the sitting room being closed, a blaring smoke alarm attracting the attention of Radcliffe's basement tenant and the rapid response to the tenant's 999 call, damage to the property was minimal.

Rubbing his arms to bring back circulation, Vinny walked quickly back to where Stefan waited, standing aside briefly as the ambulance and police car left the scene. "Excitement's over. Get the coffee and bacon sarnies on the go while I thaw out under a hot shower. There are several things I want sorted today, Stefan, and this early morning wake-up call," Vinny flicked his thumb in the direction of the fire engines, "has given us the opportunity to crack on sooner than we'd thought."

Stefan, caught up. "Vincent, did tenant who ring 999 see man in suit watching what happens?"

"No! What is it with you, Stefan? You keep on about this

bloke in a fucking suit. I'm beginning to think you and Isabelle are going the same way." Vinny tapped the side of his head then disappeared into his shower-room.

INTERESTING LITTLE EXPERIMENT. THESE BUILDINGS DON'T BURN AS EASILY AND AS RAPIDLY AS THE LAST TIME I PLAYED WITH FIRE. EASY TO UNDERSTAND WHY. THOSE WERE MAINLY CONSTRUCTED OF WOOD. AND BURNING WOOD GIVES A HELL OF A SHOW. AND ALL OCCUPANTS ARE CONSUMED IN NO TIME.

Bovey Tracey

Isabelle stepped out of the shower, pink and glowing from the scrubbing she'd given every inch of her body. She'd only had about four hours sleep but it was quality sleep — no bad dreams and no waking up with butterflies gnawing away at her insides.

Her and Shaun had talked well into the night. She'd confessed everything… Well, everything that had made sense. Telling him about her suspicions of him having an affair with some woman who worked in The Carpenter's, her anger at money spent on drink when it was needed at home, and how finding an ancient purse in the ploughed field had given her a way out. A way out of a situation that was worsening by the day. At the time, finding the treasure and then meeting Mr Conway had convinced her she was on the right track to solving everything. It was the lying, especially the lying about her health, that had been the hardest thing to admit and deep down even though she'd confessed to it, the shame still lingered.

At one point, Shaun had asked her if she fancied this Mr Conway. He'd admitted he'd followed her one evening and seen a bloke handing her something. Since then, she'd taken to wearing a man-sized ring on her thumb. Had Conway given her the ring? Without thinking, Isabelle had reached into her underwear drawer where the ring had been concealed, felt the bulk of it wrapped in white-cotton and without touching the metal, opened the cloth, explaining that it was found with the coins and her intention was to cast it back into the soil because it was cursed. She'd said too much. Immediately, she regretted showing him the ring. He'd taken it from her, read what it said inside and slipped it on his own middle finger — fitting it perfectly. She saw at a glance, he too had been caught in its spell. His eyes had lit up, his lips had smiled and his words had been so convincing. "Don't be daft, Bella, it's a beautiful old ring, and with the price of gold these days it must be worth a good few bob."

Lanzarote

Lyn lay absolutely still, focusing on the open strip by the make-shift door. Yes, she decided, it was a little lighter, daybreak had finally arrived. But it was still deathly quiet. No hum of faraway traffic, no tweeting of birds or rustlings of creatures on the ground, and definitely no sniffing or growling. She felt relaxed, completely dispassionate, lying on the mound of bedding, she and it moulded together in one smelly, comfortable heap. This state she was in, this state of absolute awareness without the uptightness of fear and jangling nerves, was due to the downing of the four remaining tablets.

After the departure of the trucks and the capture of the hound, she'd expected to fall into an exhausted, relieved sleep.

But after lying there, for what seemed like an eternity, realised she was too much on edge and in too much pain to allow relaxation to do its part. After checking her watch, she could see there were nearly two hours to go before the next planned dose of tablets but something had suddenly snapped in her head. "To hell with it!" she'd shouted into the blackness as the next flare of pain shot up her leg. "My whole life has been consumed with fear of what would happen if I didn't do what was expected of me, if I didn't do the *right* thing. Well I don't give a shit about doing the right thing any more!" She'd swallowed all four tablets with the remainder of the water Then lay back on the pillow and waited for them to take effect.

The effect was still with her. Yes, she'd slept. A deep, drugged sleep without dreams or movement — her position imprinted in the pillow as well as her memory — but payback time had arrived. She held her breath and gingerly moved the injured ankle. A definite soreness but no flaring pain, in fact no pain at all. High on relief, she goaded her dulled mind to make best use of this pain-free window of opportunity and start moving. To get out onto the single track road, where she could see and be seen. Her body however, refused to budge, preferring instead to wallow in the thick soup of relaxation, just for a little while longer.

Bovey Tracey

Shaun Thatcher waited until his wife was fully occupied in the kitchen. She'd promised a full English breakfast before *he* set out job-hunting and Robert set out for school. Slipping the phone into his pocket he mounted the stairs, carefully avoiding the ones that creaked, tip-toed into the bedroom and quietly closed the door. With fingers crossed, he punched in Vincent Conway's number.

It was answered on the fourth ring. "Conway, here. How can I help?"

Shaun wasn't expecting this brusk response from the man himself. He'd expected having to maneuver his way past a protective secretary. He cleared his throat. "Good morning, Mr Conway, Shaun Thatcher here. I'll come straight to the point. I believe you're holding property, in the form of gold and silver coins belonging to my wife, Isabelle Thatcher. As she's not well enough to collect the coins herself, and, she no longer requires your services, I'm phoning to arrange collection of them."

After a few seconds of silence, Vinny's response, "You think I'm stupid Pal? Isabelle is my client, not you, and as such, Isabelle will remain my client until the contract is terminated in the proper manner, and fees are settled by mutual consent. I'll speak to her myself, and we'll arrange a meeting."

"Like I said, Mr Conway, she's not well but I'll get her to contact you as soon as possible. Thank you, it's heartening to know that you're a man who can be trusted."

Chapter 23

Mid-morning—Lanzarote

Lyn opened her eyes. The gap by the door was ablaze with light casting a slash of heat across her lower legs. She pulled the injured foot towards her and was rewarded with agonising pain. The pain was ignored. She'd heard something. Something, she felt sure, which had brought her from the drugged sleep. Holding her breath, listening, she heard it again. Voices. Several voices, carried like falling leaves on the morning breeze.

Galvanized by panic she claws at the rough surfaces around her, desperate to gain purchase, to drag her unyielding body into a standing position. Precious moments slip by, allowing her swimming head to stabilise before she hobbles to the door. Blinding sunlight sends her retreating back, as she searches the rucksack for her sunglasses. Returning back to the gap she can see a cluster of walkers, plus two others walking ahead of the rest. They were some way off, but, "Oh thank you, Jesus! Thank you so much!" They were heading in her direction, chatting merrily as they made their way along the same road the trucks had used.

Shaking from a mixture of relief, pain and probably dehydration, Lyn rested her head against the wall and forced her mind to calm. Waiting, expecting Gran's voice rising to the challenge, guiding and reassuring, but there was nothing but the sound of her own breathing. All actions and decisions were down to her. Common sense told her she needed to be patient. Needed to wait until the forward pair were much closer. Her body was too buggered for walking and she doubted she'd have the strength for shouting.

She watched impatiently for what seemed like an age. Miniature, ant-like creatures growing larger as they inched their way closer. Then, in disbelief she saw the two leaders suddenly begin to veer in a northerly direction, heading away along a scar between two rugged valleys. "No! No! Please God, no!" she cried, grabbing at the two supporting planks that held the crude door in place, not caring that carefully applied sticking plasters were torn off, opening old cuts and creating new ones. Two weak arms were now the doors only support. She took a deep breath and pitched her body to one side. The heavy panel remained upright for a split second before falling inwards with an almighty crash. Dust clouded her view for a while. Then she saw the two leaders had stopped, turning at the sudden noise. Lyn staggered out into bright light and heat, waving and screaming for help before collapsing in a heap, tears that she couldn't afford to lose spilling down her cheeks. She began a silent prayer before raising her head. Was it just a mirage? She saw the ant-like creatures now magnified into human form. Men and women rushing towards her over the black, jagged terrain.

Bovey Tracey

Isabelle was in a quandary, as the lies she had started had now become a seemingly unsolvable problem. She was sitting at the kitchen table, had been for over half an hour, racking her brain for a solution to the predicament she'd got herself into. And she was coming to the conclusion that it was impossible.

Shaun and Robert had left together. Father dropping his son off at school before meeting up with a man regarding the possibility of temporary work. Isabelle had been content, happy to have the opportunity to clean throughout the cottage — a task which was long overdue. She'd just finished mopping the kitchen floor when the phone rang.

The call was from Mr Conway asking how she was. She was feeling good, and told him so. He'd then asked about the email. The email which said his services were no longer required, and that they'd need to meet in order to settle his account and return her property to her. To be honest, she'd forgotten all about the coins left behind at his office and suddenly found herself asking how much the coins were worth? And would it be enough to cover his fees. At this point Mr Conway had coughed a little, in fact he coughed a lot, apologising after a few seconds for the tickling in his throat and said he'd call back later after he'd made enquiries about the value of the coins. But before ending the call, in a voice still rasping from the tickle, he'd asked about the ring. Said he'd like to look at it again, if that was alright with her.

The lie had rolled off her tongue like warmed honey from a spoon. "I've thrown it back in the field, Mr Conway. It's cursed, and I'm glad to see the back of it."

Torquay

Vinny replaced the receiver and looked across the desk to Stefan, a broad grin and cheeky wink, transforming the serious look he had before making the call. "It's your lucky day, Stefan, I'm giving you one last chance with the metal detector."

"You say machine has to go back today."

"That's right, we will return it today, after we recover a certain item from the soil." Vinny explained the gist of the conversation he'd just had with Isabelle, emphasising the importance of getting his hands on that ring. Stefan listened carefully before asking why Isabelle would throw away such a valuable ring? "Because she's mad! Thinks it's cursed and doesn't want it anywhere near her. Bit like you, Stefan, sees things that aren't actually there. And as to her coins, no dealer is going to give their full worth, especially without a provenance — if you know what that word means, Stefan — so I'm going to offer her a price based on the scrap value of the gold coin and return the silver ones to her. I've done a quick calculation. My fees should just about be covered."

"And what you say to husband of Isabelle? Or maybe he mad too."

"Isabelle's the client, whatever she agrees to is fine by me. That's why I want to get over there while he's out of the way. So let's get moving. After today, I want this case wrapped up and I don't want to see that ploughed field or that metal detector again."

"I have big favour for ask, Vincent."

Vinny looked at his friend, trying to read what was behind the plea, but as usual, Stefan's face gave nothing away. "Tell me, then I'll say yes or no."

"I make promise to return this to Joe." Stefan pointed to the coin magazine, the only excuse he could think of for checking on his friend. "We drive near his home on way to field. I like to give it back today."

Reaching for the magazine that had been browsed through — phoning two dealers and promptly deciding they were rip-off artists — Vinny wondered why anyone would want it back. It was years out of date. "I'll stop and you can shove it through his letterbox, OK?"

"No, is not OK. I want to see him, to thank him and make sure he… make sure he is well. He is old man."

Vinny could see the determination on the lads face. But there was the matter of respect, and, a pecking order to be maintained. "And if I say no to this big fucking favour of yours?"

"I go anyway. Take bus to Newton Abbott. *You* search field for gold ring."

Taken aback, Vinny was at a loss for words. Stefan's face remained unemotional but determination was fixed in the eyes. Eyes that didn't waver from his own. "OK here's the deal, I give you ten minutes chatting time with your new pal. Longer than that and I'm gone and it'll be the last time you ever work for me." He threw the magazine on the desk, the force behind it sending it careering into the air-purifier. Both landing with a smack and clatter on the laminated floor. The magazine was unharmed. The air-purifier lay in bits, having just breathed its last fragrant breath. Stefan stooped to examine the breakage but was stopped by an outburst of anger and foul language. He picked up the magazine and both men silently headed out to the van.

A cold damp mist had settled over Torquay. A mist which seemed to thicken as they drove along the congested road towards Newton Abbot. Both men were silent, lost in their own thoughts. Stefan's thoughts were locked in concern for Joe. The night before while walking down to Tesco for beer, he'd phoned Joe, mainly to give, as promised, his telephone number. Joe had sounded nervous, fearful about something concerning his grandson but he wouldn't say more. Stefan had told Joe he could phone him at any time if he needed help.

On returning with the beer, he was shocked to see the same suited man he'd seen on the field. He was standing in front of a dark-coloured car, headlights full on, watching as Stefan walked slowly up the hill.

At the time, Stefan felt relief. Relief that the stalker was here. Relief that Joe had his mobile number. Stefan was young and strong. Joe was old and disabled and couldn't run far with only one leg.

Lanzarote

Suspended in a surreal state of light-headedness, Lyn was aware of strong hands lifting her body and lowering it carefully into the shade of the building she'd escaped from. Gentle words in a language she didn't understand, pleas for information she couldn't respond to. Then a bottle of water was pressed to her lips, the coolness and flavour of it better than any Champagne she'd tasted. She grabbed hold of the bottle, tilting back her head to allow free flow, but the strong hands restrained her, allowing only a few miserly sips.

More voices. Lots more, descending like a throng from heaven — angels from a foreign land where language sounded severe and guttural — all wanting their questions answered.

Suddenly one of them turning, calling out a name, "Annelie? Annelie?" Within seconds, Annelie, the queen of angels, was crouching beside her, testing a response to several words. "Are you English?" was asked after two blank responses. "Yes. Yes I'm English. Thank you, thank you…I" Lyn couldn't say more, pent up emotions flooded out as her body convulsed with sobbing.

Gradually, after more water, Lyn told how she'd been forced to spend the night, sticking only to the salient points. Annelie, a teacher married to an Englishman, translated this to her fellow German nationals, relaying *their* curiosities and questions in the same way. The first questions asked were based on why she was alone? Why didn't she phone for help? Did the wild dog bite or cause any of the bleeding that was visible on her body? She'd ignored the first question, reassured them on the question of Rabies, and explained what had happened to her phone.

Working as a team — with no apparent leader — all fourteen walkers then became active, except for Annelie who remained at her side, stroking her back, gradually allowing more liquids and translating all that was being done to help. A vehicle was on it's way which would take her directly to a clinic to treat her injured ankle, but, it's arrival could take as long as forty minutes. In the meantime two men were making a makeshift seat from the wooden planks so that she could be carried over rough ground to the road. Two women were using moist, scented wet-wipes, cleaning and dressing the wounds on hands and legs while the rest of the team set about hunting for the missing phone. Annelie had offered her phone straight away so minds could be reassured that she was safe, but Lyn had insisted it wasn't necessary, any phoning could be done when she returned to her hotel. Besides, there wasn't a good enough signal here to make a call. Annelie assured her that two of their group had satellite phones, in case she changed her mind.

The sudden shout in German was unmistakable. Someone was delighted to be the finder of the phone. Lyn knew it was bound to be smashed up, but relief that the individual parts, especially the sim card, wouldn't now be falling into the wrong hands, put a smile on her face. And before too long a tall, blonde-haired young man was kneeling beside her explaining, via Annelie, how all pieces were found and put back together. Held together in the main by clear sticky tape, but he felt sure that once she was in a good reception area she would manage with it for a while.

After the vehicle arrived, Lyn was ceremoniously carried to it, with the help of two planks and a folded towel. Her arms around the shoulders of the two men carrying her. Annelie was adamant about accompanying her, but Lyn wouldn't hear of it, she'd done enough. They'd all done enough and for as long as she lived she would never forget their kindness and their help. The driver, who spoke English, said that he would take her to the clinic, wait, and then drive her to her hotel. Only right that Annelie should continue the walk with her friends. Only right that Lyn should agree to see her that evening at the hotel where, after showering and resting, she could thank her properly in a more civilised setting.

Newton Abbot

Sitting just outside the community's closed gates, Vinny strummed impatiently on the van's steering wheel, strongly resisting the urge to bear down on the horn. He'd sat here, like some spare part, for over fifteen minutes, anger and frustration growing as each minute passed. The threat he'd given Stefan had obviously counted for nothing. Problem was, if he hooted, he knew for sure it would bring more than Stefan to the gate and he was in no mood for another confrontation with Brett Robson. What was it about this old geezer that had got to Stefan? Something had happened between them during the previous afternoon but these days, trying to get information out of Stefan was almost impossible. Well, he'd had his warning and after today, he can fuck off back to London and find some other mug to work for.

The old lady gave a heavy sigh, apologising again for having to be the bearer of bad news. She closed the door to her ground floor flat leaving Stefan alone in the shadows of the windowless corridor. He mounted the first run of stairs, eyes scanning the walls on either side. He turned on the short landing, finding the second run of stairs to be longer, higher. He stood motionless, again sweeping his eyes from side to side as they mounted each step in turn. They lingered at the third step from the top. Yes, he'd found what needed to be found.

He returned to the ground floor and pressed the large orange button on the side of the lift, watching as the door glided smoothly and silently to the open position. His attention fell on the cluster of scratches and particles of red dirt trapped in the runner of the lift's door. Emotions reared and massed forming a heavy burden in his chest. Shame, regret and especially anger, all kept in check for years, suddenly exploded within, snapping chains and opening doors that had been held fast by promises. Promises made to a father who was then murdered trying to protect his only daughter. Promises made to a mother, forced to exist in poverty while trapped in a wheelchair. Promises to a sister who should have been protected from men using her body in such a vile way. All these bad things happened because of him, because of his vanity. All the promises in the world could never change that.

Wiping his eyes on his sleeve he caught sight of the time. He cleared his throat, spitting a gob of phlegm on the gravel as he marched quickly towards the waiting van.

Vinny slammed the van door shut, barely allowing his passenger time to settle on the seat before gunning the engine and pulling away. He was determined to hold his tongue and give Stefan a chance to redeem himself. After driving at full pelt around a series of roundabouts, shooting across lights that had just turned red and brought to a sudden halt by a maneuvering articulated lorry, the determination was beginning to wither. No apologies, no explanations, absolutely nothing was forthcoming from a bloke who must surely know he was in the last-chance-saloon. He pulled over to the side of the road, killed the engine and turned to the Bulgarian. "Ten fucking minutes I said. Are you taking the piss or what?"

Silence

"What the fuck has got into you, Stefan? "Has this bloke, this Joe, got some kind of hold on you, or what?"

Stefan was sitting bolt-upright, both hands clenched into tight fists, eyes, now dry but pink and swollen, looking directly ahead at nothing in particular. Without changing his forward position he said, in a cold, clear voice. "Joe has hold on no one. Lift not working and he trip and fall down steps. Ambulance come but he already dead from fractured skull."

Vinny took a few seconds to make sense of what had just been revealed. He placed his hand on Stefan's shoulder, saying, "Sorry to hear that, mate, shall we turn back, do this another…"

"No," Stefan interrupted. "We have unfinished business. We do it today."

Vinny nodded, his attention caught by the twitching muscle on the left side of Stefan's jaw. He'd never noticed it before. But come to think of it, he'd never seen Stefan this uptight before.

Bovey Tracey

A SLIGHT SETBACK. NO MATTER, THE PROGRESSION TO MY GRAND FINALE IS STILL ON TRACK. THE DIVERSION WITH THE OLD MAN WAS FUN. NOT DRAMATIC—IT WAS TOO EASY, TOO PREDICTABLE TO BE DRAMATIC—BUT YES, IT WAS FUN. A LITTLE LIGHT-HEARTED ENTERTAINMENT TO EASE THE BOREDOM WHILST WAITING FOR THE MAIN EVENT.

Chapter 24

Wednesday Lunchtime—Lanzarote

Along with the very best care and attention, Lyn had gratefully accepted the offer of coffee and biscuits. Her stomach now however was growling for sustenance of a different calibre. The German clinic she'd been taken to by Leon, the driver, was deserted except for a doctor and his nurse, who gave her immediate attention. Tablets for the pain, X-rays to determine damage, ointments and bandages had been gently applied and all carried out in the spotlessly-clean, air-conditioned, mini-sized hospital. But outside, cheek-by-jowl to this haven of tranquility, the holiday Island of Lanzarote was functioning as normal. Aromas, wafting on the air from several nearby restaurants, were soon picked up by Lyn, as she was now starving!

Leon stopped in front of the hotel. Lyn felt she ought to offer him something — his time, his effort, his petrol, all given freely — but she thought to offer money would belittle his genuine desire to help someone in trouble. She did consider inviting him for a meal but then thought better of it. No, she would shower and eat in her room, in her present state, she couldn't guarantee her table-manners would be any better than those of a starving dog.

She was helped from the car and stood leaning on the pair of walking sticks —sticks which she'd been told would only be needed for a couple of days, provided she rested the badly sprained-ankle. Whilst holding out her hand to thank her driver, Lyn said, "I am so grateful to you Leon, and the rest of you. How can I ever repay your kindness and how can I show my gratitude?"

Taking her hand in his, he squeezed it then gave her a peck on each cheek. "You can repay us by not allowing your bad experience to cloud your judgment of this beautiful island. Do not let the fear of what happened prevent you from being spontaneous. You are a very brave woman. I hope you remain so."

For ten minutes Lyn luxuriated in the warm shower, scrubbing every inch of her body except for the bandaged foot which was encased in two waterproof bags.

The bedside phone began ringing, a forewarning of three rings had been organised by the kitchen to tell her that ordered food was on it's way, forcing her to turn off the tap. But the phone continued to ring, and ring. Grabbing a towel and wrapping it around her wet body she hopped to the bed. Snatching the phone she answered in a voice ragged from exertion. "Yes, what is it? I thought the signal was for three rings only." No response. Someone was there, she could hear breathing. It suddenly dawned on her, not everyone spoke English. The hours spent reading the Spanish phrasebook immediately paid off. "Lo siento, mi no hablar Español." (*I'm sorry, I don't speak Spanish.)*

"Seems you're able to speak the language remarkably well, considering the time you've been there."

James's voice, sounding cold and unemotional, flummoxed her thoughts. "Hello darling, how are you?"

"Well, considering I've been out of my mind with concern at not being able to reach you either by phone *or* via the hotel, I'm holding up pretty well. Perhaps you'd like to explain where you have been?"

"Lyn felt the burden of guilt bearing down. From the moment her rescuers appeared, the only thought she'd given James, was a mental note to phone him once she was back in the privacy of the hotel room. Then the need for food took precedence over everything, except ridding her hair and body of the foul-smelling hell-hole. "It's a long story, James, and I…"

A knocking on the door and a call in broken English that the ordered meal was ready, interrupted Lyn's response. "Sorry, darling, I have to go but I'll call you back as soon as I've eaten. Incidentally, how is your mother?"

"Mother died early this morning."

"Oh, James, I'm so sorry…" But Lyn soon realized she was speaking to a dialing tone.

Exeter

James threw the phone onto the sofa just as his sister arrived with a tray of coffee and biscuits. They'd spent the whole morning at the hospital, carrying out the unpleasant necessities that follows the death of a loved-one. There was still more to be done, but both felt that a break from the claustrophobic atmosphere and the antiseptic smells was needed. They'd gone back to Helen's for a spot of lunch, which neither had the appetite for. She'd served up a respectable brand of fresh chicken broth with crusty bread which had been mainly eaten in silence and without relish.

Helen lay down the tray and nodded towards his abandoned phone. "Still no joy?"

"Yes. Lyn is back at the hotel but she's just about to eat lunch and she'll call me back later."

Helen knew her brother well enough to know that now wasn't the time to delve further. Besides she had enough on her plate with losing Mother and organising a funeral. For now, she intended to steer clear of her brother's love-life. "Milk with your coffee, James?"

"No, thank you. I'll take it strong and black."

Chapter 25

Wednesday Afternoon—Bovey Tracey

The damp fog hung in the still air, deadening everything. The screeching hinges on the rotting gate, Vinny's footsteps up the path, even the three raps on the sturdy front door, all were muffled in the thick blanket of mist. Impatient, Vinny rapped again, this time louder, pressing his ear to wood in dire need of a coat of varnish. He was rewarded by two things. Pulling back from the door, head still forward from the listening stance, a large measure of condensed vapour fell from the above thatch and landed on the back of his neck, making him curse, but the listening had been worth it. He distinctly heard noises deep in the bowels of the thick-walled dwelling. Realizing suddenly that front doors in this neck of the woods were probably seldom used, he wandered around the perimeter of the cottage until he came upon another door. This door was modern, half-glazed and a hint of light showing from an inner room. His chubby hand was now hastily rubbing the glass but the thick film of condensation was not on the outside. He tried the door and was surprised to find it unlocked as he stepped into the old fashioned scullery leading to the kitchen — the room with light, the room with activity.

Vinny had parked the van, along with Stefan, at the entrance to the field — the field he was hoping never to clap eyes on again after today. His passenger had been subdued, lost in his own world, barely acknowledging anything he was told. Making allowances for the sudden death of his new friend, Vinny had repeated himself several times. Stefan was to sit tight until he returned to the van. If he returned alone, all well and good. If he returned in the company of his client or, worse-case-scenario, in the company of his client with her husband, Stefan was to make himself scarce. The last thing he wanted was Isabelle being freaked out by the guy she'd seen at the field the day before.

There was the rattle of a latch, followed by the kitchen door opening. "Hey, what's your game?" The figure of Shaun Thatcher loomed large within its frame, a poker gripped in his right hand, and for a split second Vinny wished he'd brought Stefan along.

"Come on, Shaun, put the poker down. I'm Vincent Conway, here to talk to my client about returning her coins, that's all."

"A bit cheeky, just waltzing in through the back door, why not ring first and make an appointment, that's what she'd have to do with the likes of you."

Vinny then heard a familiar voice saying, "Shaun, who are you talking to?"

Isabelle then appeared, ducking under the arm of her husband and looking a lot healthier than the last time he'd seen her. "Hello Mr Conway, please come in, "she continued as she turned to Shaun saying, "Fancy leaving Mr Conway outside in this awful fog."

Vinny apologised for his sudden appearance at the back of their home, explaining how he'd knocked several times at the front door without success.

Isabelle flicked her hand in a dismissive manner. "None of us use the front door, Mr Conway, haven't done since we moved in here. And if we're in the kitchen, well it's hard to hear anyone knocking. Shaun promised to install a bell years ago, but, you know how it is?"

Shaun tutted and lowered the poker. "We won't be needing to waste any more money on this place, Izzy, we've agreed to put it on the market straight away."

"Bella, my name's Bella, that's what we agreed Shaun. Let me take your damp coat, Mr Conway. Go on in, the kitchen's nice and warm, Shaun was just stoking up the Rayburn. I'll make us a fresh pot of tea while we're chatting."

The freshly made tea and small plate of custard creams were consumed mainly in silence. Bits of chit-chat about the weather, the rising cost of food and fuel, and the clever slipping in, by Isabelle, that Shaun had been made redundant. All mentally noted by Vinny as a ploy to get his fees down. But, if he played his cards right, he could turn *their* worsening situation to *his* advantage.

Whilst clearing his throat as politely as possible, Vinny spoke directly to his client. "Isabelle, you mentioned that you'd returned the gold ring to the place where it was found?"

Isabelle turned to Shaun, saw his look of incomprehension and promptly changed the subject by asking, "Who would like more tea?"

Undeterred, Vinny persisted "I know you're a bit, how can I say, spooked by the ring." Silence and frowning faces from the other two. Vinny hurried on, "I read somewhere that women are more sensitive to vibrations left from previous wearers of things like jewellery and clothes. Maybe the previous owner suffered in some way."

A sound erupted from Shaun that couldn't be described in

words, but words followed. "'Course they bloody suffered. Hadn't they lost a purse that probably held all the wealth they owned; wouldn't you be pissed off?"

"Shaun, please, mind your language and let Mr Conway finish!"

Wishing for the umpteenth time that he could speak to his client alone but knowing that it wasn't going to happen, Vinny got straight to the point. "Just show me the place where you threw it, I'll do the searching and if and when I find it, I'll be happy to take the ring in part exchange for my fees."

"Oh I bet you will!" Shaun blurted out. Turning to his wife he continued, "Izzy...I mean Bella, tell me you haven't done such a daft thing as throwing the ring away?"

Isabelle slumped in her chair, head down. The men looked at each other, both preparing for an outpouring of tears but she was dry-eyed when her face lifted to answer. "Sorry I lied to you, Mr Conway, It's true, I was obsessed with the ring at first but now I can't bear to touch it. My intention *was* to fling it back into the dark earth were it belonged. But Shaun's taken a fancy to it, says he'll sell it to help our situation, but," she looked at her husband, "I feel strongly that nothing good will come of it. Anyway, I've got a pile of ironing upstairs to get through, so I'll leave the two of you to sort it out. I've got no money and I don't even know how much you're owed. It can't be much but I do understand you need to get paid before handing back my coins." Isabelle held out her hand, smiling as chubby fingers closed around her own and squeezed gently. Then she turned to leave.

Feeling that the opportunity was slipping away, Vinny called after her, "May I see the ring again, Just one more time? Isabelle left the room without answering and closed the door behind her.

Shaun jumped up, rummaged on a shelf under the kitchen sink where a blue curtain was doing it's best to hide an assortment of paraphernalia, found what he was looking for and tossed it on the table. "I take it this belongs to you?"

Vinny scrutinized the square of plastic, measuring approximately 40mm by 35mm. It was a very sophisticated and expensive listening device. He'd seen them in his Spy Store Magazine but had never actually handled one. "What makes you think it belongs to me?"

Shaun Thatcher leaned in close, talking through gritted teeth. "You're the private detective, you're the one who's been following my every move, you're the one who thinks he can just waltz in here at any time and set up this, this whatever it is, to eavesdrop on what's being said. Izzy may think the sun shines out of your backside, but you don't fool me. You're a nasty piece of shit and I'm sure this kind of thing is illegal." Shaun tapped a finger aggressively on the device, so aggressively that Vinny was afraid it might break and he didn't want that. The bit of plastic with its enclosed sim card was worth over five hundred quid. How the hell did it get here and who was responsible for hiding it?

The kitchen door opened and Isabelle sauntered in placing a small, tissue-wrapped bundle in front of Vinny, her eye's falling on the square of plastic. "Is Shaun accusing you of hiding that in the kitchen's plug extension bar?"

Vinny looked at Shaun before answering. "He didn't actually accuse, no, but naturally he is concerned, but I swear to God, I've never been in here before today. Let me ask, did you buy the plug extension from new? Maybe if it had been bought second hand…"

Shaun opened his mouth to speak but Isabelle beat him to it. "Robert uses it when he's on his laptop. He bought it new from Tesco. With the kitchen being the warmest room in cold weather, it's been plugged in down here for a while."

"Could it be your son, having a joke maybe?"

"No! Fired Shaun. Robert wouldn't dream of doing such a thing, besides he hasn't got money to waste on such things."

Isabelle began to reprimand her husband for not taking her suspicions seriously and then mentioned the foul smells, the man in a cloak and the footprints she had seen in front of the Rayburn. Vinny wasn't really listening, his mind was on more important things. He'd unwrapped the bundle in front of him, surreptitiously slipping the ring onto his finger before dramatically coughing. he continued with the coughing charade, whilst closing his hand and shoving it in his jacket pocket to pull out a fresh white hanky — the hanky holding the replica ring he'd received from Taffy.

Isabelle jumps up and rushes over to the sink, returning with a glass of water, which Vinny accepts with a smile of satisfaction. The rings had been successfully switched!

Isabelle pushed the glass of water to one side and nodded to the ring which Mr Conway had rewrapped in the tissue. "So how much do you think it's worth?"

Vincent, dreading that the switch might be discovered, picked up the wrapped bundle and bounced it on his palm. "Well, even as scrap you'll get several hundred pounds, but if you could find a collector of this kind of ring, obviously you'll get more."

All she wanted was to get back to normality. Cooking, housework, washing and ironing. Just the thought of it filled her with joy. But she needed to pay his fees. She'd hired him and it was her responsibility to pay him and so she asked, "Can I see the invoice for your fees, Mr Conway?"

Temporarily lost for words, Vinny wondered how to overcome the fact that there was no invoice. He'd fully intended to scribble one out that morning but after being woken early by the fire brigade, and everything else that followed, it had gone straight out of his head. "Look, Isabelle, I know all this business has taken its toll on you. Forget the invoice and forget the fees, Shaun and me will work something out between us. You carry on with your chores upstairs, I'll say cheerio now because I have to leave soon for another appointment."

A flood of relief helped propel her up the stairs to the overflowing basket of ironing.

Shaun leaned back in his chair, arms crossed and a smile on his face. "That's very generous of you, *Mr Conway*, writing off your fees like that."

"That's not what I said, Shaun, and you know it. Isabelle's health has improved no end and neither of us want to see that reversed. As she's got no money of her own, we have to do a trade with something she has got."

"Right, cards on the table time." Shaun leaned forward, resting his folded arms on the table and his face turning serious. He didn't trust this guy at all. "I want to see the coins Izzy found," winking and following with, "And she has described them in detail, just in case you've been tempted to swop them."

Vinny reached into the inside pocket of his jacket, lifting out the coins which were all individually placed in sealable, plastic bags. Without removing them from the bags, he lay down the two silver coins and shoved them under Thatcher's nose, keeping back the gold coin.

"I reckon this little gold coin will just about cover my fees," said Vinny, placing his index finger on one corner of the coin's plastic bag.

"And *I* reckon you must think I'm stupid. I've done my homework. Old coins, especially gold ones in good condition, are reckoned to be quite valuable." Shaun placed two fingers on the opposite corner of the bag in question and dragged it towards the others.

"Shaun, without a written provenance, you'll get scrap value only. There's a minefield of rules and regulations out there."

Shaun had his provenance. They'd been living in it for years. His grandfather told him many a tale of coins and valuable spoons hidden in the thatch of old cottages. 'Bout bloody time the place offered up something other than crippling energy bills. As quick as a flash, he opened a drawer in the side of the table they were sitting at, scooped all the coins and the ring into it then dragged his chair forward, using the weight of his body to prevent it being opened by anyone.

"Here's the deal, Conway." Shaun reached across to the listening device which sat half-forgotten at the other end of the table and flicked it toward his flabbergasted opponent. "This looks like a pricey bit of kit but you say it doesn't belong to you. In your line of work, I'm sure it would come in very handy and I suggest you take that in leu of your fees. Now fuck-off and if I see you around here again I'll be reporting you for breaking and entering."

There was a time when Vinny would have floored the bastard but he was a business man now and thinking about it, he was still up on the deal. He couldn't help having a final dig, however with, "And what do you intend doing with the proceeds of Isabelle's good fortune? Piss it up the wall? Spend it on the tart behind the bar?"

"You've got me completely wrong, Conway. Now take your listening device and be on your way."

Shaun followed the private investigator to the scullery door, locking it behind him. On returning to the kitchen, he opened the table drawer smiling. Things were starting to look up for him and his family. Thanks to these few bits of metal, he felt sure he could make a fresh start and picking up the phone, he tapped in Benny's number.

"Hi Benny, it's Shaun. I might well be interested in your brother's steam-cleaning business, provided of course we can cut a realistic deal. Can you arrange a meet?"

Lanzarote

Feeling groggy and disoriented, Lyn rolled off the bed and groaned out loud looking at her watch. The promise of a return call to James within half an hour had been broken ages ago.

After the tray of food had arrived, she'd resisted touching it long enough to swallow two of the prescribed tablets from the clinic. That done, she'd eaten her way through everything on the tray, shamelessly licking the plates of the main course and dessert and downing the large glass of chilled orange juice. All that she remembered, after eating the best meal ever, was a deep sense of satisfaction and relief.

Now, what to use as an excuse for breaking her promise to James? Telling him the truth meant telling him everything and she had no intention of doing that. She'd already unburdened the whole sorry tale to Annelie, and that had been fine as she was emotionally detached. Annelie wasn't sitting in judgment.

Picking up her phone she half-expected guilt to descend, chasing away the carefree mood. It didn't. His phone rang seven times before James' voice cut in with a recorded message stating the obvious — he was unavailable at the moment but a message could be left. Lyn declined the offer, hobbling over to the mini bar area of her suite to make use of the coffee-making facilities.

Taking the mug of strong coffee out onto the terrace and congratulating herself that no spills were made, she adjusted the footrest of the lounger to accommodate the bandaged foot before carefully lowering her body with a sigh of satisfaction. Beside her on the terrace table, were her mobile, notepad, pen and a fully-charged laptop computer — a loan from reception which was brought up with the meal, and necessary for her plan.

After taking a few tentative sips of the hot brew, she decided to try ringing James again. After three rings she heard his voice; a very strident voice.

"That was an extremely long lunch."

Determined not to apologise — she was always apologising even when things weren't really her fault — she arrested the 'sorry' that was about to begin her response. "It was strange", she began in a casual, lighthearted way, "I just fell into a deep sleep after finishing the meal. Mind you, I hadn't slept or eaten properly for nearly twenty-four hours." Silence followed, soon to be swallowed up by squeals of delight from the pool area as an unsuspecting father was pushed into the water by his two young sons.

"Lyn, where are you? What's happening? What do you mean, you've hardly slept or eaten in twenty-four hours?"

I'm right here where you suggested I stay. I'm at the hotel, sipping coffee on the terrace. All that jollity you can hear are couples and families enjoying themselves by the pool. Unfortunately, I've had an accident. I was on the rocks by the beach late yesterday afternoon, just about to make a phone call to you actually, when I slipped. My phone got smashed and my ankle got badly sprained. I finished up spending hours at the hospital and after X-rays, bandaging and dosing up with pain-killers, arrived back at the hotel this morning."

"But I phoned the hotel several times last night. Didn't it occur to you to leave a message for me at reception?"

Again the urge to apologise was resisted. "Nothing occurred to me. I was in far too much pain to think of anything except my predicament. I'm getting about on two sticks at the moment but should be more mobile in a couple of days. I'm about to search out a suitable flight for returning as soon as possible."

"You might as well stay the week, rest up for as long as possible. Besides, it'll be much easier for me, picking you up from Exeter Airport rather than driving at least a hundred miles to another airport. I've got a lot on my plate this end, what with helping Helen to arrange the funeral and tracking down other members of the family."

"I'll think about it James. And please, give my condolences to all the family."

The connection was cut leaving Lyn uncertain which one of them had ended the call first; tablets were playing havoc with her brain.

Bovey Tracey

Walking at a steady pace Vinny headed back to where the van was parked. His mind, like the weather, was in a fog. How come he'd allowed Shaun Thatcher to pull a stunt like that? He had a sneaky admiration for the bloke however, and how he'd carried it off. he saw a lot of himself in the way that Thatcher operated but the man was right. He had got him completely wrong and as for Isabelle, well the word *nutter* quickly sprang to mind.

He stopped suddenly. There it was again. The sound of footsteps from behind, stopping when he stopped but leaving behind a short overlap. After a quick look behind, he turned up the collar of his jacket and crossed over the road, cursing the fog for hiding whoever it was following him. After several minutes of walking at an increased pace, he halted again. There were no footsteps to be heard, just a strange, deep-throated chuckle from somewhere ahead.

Stefan halted his search and was now looking down to where the van was but he could see nothing. The grey fog was covering the whole of the lower part of the field. He'd made one trip back to the vehicle, running the risk of blowing his cover. Assured that Vincent would sound the horn on his return, he continued swinging the detecting machine over the flattened soil. The effort, and the risk, had paid off, as he now had five more coins in his pocket.

Unbeknown to them both, when they'd parked the van in the usual place, a hive of activity had been going on less than half a mile away. Vincent had left quickly, giving a stark warning to Stefan to make himself scarce if he returned with Isabelle. The air had been still and the fog had thickened, lowering visibility to no more than fifteen metres. Sitting in the passenger seat, devoid of any visible stimulus, Stefan's thoughts had wandered back to Joe and the cause of his death. Determined to resist going over what couldn't be changed, he'd opened the van's door and the grey murky air reached his nostrils and the sound of something familiar reached his ears.

Within seconds, Stefan had realized the sound was coming from the movement of a JCB. He'd grabbed the bright-green workman's jacket and rolling it tight had stuffed it in his pocket. After closing the van door, as quietly as possible, he'd headed along the hedge of the field in the direction of the noise. As the field rose, the fog became thinner, gradually revealing the backward and forward dance of the giant earth-mover. With mixed feelings, Stefan had watched as the mound of soil containing the remainder of the coins, was pushed back into the previously opened trench and tamped down. He'd moved as close as he dared, without risk of being seen before slipping on the jacket and boldly walking further up the hedge until he was in line with the diminishing mound. With his back to the activity, his stance had taken on that of a workman taking a piss. In reality he'd been grinding the heel of his boot in the soil and making a cross — marking the spot for his return. Retracing his steps along the safety of the hedge he'd listened intently, stopping when he'd heard the faint sound of voices and cautiously moved towards them.

In his native tongue, he'd whispered a thanks to the God of good fortune. The ghostly figures of at least eight men were hard at work with shovels. All in bright-coloured jackets — some green, some orange — and most were speaking in a language similar to his own.

One man had broken away, headed toward the hedge to do what Stefan had just pretended to do. He'd waited, giving the man chance to relieve himself before wandering over and asking what was happening down this end of the field. Stefan had his story ready — he'd brought out a replacement part for the JCB driver — but the other man couldn't care less, he just wanted to get the lower trenching done for pipes arriving the next day, pipes leading to a soakaway at the lowest point in the field. Stefan wanted to know more, but the man was eager to get back to work and get the job done. He was eager to swap this foul weather for warmth, beer and television.

Within minutes, Stefan had been back at the van but there was still no sign of Vincent. Removing the spade and the metal detector, he'd returned to the marked spot. More good fortune. The JCB had finished filling the area of the mound and was trundling it's way down to dig out the required soakaway. Without hesitation, and thankful for the natural cover of fog, Stefan continued his quest for more coins. An obsession was taking hold, an obsession to right the wrongs committed by a fifteen-year-old boy.

Vinny was almost at running pace when the blur of his van came into view. He heard the snap of a twig to his left, the side where the tangled hedge dripped its burden of fog. He kept to the right, fumbling for keys that weren't needed. He'd left the van unlocked and left Stefan in charge of it. Where the hell was he?

Three things happened simultaneously. Vinny's heightened awareness blossomed into terror as a heavy weight from behind suddenly pinned him to the driver's door. His left cheek pressed firmly against cold, wet metal, the keys from his right hand were plucked easily from his fingers, and a knife, blade long and slender, glistened in the limited range of his vision. Somewhere in the distance he heard voices, voices and machinery but the fog made him blind. Then he heard another sound. This one close to his ear, began speaking, no not speaking, growling.

"HELLO CONWAY, WHAT A LOVELY POSITION TO HAVE YOU IN."

The steely pressure of the weight gave no room for manoeuvre, but Vinny was oblivious to any physical pain. His mind was reeling, stunned by what he'd just heard. Not the words, their meaning hadn't yet sunk in. It was the deep gravelly voice that brought terror and in a flash he was reminded of childhood nightmares.

Cold lips oozing hot air pressed even closer to his one exposed ear.

"CAT GOT YOUR TONGUE, CONWAY? FINDING IT DIFFICULT TO SPEAK? WE HAVE SOMETHING IN COMMON THEN."

As fear and anger took hold, Vinny made a desperate attempt to wriggle free from the powerful hold. The door he was pushed against began to slide open and as the pressure diminished one arm was pulled free allowing him to reach the steering wheel and bear down on the horn in its centre.

Stefan was down on one knee, retrieving yet another coin, when the blast of a horn cut through the air. The blast, definitely from the van, went on and on and on. He was quite used to Vincent's moods and his lack of self-control when angry, but the man was no fool. Something was definitely wrong and Stefan was already dashing towards the hedge. He tucked the detector well into the bushes, throwing the green jacket over it and with spade dragging behind, cantered along the hedgerow, stopping abruptly as the van came into focus.

With three fingers pressing continually on the horn the balance of the hold shifted in Vinny's favour and the throaty-growl became more erratic.

"YOUR DAYS ARE NUMBERED, CONWAY. BEAR IN MIND EACH TIME YOU WALK INTO YOUR FLAT. I HAVE THE KEYS TO IT. AND I HAVEN'T WITNESSED A GOOD EXPLOSION IN AGES."

Vinny's fingers were beginning to cramp but he still bore down as the deafening noise continued. Voices were coming closer and shouts in a language he couldn't decipher but the very fact that they were there was manna from heaven. Suddenly the pressure on his back lifted and again the flash of the long-bladed knife. He closed his eyes expecting the worst just as three strong men arrived, still hollering in a foreign tongue. The dark shape bent low, thrust the knife deep into the front tyre. The cramped fingers lost their hold and the deafening noise stopped abruptly a hissing sound taking over. Vinny turned and watched in disbelief as the long-coated shape fled to the back of the van, stabbing at the back tyre before disappearing into the hedge.

The horn stopped just as Stefan came upon the scene. He crouched low trying to read the situation. Vincent had slumped to the ground, shaken but unhurt as four men appeared on the scene. Stefan's eyes were now shifting in another direction. Following the shape that was slipping from view into the hedge a few meters away. A man wearing a long coat and hat pulled down low on his head. The same man he'd seen the evening before.

With the stainless-steel spade gripped firmly in both hands, Stefan followed as stealthily as he could. The warning call of a bird and twigs broken underfoot led him in the right direction. The rustling and snapping stopped, leaving only the relentless sound of the startled bird. And there he was. Vincent's attacker, sitting on the stump of an old felled tree. His coat spotted with moisture and flecked with greenery. The hat pulled down too far on his head, but not so far that Stefan couldn't see that the face was badly disfigured. The man beckoned to him in a voice more hideous than his looks.

"COME CLOSER, PLEASE, LET ME SEE YOUR FACE."

Stefan held his ground, remembering how his father was led into a trap by a sweet-talking assassin, and how two minutes later he lay bleeding to death, while his eldest son trembled in his hiding place. This murderer also carried a knife, he'd seen it cut easily into the van's rubber tyre, but the spade gripped in Stefan's hands had longer reach. The memory of his father's brutal murder filled his mind. In one powerful swing the business end of the spade made contact with the side of the stranger's head, releasing a loud clang that seemed to go on resonating until the body fell sideways onto the carpet of undergrowth.

"Stefan! Stefan, where the fuck are you?" Vinny shouted, after hearing a loud noise somewhere in the hedge. He followed the shouting with a punch on the horn. There was a rustling noise nearby and for a split second he was tempted to run back to the safety of the Polish builders. Then Stefan emerged still holding the spade.

"Where the fuck were you while I was being attacked and the van's tyres ripped to shreds?"

Stefan remained silent whilst he examined one tyre and then the next.

"Is spare wheel in good condition?" he asked.

"'Course it is, but we can't fucking get home on three wheels, can we?"

"There is small garage in town, repairs only, maybe they help us."

"I ain't going anywhere in this fog. Not with a dangerous maniac on the loose."

"I go for help to garage. Or lock van and we go together."

Vinny suddenly realized something, and that realization made his guts cramp with fear. The maniac had taken his bunch of keys — keys to the van and keys to his flat. And for the first time ever, he was considering calling the cops.

"Oh shit, Stefan, we're in the worst possible fucking mess, I think I'm gonna have to report this to the police."

"No! No police. Is not necessary."

Having no choice, Stefan gave a brief account of how he'd followed the long-coated man into the hedge and bashed his head in with the spade. He also said how they could bury him in the trench after the workmen left, and no one would be any the wiser. He'd been a fool not to search the man and they must do that now to find out who he is and take back the keys.

Placing a hand on Vincent's shoulder, Stefan said, "Wait here, my friend, I will bring back your keys."

Vinny pushed back his shoulders. "I want to see him. I want to see the bastard's face, and I want to get to the bottom of how he knew my name and where I live."

Stefan led the way back to the old felled trunk a strong sense of foreboding increasing by each step. On reaching the spot, they found there was no body there. Nothing was there but the two words that had been crudely carved on the top of the tree stump.

SLEEP WELL

Chapter 26

A light breeze, coupled with a steady drizzle, were gradually dispersing the fog that had lingered for most of that day. It had been a source of misery for many — causing several minor road accidents in the area — but, for two men, it had been a blessing and a reason for rubbing their hands in glee. Jack and Ted Wilcox, brothers and partners in Bovey Tracey's only garage that dealt with repairs, had their busiest day since last winter's sudden overnight plunge in temperatures.

Vinny and Stefan sit in silence in the steamed up van, stinking of fish, chips and vinegar. The windows were closed against the rain and both felt slightly out of kilter due to the lopsidedness of the van having two completely flat tyres on the driver's side.

Vinny shoved the last few chips into his mouth, rolled up the paper, squeezed it to a tight ball and lobbed it over his shoulder. Stefan gave him a meaningful look.

Vinny bridled. "What? You don't expect me to go looking for a fucking waste bin in this weather? Besides, it's pitch black out there. That maniac could be lurking anywhere. Where the fuck are those guys with the new tyres? I gave them an extra twenty quid for a speedy response. How long does it fucking take to pick up two tyres, drive here and fit 'em on? I knew I should have called the AA; we would've been back home by now!"

Stefan finished his food, bending the paper into ever decreasing folds until it was small enough to fit into his jacket pocket. "Vincent, is like the man at garage say, lots of accidents because of fog. I think if you wait for AA you probably wait all night."

The sound of Vinny's phone suddenly filled the cramped airspace. He snatched it from the dashboard. "Yeah, who else would it be? You promised to get those tyres to me asap. I've been hanging around like a spare part for nearly two hours." Vinny, scoffing inwardly at the apologies and weak excuses, gave the caller his exact position and reminded him that light was needed and because of the stolen keys, means to restart the van's engine.

The man of many names raised his head from the narrow camp bed and looked about him. All seemed in order. The barricaded door, still intact. The alcoholic, whose place this was and whom he'd once traded twenty-pounds for a stinking cloak with a large hood, lay dead in the corner. He had lain there for four days, his body slowly turning to foul-smelling liquid under the same hooded cloak. *Shame he'd turned nasty, his company was quite amusing.*

Easing himself into a sitting position, *Nicholas* (reminding his traumatized brain of his latest identity) lifted his hand and felt the place where the spade had made contact. There was damage. But not enough to stop him carrying out what needed to be done. There was also pain but pain meant nothing to him. He'd suffered excruciating bouts of it in many of his roles — even in boyhood. He had learned to utilize pain and use its power for exacting revenge against those who deserved it.

His first steps faltered. Then, shrugging into his long coat and pulling down the hat — grinning as the pain intensified — he shouted to the cob-webbed ceiling.

"YOUR TIME ON EARTH IS ALMOST OVER, CONWAY!"

He was driving his expensive black car, the only luxury he afforded himself these days, the windows tinted black against a world of ignorance. The vehicle, which was part home, part workshop and part office, was all he required for performing any task he set himself.

As Nicholas waited to turn left onto Bovey Tracey's main road, a repair truck came hurtling along. He could easily have cut in front of it, delaying the driver a few seconds, but thought better of it. He would need all the concentration he could muster to carry out his mission. Recklessness was counter-productive. Pain was one thing but losing the ability to wreak a greater havoc would defeat his objective.

Lanzarote

Lyn was putting the finishing touches to her make-up, trying her best to conceal the abrasions on her face. She'd arranged to meet Annelie for a couple of drinks at the terrace bar and was anxious to show her that she didn't always look like she'd been dragged through a hedge backwards.

Having spent a positive afternoon on the laptop, initially to find an appropriate return flight, as only Sunday flights are available for Exeter. She soon realized that flying to one of the

London airports was the best choice. Flights were much more frequent and all had easy links to the rail network. Once she arrived at Torquay Station, she could easily grab a cab home. She congratulated herself on insisting that they travel light, as she was now seeing the benefits of less luggage. In spite of her bad foot, she was confident she would manage her handbag and one small case. She was also confident that she wouldn't need anyone's help to get home.

Gentle music from a solo pianist drifted up the wide, open stairway as Lyn made her way to the lift, her sticks tapping almost in tune on the polished marble floor. On reaching the ground floor she could see garlands of tiny white lights wound around several of the coconut palms, adding a celebratory feel to the elegant, sub-tropical surroundings. Most of the terrace bar tables were already occupied. She made a beeline to the only one remaining close to the bar and backed by a wall, where she could securely lean the sticks. It also offered a superb view across the ocean to Fuerteventura — flecks of light indicating another idyllic tourist spot enjoying the lovely warm evening.

Annelie and a waiter arrived simultaneously and Lyn was pleased, and relieved, that she'd come alone. After establishing that neither wanted a full-blown meal, the women decided on sharing a bottle of white, Lanzarote wine served with a selection of nibbles. They touched glasses and smiled, words weren't necessary to convey the obvious. Sitting here in this delightful hotel and feeling the embrace of the warm sea air, it seemed like a million miles from where they'd first come upon each other, and neither made a reference to it.

Between nibbling and sipping, each learned about the life of the other. Childhood aspirations, jobs, relationships, marriages, births and deaths, all were covered, all easily discussed as though they'd known each other for years. When the bottle was empty and the food consumed, they promised to keep in touch, even if only by email.

Deciding that the three glasses of wine would be sufficient for a good night's sleep, Lyn tucked the pain-killers into the bedside drawer and reached for her mobile phone. There were three 'missed calls' from James but no messages were left. After making a comfortable nest with the pillows, she dialed his number.

Torquay

James replaced the receiver of his office phone, underlined the name and number of uncle Gregory, and moved on to the next relative on his list. He took a large sip from his glass of red wine and reached for the phone again — just as his mobile began to ring.

The call was from Lyn, but before answering, he took another sip of wine.

"Hello, Lyn, I thought you said your phone was fixed."

"It is, but it's not a permanent attachment and I was down on the terrace sharing a bottle of wine with a new friend I've made."

"Oh?"

She waited, but nothing more was added, even though the inflection of his response, held many questions. After the long pause, she asked. "How are things going your end?" An apology for missing his three calls wasn't forthcoming, nor was any further mention of her new friend.

"Should you be drinking wine whilst on pain-killers? I mean, you wouldn't want to slip over and add to your woes."

James heard the sarcasm in his own voice and attempted to mollify it with a forced laugh.

"You know from experience, James, whether the pain is mental or physical, a couple of glasses of wine are far more preferable than pills. And before my credits are completely wiped out, I was phoning to let you know that I'll be back by Friday at the latest."

James bristled but kept his voice even. "Where are you flying into and on what day, and what time, is your arrival?"

It was Lyn's turn to laugh, a meaningful sound that sent James's free hand reaching for his glass. "Like I said, I'll be back by Friday at the latest. If my foot can bear it, I might leave tomorrow. There are plenty of available flights to the London airports but I'll make my decision tomorrow. How are you coping with things at your end?"

"Lyn, forgive me for saying, but I don't think you've thought this through properly." His voice sounded tense and impatient. "How can I be expected to collect you from the London area at such short notice?" There was a pause, punctuated by a sigh. "I could probably arrange for Vincent to pick you up but surely staying put, resting your injury and returning on the booked flight is the more sensible option?"

"There are times, James, when the sensible option just doesn't suit me." Believe me, sweetheart, I have thought it through, I've spent all afternoon thinking it through. Arriving in London gives me easy access for a train to Torquay, from there I'll take a cab home. I certainly don't expect you to be dragged away from your mother's funeral arrangements, and thanks for the offer, but the last thing I need is to be travelling over two hundred miles sitting beside Vinny Conway."

Torquay

There were just two names left on James's list that he hadn't been able to contact, both from his father's side of the family, and both, he suspected, spending the winter months abroad. His father was from wealthy stock, but was virtually ostracized from his immediate family when he fell in love and married a woman below his class. His father then went on to spend the bulk of their married life, sacrificing every luxury in order to give James and his sister an education that *he* had taken for granted — a merry-go-round of money, position, stifled lives and children burdened with guilt — and to what end? He scored a line through both names and reached for the phone.

After four rings Helen's voice, sounding tired and weary. "How's it going, James?"

"I've managed to contact everyone bar two, father's youngest brother and the nephew. I feel sure that at this time of year they'll both be abroad until the spring, and I feel even more sure they wouldn't be attending Mother's funeral even if they were residing in Devon."

"Come now, James. It's not the time to become all bitter and twisted. It's only right to let everyone know and then leave it up to them whether they wish to pay their final respects. As you know, there's hardly anyone left of mother's family, and the number of friends and acquaintances have dwindled to single figures. Monday morning is going to be a very poignant time. Changing the subject, I've decided to stick with tea, coffee and sandwiches for anyone wanting to return to the house. Since father died, mother never allowed alcohol in the house and it wouldn't seem right breaking that rule straight after her death. Are you in agreement?"

"Yes of course, whatever you decide is fine by me. Will you need my help preparing the food?"

"No, not really. Making sandwiches is more of a woman's thing. Maybe Lyn would like to come over before the funeral and lend a hand…well keep me company really. I take it she is coming to the funeral?"

"Of course she is."

"So you have spoken?"

"Naturally. I was speaking with her just before I rang you. She had a slight mishap, slipped on the rocks, spraining her ankle and smashing her phone. She'll be back by Friday at the latest."

"Can I still count on your help in dealing with the undertakers tomorrow? I think all the decisions should be made jointly."

"I promise to be there, as arranged by ten. Lyn will be flying into London and taking a train to Torquay."

"Good for her! Good night, James, see you tomorrow."

Vinny pulled up in the only available space large enough to avoid too much shunting back and forth and running the risk of the engine stalling.

"Stefan, go and see if there's any sign of the bastard inside the flat. If there isn't, I'll drive around the back, shine the headlights on the back door and unless there's an open window, we'll just have to break in. Please reassure me Stefan, that you didn't bolt the back door this morning." *Ever since the scattering of the food that Fairbank had left by the back door, the Bulgarian had been spooked and over-cautious when it came to locking up.*

Before answering, Stefan jumped down onto the wet road, four doors down from Vincent's flat — a miniature river was flowing in the gutter, carrying any litter dropped in the daylight hours. "I sure, I don't push bolt on door, I also sure no windows are open," he said, leaving the van door slid open and stealthily moving off. The night seemed darker than usual. He raised his head and understood why, the street light closest to the flat was unlit. He edged closer, feeling fragments of glass splinter beneath his heavy boots, reminding him of Joe, but he pushed the thought away. Up ahead there was a pool of light rising from a basement flat — Vincent's basement flat.

Shielded by shadow, he crept closer and peered down the run of steps leading to the front door. The door stood slightly ajar, the passage light winking an illuminating glow on the bunch of keys swinging from the keyhole. Stefan moved even more slowly down the steps, listening for the slightest sound. Nothing. He eased the keys from the lock and turned off the light while closing the door, in fluid, almost silent movements.

The sudden sound of a car starting up spooked him. He turned and the air was filled with diesel emissions. The roar of its powerful engine, a blast of a horn and a flash of light and it was gone. Deathly silence surrounded him as panic set in!

Stefan ran back towards the van, refusing to allow his mind to think of what might have happened. "Vincent! Vincent, are you OK?"

Alarmed at the sudden appearance of the dark car with no lights, Vinny had stalled the engine, doused the lights and ducked down below the windscreen.

The car roared past with a wink of the indicator light and a toot of the horn.

The fucking bastard's playing with us, he thought, as he rolled out of the open, off-side door, concerned about Stefan and dreading what might have happened to him. He ran towards his flat, hollering in panic. "Stefan! Stefan, where are you?"

They collided, arms wrapping round each other, a mingling of words, of both English and Bulgarian profanities saturated with great relief!

Grinning, Stefan held up the keys. "I go lock van, then we look together inside flat, making sure bastard leave no surprises, yes?"

Chapter 27

Wednesday Night—Torquay

It was a great relief for Vinny to be reunited with his bunch of keys. The keys that were indispensable for most of his business and private life. The fear of their loss had prompted him to make sensible changes, to have them separated and copies made of the most important ones as soon as possible. The fact still remained, his property had been invaded by a dangerous lunatic who had threatened him. Threatened him with some kind of explosion. They'd opened the flat door very slowly and very carefully, both flinching and turning their backs as the light switch was flicked on. A foul smell had hit their nostrils setting off a stream of cursing and gagging. Footprints, laying down a dark, foul-smelling liquid, made it easy to plot the course of the invaders movements. *Was this a deliberate attempt to deceive? Or was this person truly a half-wit?*

From what they could see, three steps took him to Vinny's office door which was always kept closed when not in use. It was now wide open but with no indication of the intruder entering. He'd then walked the length of the passage to the kitchen, leaving a cluster of prints where the boiler was housed and then a straight path back to the front door. Neither of the two bedrooms, nor the bathroom, showed signs of entry; that didn't stop them giving these rooms a thorough search — any idiot could easily deceive by removing the soiled shoes. That done, Stefan busied himself with mop, bucket, disinfectant and bleach, while Vinny scrutinized the boiler cupboard for any interference or sign of surplus wiring. Finding nothing untoward, it was deemed safe to make a brew.

As Vinny made his way into his office, mourning the fact that his air-purifier was lying in bits on the floor, he bent down to gather up the damaged parts. "Well I'll be fucking damned," he heard himself say. Clamped inside a piece of the housing, was a listening device of similar size, colour and make to the one that Shaun Thatcher had given him.

Bovey Tracey

I AM LOSING POWER. THE METAL PLATE IN MY HEAD FEELS LIKE IT HAS SHIFTED AND IS CAUSING PRESSURE ON MY BRAIN. I WILL NOT GO TO HOSPITAL. I WILL NEVER AGAIN ALLOW SUCH PEOPLE TO USE ME FOR VANITY AND EXPERIMENTATION. I WOULD RATHER DIE. AND SOON I WILL DIE. BUT NOT BEFORE MY MAIN QUEST IS COMPLETED. I WILL THEN WALK INTO THE FIRES OF HELL WITH VINCENT CONWAY — THE LAST OF THE DECEIVERS.

BUT TONIGHT I MUST REST. MY RIGHT HAND IS OUT OF CONTROL, TREMBLING LIKE AN OLD MAN'S. I COULDN'T MANIPULATE THE EXPLOSIVE AND TIMER. COULDN'T EVEN HOLD THE PHONE PROPERLY WHILE UNLOCKING MY CAR. IT'S LYING IN THE GUTTER WHERE IT FELL.

TOMORROW I WILL NEED HELP. HELP TO ACHIEVE WHAT I AM NOW INCAPABLE OF DOING ALONE. BELLA WILL BE MY ASSISTANT. YES, BELLA WILL BE PERFECT.

Chapter 28

Thursday Morning—Torquay

Totally unaware of the time, Vinny shuffled through the eight pages of downloaded documents he'd printed off the internet and began slipping them into an envelope, changed his mind, and started reading them again. After finding the listening device, his mind had gone on a rampage of all the possibilities behind such an infringement of privacy coupled with the threat on his life. One person had sprung immediately to mind — Victor Carlson — a man with many identities and no scruples. A man with millions tied up in flashy properties he'd acquired around the world — aided by the position he'd held at several banks. A man who, once crossed, wouldn't rest until he'd exacted revenge. But Carl, the name Vinny knew him by, was dead. Died alongside his whole family in Norway as they were celebrating an important anniversary. A massive explosion in the vicinity of the gas boiler and the fire that followed, razed the large, timber dwelling to the ground before fire-fighters could get there. The bodies were burnt to unidentified crisps, with only important DNA proving their identities.

Vinny had read all about it several months ago in a Sunday newspaper, and clearly remembered celebrating Carl's demise that same evening. The corrupt banker had wanted to add Fairbank's property to his collection, but a deal struck between the solicitor and Vinny, had scuppered his plan, placing Vinny on Carl's list for payback.

The article, now in front of him, described how Victor had cheated death only a few months earlier than the explosion. Apparently, Carl was on his way to Heathrow Airport — returning home to attend his mother's funeral — when his car, being driven in the wrong direction down a slip road, was hit by an articulated lorry. Both vehicles had swerved resulting in a clip to the offside. Even so, a team of London doctors had fought relentlessly to save his life, *and no doubt relieve him of a pile of his money,* thought Vinny, as he scanned the article once again. The evidence of Victor Carlson's presence on that fateful night in Norway was his car, containing passport and further documentation, found parked, in a nearby road. Also, he had not shown up for any further scheduled hospital appointments.

After sliding the documents into the envelope Vinny stood and stretched. His stomach rumbled and his neck ached. Glancing at the clock he was amazed to see it was not yet seven-thirty and still dark outside. Apart from about three hours sleep they'd spent most of the early hours checking and rechecking every possible hiding place for explosives, scanning the internet for information on Carl and drinking loads of coffee. Now out of milk, Stefan had gone looking for an open shop to buy some. Overdosed on caffeine, a sudden thought propelled itself into Vinny's mind.

What if the bastard's planted something in the van? It was empty and unlocked when he arrived back from the Thatcher cottage. Fucking hell, Stefan, where were you? Anybody could have climbed aboard and…

Vinny leapt to his feet, grabbed the van keys and a torch before heading for the parked van which was still four doors away. Before even attempting to open any doors, the torch swept each individual wheel for any signs of a car bomb. Gingerly, the back doors were opened and Vinny climbed in. All seemed in order as the torch beam waltzed back and forth across its width. On the final swing, the torch beam picked out an inch of bright-green, luminous material poking out from the back of the passenger seat. Intrigued, Vinny pulled carefully, soon realizing that it was the waistcoat that was usually draped over the back seat; an item of clothing required to be worn when fitting locks on new-build-properties. The jacket was rolled tightly and felt heavy. Suddenly feeling on high alert, generating nervousness and perspiration, he very slowly unrolled the jacket. The weight was in the pockets and as his hands probed further and his torch shone nearer, Vinny found he was holding two fistfuls of coins. All were silver and, as far as he could tell, the majority looked in very good condition.

The sky was just beginning to lighten as Stefan reached the steps leading down to the basement flat. Fragments of glass littered the pavement near the steps and Stefan's bag, containing milk, bread and bacon, swung from his hand as his right boot brushed the glass into the gutter. Something caught his eye. Stooping down he could see it was a mobile phone, scratched but not smashed. He picked it up, looked around then shoved it in his pocket.

A light tapping on the door and it immediately swung open.

"I find something that may be important, Vincent."

"I know you have." Vinny grabbed the bag of food from Stefan's hand and shoved the rolled up jacket in its place, the weight of it proving the coins were still in its pockets. "How come you never mentioned these before now?" Without giving Stefan time to respond, Vinny continued stoney-faced. "I never trusted foreigners, Stefan, until I met you. Seems I was right all along." The look of hurt developed into a sneer. "There you were, telling me all you were finding on that field were ancient bullets and bits of lead."

For the first time in years Stefan felt embarrassed. Heat rose from his chest, spreading upwards to his neck, face and ears. Always as a young teenager, embarrassment would send his face and ears a vivid red. He was no longer a teenager and as a man he must stand tall. "I sorry for keeping secret. But I no sorry for keeping coins for myself. I work hard to find them and you have already made good profit from the treasure Isabelle find."

"What the fuck do *you* know what I've made? Besides, I thought we were mates. Well I'll tell you what I've decided, *mate,* you can consider the cost of hiring the metal detector as your wages. It's going back today and *you* can piss-off back to London!"

Having been reminded of Isabelle's gold treasure, Vinny rifled through the pockets of the jacket he'd worn the day before and found the tissue-wrapped ring — the genuine ring — and walked out the door, slamming it behind him. Although it was early, a light shining in one of Jimmy's upstairs rooms, showed he was up and about.

After knocking several times on the solid oak door and hearing nothing, he pressed the highly-polished, brass bell push. The ring resonated throughout the building. Above his head he heard the sound of a sash window opening, followed by the solicitor's polite but stern voice.

"Excuse me, the office hours are clearly printed for all to see…"

Vinny stepped back from the front door, allowing Jimmy to see who was calling and cutting off his rebuke. "Morning, Jimmy,"I could see you were up and about. I got something for you."

"Good morning, Vincent. Look, whatever it is, can't it wait? As you can see I'm not yet dressed."

What Vinny *could* see, was a man dressed in black silky pyjamas with a deep red, expensive looking dressing gown slung on top — *what a poser*. "You look descent enough to me, Jimmy. Besides, my working day starts earlier than yours."

After a heavy sigh, the window slid shut. Within seconds, Vinny heard the sound of footsteps descending the stairs and locks being undone. Then the appearance of the solicitor, whose lavish night apparel must have cost as much as Vinny earned in a week.

"Vincent, I don't mean to be rude, but it's Mother's funeral on Monday and this morning I've a eulogy, to compose, that's a speech to be read at the funeral, several people to contact and a meeting with my sister at the undertakers. So can you please be brief. And I'm sorry but there'll be no coffee on offer."

Vinny could easily forego the coffee but he'd come to learn that coffee episodes lowered the professional guard of this man, making him less reserved, almost friendly, and he was in dire need of a friend right now. He needed to unload the swirl of fear and anger that filled his head. Disappointed, he blurted out, "You need your wife-to-be by your side at a time like this, Jimmy. Still, at least someone is getting their fair share of relaxation. She'll look lovelier than ever with a healthy suntan as she stands amongst the pale faces of the mourning Fairbanks. Oh yes, before I forget." Vinny delved into his pocket and produced the small bundle. He cleared his throat and in a flurry tried to reproduce the tone of an antique dealer who was wooing a prospective buyer. "The original ring that was lost, or buried, over three hundred years ago."

James reached for the bundle and leaving Vincent standing in the porch turned and walked into his office. With the help of a magnifying glass, he read again the poignant inscription and checked the mark of its maker.

When he turned, Vincent was behind him.

"So, we have a deal, yes?" Vinny caught the uncertainty on the solicitors face and was determined not to let his run of bad luck spill over into this deal. "The finder did have other offers, Jimmy, one even better than yours, but when I explained that the ring was being used as a wedding ring and the groom belongs to a fine family who have resided in South Devon for generations, well, who could resist that? I don't suppose you've got the cash to hand? I'm a bit strapped at the moment."

"No, Vincent I haven't. My profession doesn't involve dealing in cash, however I'll pay you when the funeral's over. Besides, I thought you told me you had lots of work on at present and that's why Stefan was hired for the full week?" James noticed Vincent's body language change at the mention of Stefan's name. He also noticed the clock relentlessly eating up the time. "Now I really must get on but thank you for this," James held up the ring, "and of course you are right, a deal is a deal."

Bovey Tracey

Isabelle continued from where she'd left off the day before, cleaning the cottage from top to bottom and clearing out all unnecessaries in preparation for selling up and moving on. At present, she was rifling through her wardrobe, filling a sack with cast off clothing for the charity shop. She was feeling good, better than she had done in years.

Shaun had left early for Exeter Station. He was off to London to sell the coins, convinced he'd be able to raise enough money to start his own business. He was so happy, so full of hope for the future. A shout from Robert cut across her thoughts.

"I'm off now, Mum, but I've got a free period this afternoon so I'll be home for lunch, OK? And remember what you promised, no contacting Mr Conway or… or anybody else."

She'd overheard Shaun and Robert whispering, heard Robert agreeing to keep a close eye on his mother while Shaun was in London. Isabelle walked to the top of the stairs and called back. "Don't worry sweetheart, I've got enough to keep me busy for days. I'll have a casserole on the go for when you get back. Enjoy your morning." She heard the back door close and his key turn in the lock, before returning to her task.

I HAVE SLEPT TOO LONG. DAYLIGHT IS ALREADY HERE AND THERE IS MUCH TO DO. EVEN THOUGH ONE HAND IS ALMOST USELESS, MY MIND IS STILL STRONG AND MY WILL EVEN STRONGER. AS ALWAYS I WILL CARRY OUT THAT WILL!

With radio Classic FM for company, Isabelle moved from the cleared-out wardrobe to the bedside cabinets. Her cabinet barely took five minutes to tidy as she'd recently tossed out old makeup, cheap costume jewellery and sentimental oddments that she'd clung to over the years. She moved around to Shaun's cabinet and opened the drawer, her eyes fixing onto the small tissue-wrapped package. *So, he had decided to keep it.* Her first instinct was to close the drawer, leave the clearing of this private space to Shaun but hadn't she promised him she'd be strong. That she would carefully and rationally think through all that made her nervous, all that made her scared. She reached for the tiny package, slowly peeling back the tissue paper until the ring was revealed — taking care to keep some tissue between it and her fingers. Flicking on the bedside light, she read again its charming line of poetry, turning further she noticed something odd. *Oh my God! what has happened? Am I really going mad?* The two letters, NP, had changed to one. The letter R. She checked, then double-checked using a magnifying glass. The R remained the sole letter.

Beautiful choral music filled the room commanding her to calm her nerves and rationalize her fear. Nicholas had stated that she was promised to him and the ring proved it, so who was R and was she now to assume she was promised to him?

"Of course! Of course, I understand now," she called out triumphantly over the crescendo of music. "I'm promised to Robert — my son —promised only this morning that I wouldn't make contact again with Mr Conway or Nicholas."

Full of relief, she flung the tissue in the rubbish bag and kissed the ring before slipping it on her thumb, making a mental note to get it altered to fit as soon as she could afford it. Checking the clock, she decided she had just enough time to drop the clothes and oddments up to the charity shop before preparing the casserole.

With collar turned up against the chill breeze, and two

large bags pulling at her arms, Isabelle bent forward intent on her short journey. A black car, with blackened windows, went unnoticed as it slowly followed twenty yards behind.

Torquay

Stefan was packed and ready to go but there were explanations required and words needed to be said; to forgive and be forgiven was so important to him.

His stomach growled with hunger and he knew Vincent must be feeling the same. The bag of groceries still lay abandoned by the kitchen door. He emptied its contents and set to work.

The smell of brewing coffee and frying bacon pulled Vinny's attention away from the problem of the listening devices. He'd phoned Isabelle twice in the last half hour, in the hope of gaining knowledge about the mysterious hooded bloke who stunk to high heaven and, to ask who she felt was responsible for hiding the listening device in the cottage, but there'd been no answer. He could kick himself for not mentioning it to Fairbank. As he'd been sent one of the free air-purifiers, the odds are he's bugged too There was also bad blood between Carl and the solicitor a couple of years ago. *Could the bastard still be alive?* The thought made him shudder.

There was a tap on his office door and there was Stefan, sheepish, standing with a tray holding two mugs of coffee and a plate of bacon sarnies. Without saying a word, Vinny stood aside and let him in, moving some paperwork to allow for the tray. Both men ate and drank, amidst a lot of slurping and smacking of lips; but without speaking and very little eye contact. Vinny was the first to finish and the first to speak.

He lifted his empty mug. "I need a refill. What about you?"

"Yes. Thank you."

On his return he saw a scratched mobile phone on the tray. He reached for it and turned it over before asking, "Whose is this?"

"I find outside when I go for milk. I think it belong to the one who wants you dead."

Vinny suddenly realized that this was what Stefan had wanted to reveal on his return. "OK, I jumped to the wrong conclusion, but you still tried to cheat me out of a fair share of those coins."

"Every coin was found by my skill and in my time, and, as you tell to me, hiring of machine will be my wages." Stefan bowed his head, waiting for the next bout of abuse. But Vincent remained silent. Raising his head he looked him in the eye. "The coins are to help repay to my family, in Bulgaria, the murder of my father and the damage, through rape, to my sister, Elena. Both these things happened because of me. Because my father entrusted to me a secret which I didn't keep. He too found a hoard of coins. A massive hoard of coins. By accident one fell into my trousers and I show it to a friend — boast that we now richer than his family. My words moved faster than the wind in our small community and when my father used some of coins for Elena to travel to England for more education and better job, a criminal gang take her and send threats of her death if my father don't pay them large sum of money."

Stefan swallowed hard in an effort to keep his voice steady. He looked at Vincent with eyes moist with anguish. "My father ordered me to stay and watch over family while he went to plead with head of gang. I disobey again and follow him. Standing behind an ancient tree, I watch, cringing like coward, as they laugh at his pleas before cutting his throat. Then they drive, in fast car, to my family home. By time I get there, panting from running, my mother already give to them what they want — all the coins in exchange for her children's lives. Overnight, I become man of family. I spend day and nights using detector to find Grandfathers buried gun, while my family go without food and medicines. I finally realize my revenge and my guilt would soon lead to my families death.

So now I work hard. I take only what I need to survive. The rest is sent home to my sick mother and younger brother. Elena, she do the same. Money from selling coins will make big difference to their lives and, help me sleep more peacefully."

Vinny was lost for words. But words were soon found when he switched on the mysterious mobile phone and found just three numbers in the contacts list: one under Conway, the next under Fairbank and the remaining one under Bella. "This is it, Stefan. These are the numbers to the tiny sim cards embedded in the listening devices. All I have to do is dial each number and I can hear any conversations in the vicinity of each hidden device. Very clever. And I hold two of the devices in my hand, neither of which is linked up to any explosives."

"Maybe Mr Fairbank is target. If his place explodes, you be crushed down here in rubble."

"And how would this bloke have got in there? Fairbanks place is as secure as a prison, besides, Lyn Porter has the device in her studio, and if our mystery-man has been listening in since these air-purifiers arrived, he'd probably know that." Vincent thought for a minute then continued even more animated. "Fucking hell! That would be even worse! Her studio is just above my office!"

Bovey Tracey

Isabelle sat perfectly still on the back seat of the black car, both hands holding onto the box of fragile cakes while her brain tried to make sense of what she was being asked to do. What would Shaun think if he could see her now? He'd drummed it into her that there was no such thing as reincarnation. But according to Nicholas, the man drifting in and out of consciousness on the seat in front of her, he was living proof. Apparently, Bella had shared his life centuries ago; a life cut short by treachery and violence. Nicholas explained that *he* couldn't move on like she had. There was something he desperately needed her to do before he could leave behind his endless pain and torment. He looked in a terrible state. Dried blood matted his hair and covered some of his fingers. Fingers that trembled like the body of an injured bird. He was close to disappearing for good. Yes, those were his words, disappearing, never to return; the very sound of those words filling her with joy. Then he fell silent, head slumped forward. She reached forward and touched his shoulder, lost for words, filled with wonder and compassion. What should she do?

On leaving the charity shop to return home, she'd cut through the car park and was suddenly aware of the large black car blocking one side of the exit. Thinking it was a stranger needing directions she'd approached the rolled down window of the empty passenger's seat and peered in. A deep, persuasive voice, calling her by name, had instructed her to climb aboard and, as if by magic, the back door had clicked open. She'd hoped she was being given a lift home, but the car had sailed by the cottage at a slow, sedate pace, winding its way through town, down the country lanes and around to the top end of the ploughed meadow; coming to rest inside an obscured gateway which looked down over the whole field. The field which had changed her life.

He'd handed her a box of cakes and she recognized the wrapping of the homemade cakes from the best bakers in town. He told her she must hold the box very carefully and upright, to prevent it's delicate contents. In between lapses into semiconsciousness, he'd explained how he could no longer risk driving any distance, and *she*, *his* beautiful Bella, would have to do this final task alone. The deep persuasive voice droned on about Mr Conway and how because of this man, he'd been able to find *his* Bella again. And this gift, this token of *his* appreciation must be delivered to Mr Conway's place of abode within the hour. Only by doing as he asked, would all earthly debts be cancelled. Telling her all this had tired him and he'd lapsed once again into sleep.

Birdsong in a nearby tree cut through the silence. She'd thought of her son, remembering the casserole. She tried the door and found it locked!

Nicholas suddenly roused himself and checked his watch before rummaging in the glove compartment. Grabbing a handful of money, including tens, twenties and even one fifty pound note, he shoved them into her hands, telling her she was to make sure Conway was home. A mobile phone seemed to appear from nowhere and with slow deliberation, she watched as a trembling finger pressed the keys. Ringing could be heard as the chill of the plastic phone was pressed into the side of her face and his low scratchy voice, telling her what to say. Another call was made to the local taxi firm, asking for a car to come straight away to take Bella to The Terrace, Torquay.

Torquay

When Vinny replaced the receiver, he wasn't sure whether to smile or frown. A truce had been forged between him and Stefan and they were just about to leave and complete a security job that needed two pairs of hands.

Stefan sensed the phone call had altered their plans. "What is happening?"

"An important delivery, Stefan. I need to hang on here till eleven. You take the van and get started, I'll join you as soon as I can."

"Who make call? Remember, maniac is still free."

That too had crossed Vinny's mind until everything suddenly fell into place. "It was Isabelle. She wants to say *Thank You* in person. She has a little gift for me." *And I think I know what it is — a heavy gold ring that's worth quite a few bob!*

Bovey Tracey

BELLA IS PUTTY IN MY HANDS. SHE HAS LEFT TO DO MY BIDDING. NOW I CAN REST. WHEN I WAKE IT WILL BE DONE — I WILL TURN ON THE CAR RADIO AND HEAR ALL ABOUT THE MAYHEM I HAVE CAUSED. MY WHOLE LIFE HAS BEEN DOMINATED BY DECEIVERS —EVEN MY OWN MOTHER — AND THE LAST OF THEM WILL SOON BE GONE. I WILL DIE A HAPPY MAN, HERE IN MY CAR.

Chapter 29

Thursday Afternoon—Arrecife Airport—Lanzarote

After a good night's sleep, Lyn had woken with the overpowering urge to return to Torquay. Sitting around doing nothing, while James was grieving and bombarded with so much to do, didn't sit well. She'd tested her ankle by gingerly pacing the room — an initial gasp of pain, then relief as it became more manageable. A flight to Gatwick was booked before doing anything else; leaving at twelve-twenty-five to arrive at four-fifteen, giving her ample time for getting back to Torquay under her own steam. But in spite of the two pain-killers, by the time she'd checked in, she was regretting leaving behind the sticks she'd been loaned; keeping one to alleviate the pressure off her bad foot would have been much more sensible. She'd overcome this problem by purchasing a stout umbrella in one of the airport's shops, hoping that it wouldn't be regarded a *lethal weapon* by the airport security.

With the umbrella now safely stowed in the overhead compartment, Lyn gazed out of her window as the plane soared above Lanzarote's volcanic mountain range — a diminishing scene of craters and tracks, dotted with tiny, isolated, white buildings. Turning from the sight, she wondered if she'd ever be able to visit this place again.

Exeter

James read again the letter he had found amongst his mother's private papers. He was in Helen's home office sifting through documentation that spanned decades. The first cursory glance of the letter had been interrupted by Helen offering a coffee-break, which he'd declined. Alone once more he assimilated the written thoughts and feelings of the woman whom he'd always regarded as completely dependent on her husband, until after his death over ten years ago.

It was difficult to remain impassive as line after line revealed a strong personality, possessing ideals far removed from those of her spouse. Opposites, was the obvious attraction in their long-standing marriage. Partially disguised within the heart-felt words were apologies to each of her children. Apologies for allowing an antiquated class system to shape their lives, but on this, her husband's most vociferous wish, she had acquiesced, rationalizing that a private education would guarantee independence for each of them.

The final paragraph, added more recently and mainly aimed at James, was more difficult to read — deterioration in the writer's co-ordination coupled with the blurring in the reader's moistened eyes — changing James's mind about the coffee. Carefully replacing the letter in the envelope, he slipped it in his jacket pocket and followed the welcoming aroma to Helen's kitchen.

Helen pushed aside the book of HOME RECIPES and reached for the coffee pot. "I'll make us a fresh one."

"No, I'll do it. My fault I didn't come earlier."

"Didn't expect you to when I saw what you were reading."

Helen caught his accusing look. "Don't worry, I wasn't peeking and I had a letter too."

"Were you surprised by any of its content?"

"No, not really. It's quite natural when you're coming to the end of your time to stress how much you love your children and to apologise and ask for forgiveness for the conditioning foisted upon them. But, I would have preferred it straight from the horses mouth instead of a few scribbled lines."

James looked at his sister, searching for signs of anger or frustration. "That's a bit unfair, isn't it?"

"How can telling the truth be unfair? I am my mother's daughter — upfront, out-spoken and independent. Whereas you, dear brother, are a carbon-copy of dad, who always thought women were vulnerable and in constant need of masculine strength and guidance. When did you say Lyn will be back?"

"Sometime tomorrow, probably the evening. Why?"

"Because I'm taking full advantage of my enforced leave from work. I'm treating my family to an old-fashioned, home cooked meal and *you* are invited. As I intend to serve a different wine per course, I'll make up the bed in the spare room for you."

Chapter 30

Thursday Evening—Torquay

Vinny heard Stefan maneuvering the van into the flat's parking space at the rear of the building, not an easy thing to do with Lyn Porter's car sharing half the bay. A cloud of guilt descended.

Vinny had promised to join him after Isabelle had left. Trouble was, she'd never arrived for the eleven o'clock appointment. Annoyed, he'd given her till eleven-thirty and then grabbed the phone, fully prepared to let off steam and change the appointment to another day. But several tries had resulted in the same thing — her home number was unobtainable. He'd been disappointed, sure he wanted the ring, but even more, he wanted to find out all he could about this, so-called, hooded man. He was scared. So scared he'd spent the afternoon rechecking every inch of his flat for signs of planted explosives.

A knock on the back door was followed by Stefan's voice, "Is only me, Vincent."

Vinny drew back the bolts, slapping his friend's shoulder as he entered. "Sorry I didn't join you, mate. Isabelle, didn't show and I, well to be honest, Stefan, I've been combing the place again. I can't get the bastard's threat out of my head. We'll get an early start tomorrow and the job should be done by lunchtime."

"Work is finished," Stefan said with a smile, I late because I wait for boss to arrive and give cheque for you." A brown envelope, addressed to VC Securities was then handed over to Vinny.

"You are a diamond, Stefan. And to show my appreciation, I'm taking you down the pub for a couple of pints and no cooking tonight; on our way back we'll pick up something special to eat."

First Great Western Train to Torquay

Her careful planning had paid off, up to a point. Lyn was aiming for the five-thirty three to Paignton, the only train without changes and the only one getting her home at a reasonable hour. No sooner had she arrived at Gatwick, a connecting train had whisked her along to Paddington. Ignoring the mounting ankle pain, she'd hobbled, elbowed and then almost sprinted to the platform, clambering aboard the nearest carriage by the skin of her teeth. The train was rolling along before she realized the carriage she'd entered was first-class and full. The next two carriages were struggled through and one woman confronted. A woman who had plonked her shopping on the seat beside her before closing her eyes and feigning sleep. A sharp nudge on the shoulder and Lyn was allowed to squeeze past her and deposit her gear under the table — a space to accommodate four pairs of legs.

With a sigh of relief, Lyn eased her throbbing ankle onto the vacant seat in front of her, fumbled in her pocket for two painkillers and washed them down with the remaining content of a small bottle of water. The packed Paddington train had just emptied by at least fifty-percent. She wasn't familiar with the town of Newbury but after the mass exodus, she realized it was a place with a high percentage of commuters.

There was now time enough to rest, but first she checked her phone for messages. Nothing. Not for the first time, she regretted having left her phone's charger at home — the power indicator had been down to one digit before leaving the hotel. She had rung James at the office as soon as she'd booked her flight. There had been no answer, and so she had left a quick message stating she'd be back late that evening. Ignoring the pangs of hunger, she closed her eyes and allowed the rock and roll of the carriage to lull her into sleep.

Bovey Tracey

The saucepan-lid clattered loudly as it hit the tiled floor of the scullery. Robert's voice followed its echo, "Sorry Mum, hope I didn't wake you."

Isabelle, sitting in the rocking chair facing the stove, roused herself. "It's all right love, I was just relaxing, I'm not sleeping." The truth was, Isabelle wasn't sure anymore what was reality and what was dreaming.

Had she been dreaming when Nicholas had driven her to the top of the ploughed field, revealing in fits and starts his cruel and violent past? Had she been dreaming when she'd spoken on the phone to Mr Conway, telling him she'd be arriving before eleven with a thank you gift? Had she been dreaming when hearing a car stop on the other side of the hedge, beckoning by hooting its horn, and the door lock was suddenly released beside her? And, had she been suddenly pulled from this dreaming when a blast of refreshing cool air and the sweet sound of a robin greeted her as she'd pushed open the door? Uncertainty had vanished like a puff of smoke when she touched the ring to her lips and filled her mind with Robert. Yes, her allegiance was now to him and his father. With the back door wide open, fresh air banishing the strange, stifling atmosphere, she leaned forward, intent on confronting Nicholas with her new found certainty, but he'd lapsed once more into an unconscious state. Stroking her fingers softly over his scarred, pale face, she'd whispered goodbye, placing the box of cakes she knew she could never deliver, under his seat. Mr Conway didn't need fattening cakes, he was already a little overweight, and besides, she'd made a promise to Robert and she must honour that promise. Gently pushing the door closed, she'd headed for the waiting taxi, changing the destination from Torquay to Bovey Tracey's high street.

She stretched and looked about her warm kitchen. The aroma of lamb casserole, roasting potatoes and burning candles filled the air. Robert smiled as he lay another place mat. "I just got a text from Dad. He should be home in about half an hour. He said he had done well on the sale of the coins. More than enough to get started in the steam-cleaning business. I warned him about the power lines being down and the diversion at the top end of the town."

Isabelle sat down next to her son and reached for his hand. "Everything's going to be fine, Robert. We are fortunate to have the benefit of the Rayburn. we have warmth and we can cook." She caught sight of the ring, snugly fitting her thumb, mentally vowing to wear it every single day.

Robert followed her gaze. "How come that ring fits now? I didn't think you had the money to get it altered."

"Money, like everything else, always has a way of appearing when you need it most. The jewellers in the high street have an in-house workshop; they told me to go and have a coffee, and it would be sized on my return. Such a lovely, helpful man he was, and true to his word." Isabelle held up her hand to allow the candlelight to flicker across the richly polished gold, remembering how the explosion could be heard just as she'd pushed the sized ring back onto her thumb. Everyone was in a panic as shop lights blinked out and burglar alarms sounded. But she'd been content as she'd walked back home to prepare the casserole — sensing the long nightmare was over.

Snippets of news had filtered from Robert's little portable radio throughout the afternoon. Early impressions that groundsmen, excavating and laying pipes in a field due for development, had ruptured a gas main, resulting in the massive explosion which had brought down power lines and uprooted trees. The investigation and its findings however, were still progressing. In the meantime the disruption affecting overhead cables, both electrical and telephonic were hopefully going to be fixed within twenty-four hours.

Torquay

With a sigh of relief, tinted with a little shame, Lyn beat the elderly woman by a short head to the last waiting taxi. She was tempted to offer it up, but her foot throbbing, starving hungry, and her bursting bladder kept her going.

The taxi pulled away with a brief pip of its horn, leaving

her and her baggage in complete darkness. There was no welcoming light in the porch, no sign of life in James's place and most annoying of all, the street lamp that should have helped illuminate the front door, was unlit. She part hobbled, part dragged herself and her belongings to the porch door, fumbling for the keys whilst feverishly holding onto the contents of her bladder. Once opened, she flicked on the light, and with another key in hand attacked the lock on the inner door. Warm air greeted her; at least her boiler was faithful. Everything, apart from the walking-stick-umbrella, was dropped or kicked into the hallway before Lyn made a limping dash to the toilet at the back of the building.

With collars turned up against the damp chill coming off the sea, Vinny and Stefan marched up the incline of The Terrace, eager to get back in the warmth and tuck into the extra-large portions of fish and chips they had stuffed inside their coats, the only takeaway food available. In perfect synchronization, they stopped, looked in the direction of the property above the flat— door ajar and all lights blazing — and cursed.

Keeping his voice low, Vinny hissed, "He's back! Fucking hell, Stefan, I was right, his intention is to create an explosion from Lyn Porter's side of the building."

"Maybe is Lyn Porter inside?"

"No, it's him alright. Fairbank told me she won't be back until tomorrow. And there's no way Jimmy would have left his doors unlocked and open at this time of night. Don't forget Stefan, this psychopath has been able to listen in on conversations. Wait here, I'll be back in a second." Vinny shot down the steps to his own flat, retrieving a two-by-four inch length of wood cleverly concealed in a sharp angle near the door. He also pulled a balaclava from his pocket and slipped it over his head. With him leading the way they moved toward the open door.

After the relief of using the loo, Lyn's next priority, apart from phoning James, was satisfying her growling stomach. The tip of the umbrella clonked across the wooden floor of her kitchen as she hobbled from filling the kettle to surveying the fridge, disappointed at what she found. She was sick to the back teeth of cold sandwiches and sugary snacks; what she needed was hot, hearty food and there was only one easy way to get it. She could order a takeaway meal and then phone James, while she waited for it to arrive. Carefully carrying the mug of hot tea she leaned on the umbrella and slowly hobbled out of the kitchen.

Vinny and Stefan were partway down the hall, anxious to discover what lay beneath the dark jacket. Part of a rucksack was showing, but something larger in shape was completely hidden. A rush of water and a rhythmic knocking sound froze the pair in their tracks. *The bastard*, Vinny thought, *he's in Porter's kitchen, preparing to sabotage her boiler*. He gripped the five-foot-length of wood in both hands and crept ahead. Stefan grabbed his arm, pressing a finger to his lips as Vincent halted and turned. The rhythmic knocking was getting louder and, coming closer. Stefan opened a door to their left, both slipping inside and closing the door as quietly as possible.

A stream of cold air met Lyn as she turned into the hallway. *Bloody hell, James would have a fit seeing those two doors left open,* she thought, *still, better a bit of cold air than a puddle of pee on the floor.* She utilized the umbrella to slam each door shut, then hobbled back, stopping at her studio door. She opened it, flicked on the light and all hell broke loose!

A large shape holding a long piece of...of something, was behind the door ready to attack. Instinct kicked in as her loud scream rent the air. Both mug and contents were then flung at the masked face. The umbrella, having become an extension to her arm for most of the day, was raised at lightning speed to block the attack. The injured ankle, lacking support, sent an excruciating reminder of how badly it's treatment of late had been, causing Lyn to stagger to one side. The attackers weapon hit the wall beside her as the point of her *arm-extension* jabbed him in the groin.

Helped onto a chair by Stefan, whilst Vinny, red-eyed from the hot liquid, nursed his bruised genitalia, Lyn was given a fractured run down on how they came to be on her premises. Protecting *her* interests, Vinny insisted between lapses into the moans and groans of not ever being able to father a child.

A waft of sea air was suddenly released from the air purifier, trying its best to cancel out the delicious smell that was permeating the studio. Lyn pointed to the package on the floor by the discarded length of wood.

"Are they fish and chips?"

Stefan responded first. "Sorry, we take them away and..."

Vinny interrupted. "It's like I said, we were coming back from the harbour chip shop when we saw your door open and the lights on. We thought the worst and acted like any good neighbour would. Jimmy'll go berserk when he finds out "

Lyn looked him straight in the eye — his red, watering eyes. "Tell you what, lets all agree that nothing more will be said about what happened here." She waited for their nods. "I'm starving, do you reckon there's enough fish and chips there for three? I'll provide the wine or beer to go with it."

Vinny thought about it, then smiled as he picked up the length of wood. "Let me get rid of this and slip on some dry trousers. Stefan, you help Lyn set up the table, I'll be back in five minutes."

Vinny, sitting at his desk, removed the scratched phone that held the three numbers in it's contacts. He dialed the one allocated to Fairbank. Within seconds, the clatter of cutlery and crockery filled his ear. Then he heard Lyn Porter's voice loud and clear as she asked, "How's Elena, Stefan, is she still working for Candy full-time?"

Stefan, clearing his throat. "She taking a month off for Christmas. We both go home to Bulgaria. I have very special present for my family."

"Sounds intriguing. Is it a secret?"

"Yes. Is secret."

Stefan's footsteps were heard receding to the kitchen.

A satisfied grin appeared on Vinny's face as he pulled on a pair of clean chinos.

Epilogue

Somewhere in the distance a church clock chimed ten o'clock. It was Monday morning and four days after the explosion. Isabelle was standing as close as she could get to the area where the black car had parked. As to the cause of the explosion, the enquiry was still not completed. According to the news bulletins, it happened in close proximity to the petrol tank of a parked car, causing a huge fireball and blasting the car to smithereens. But so far, no car or person had been reported missing. Apparently, such was the devastation, that several months would be needed to piece together exactly what happened — delaying considerably the planned development of the site.

For Isabelle, memories of that day, and the preceding week, were all but gone. Just a few wisps of happenings here and there — snatches of dissipated dreams clinging on to a mind that, according to her menfolk was hypersensitive and easily influenced. She hadn't argued, it had become easier not to. But what they couldn't deny, was the beginning of it all. The finding of the ring which now sat comfortably on her thumb. The coins found with it, sold for a handsome amount of money which would help turn their lives around.

She was here simply to say goodbye. To whom, or what, she wasn't sure. All she was sure of was the fact that she'd never walk across this field again. The estate agent would be around in an hours time with a couple from London, eager to look over the cottage. She was ready to move on. Taking a deep breath she looked around, her eye catching the movement of something gold caught up in the hedge. Moving closer she could see it was a length of gold-coloured ribbon trembling in the breeze, the sort of ribbon the baker's used to gift-wrap their cake boxes. She reached out to touch it but thought better of it and picked up a stray twig instead. A little poking and the ribbon fluttered free. Carried by the wind it rose and fell, dancing across the cold, dark earth while Isabelle headed home.

Vinny stopped outside of the Torquay Central Railway Station and wished his friend a safe journey back to London. "Give my best wishes to Elena and Candy," he called, feeling a pang of loneliness as Stefan disappeared into the mouth of the ticket office. The feeling didn't last long, his mind already busy on the next job in hand — returning the metal detector. He *had* toyed with the idea of hanging onto it for a while, he knew the approximate area where Stefan had been lucky, but after all the news reports of the explosion on the very field in question, he knew it would be a waste of time. Police were desperate for information on a car parked in the area at the time. But no one had yet come forward, and Vinny felt pretty certain that no one would. His conclusion, the maniac — whoever he was — had accidentally blown himself to bits whilst preparing his next assault.

Before driving off, he took the scratched phone from his pocket and punched in the number for Fairbank. The silence, apart from faint, background seagull noise, told him that Lyn and Jimmy had already left for the funeral. He'd assured

Stefan that he'd inform the solicitor of the hidden device. After thinking about it however, he knew Jimmy would find it as soon as a refill for the air-purifying was needed. In the meantime, Vinny could practice and expand his skills on surveillance. After all, how else is a private investigator supposed to learn.

There were no more than a dozen people in the church where Lyn sat listening to James. The eulogy, lightening the sad occasion by referencing small anecdotes of childhood, was executed perfectly whilst emotion was held at bay. She loved him dearly. He was her knight in shining armour, offering stability at a time when her life was filled with uncertainties. But now, it was time to find her own way.

Yesterday was James' fiftieth birthday and because of his mother's death, celebrations had been postponed. Nevertheless, Lyn had insisted on marking it. A bottle of Champagne was opened and uplifting floral arrangements made for his sitting room, office and bedroom. They'd spent a lot of time talking. Communicating on a level that neither had hitherto touched upon. Each sensitive to the uncertainties of the other. Each knowing that a wedding ceremony couldn't guarantee anything. She'd accepted his ring on the basis of love, friendship and mutual respect. Marriage wasn't necessary for that.

As James turned to the coffin, whispering his final farewell to a mother whose most important wish was to see her children happily married, Lyn thought of her own small family. Her parents, who until recently were presumed dead, her daughter and two-year-old grandson, all living thousands of miles away in Australia. Her heart swelled with happiness and excitement at the thought of seeing them. Sharing three months with them. Experiencing for the first time, Christmas with four generations of *her family.*

Much appreciation to:

Barry, for his constant support.

Lil, for giving her time and effort pointing out and editing my flaws.

Roland, for helping me to find the perfect scene to photograph for the cover.

Jackie and Dan, two friends who, like me, enjoy walking in the majestic terrain of Lanzarote and were present when the first glimmer of an idea for HOUNDED was born.

Against All Odds

First in the Psychological-Thriller-Trilogy

ISBN — 9780955971020

Lyn Porter is a redundant florist on the verge of bankruptcy.

James Fairbank is an eminent, long-established conveyancing solicitor who owns properties in one of Torquay's most prestigious areas.

A chance meeting between the two, begins a catalogue of discoveries and plots which could, potentially find Lyn homeless, and James swindled out of one of his properties.

Behind the scenes and pulling the strings, lies a rogue banker and his greedy accomplice. The former, delights in wrecking people's lives. The latter, is stupid enough to believe he is improving his own.

To place your order P&P free in the UK email
shorelinespublishing@hotmail.co.uk

Blind Truth

Second in the Psychological-Thriller-Trilogy

ISBN — 9780955971037

One year on, and the chance to uncover the truth surrounding Lyn Porter's parentage, compels her to travel to the other side of the globe, putting at risk her recently acquired sense of security.

A traumatic journey, followed by castigation from her own flesh and blood, leaves Lyn wondering if the sacrifices made have been worth it.

Meanwhile, back in Torquay, corruption expands into marriages of convenience, kidnapping and attempted murder. Can a well-respected, long-established solicitor afford to get involved? James Fairbank doesn't really have a choice.

To place your order P&P free in the UK email
shorelinespublishing@hotmail.co.uk